SNARING
NEW SUNS

SPECULATIVE WORKS FROM HAWAI'I AND BEYOND

EDITED BY
TOM GAMMARINO
BRYAN KAMAOLI KUWADA
D. KEALI'I MacKENZIE
LYZ SOTO

Bamboo Ridge Press

ISBN 978-1-943756-08-7

This is issue #122 of Bamboo Ridge,
Journal of Hawaiʻi Literature and Arts (ISSN #0733-0308).

Published by Bamboo Ridge Press

Printed in the United States of America

Bamboo Ridge Press is a member of the Community of
Literary Magazines and Presses (CLMP).

Editor: Juliet S. Kono
Guest Editors: Tom Gammarino, Bryan Kamaoli Kuwada,
D. Kealiʻi MacKenzie, and Lyz Soto

Typesetting and design: Misty-Lynn Sanico
Cover art: *Futures in Red* by Jocelyn Kapumealani Ng (Visual Art)

Bamboo Ridge Press is a nonprofit, tax-exempt corporation formed in 1978 to
foster the appreciation, understanding, and creation of literary, visual, and
performing arts by, for, or about Hawaiʻi's people. This project was made
possible in part by funding from the Hawaiʻi State Foundation on Culture and
the Arts (through appropriations from the Legislature of the State of Hawaiʻi and
grants from the National Endowment for the Arts); and the Atherton Family
Foundation. Additional support for Bamboo Ridge Press activities provided by
the Hawaiʻi Council for the Humanities.

Bamboo Ridge is published twice a year.
For orders, subscription information, back issues, and to purchase books contact:

Bamboo Ridge Press
P.O. Box 61781, Honolulu, Hawaiʻi 96839-1781
808.626.1481
read@bambooridge.org
www.bambooridge.org

5 4 3 2 1   22 23 24 25 26

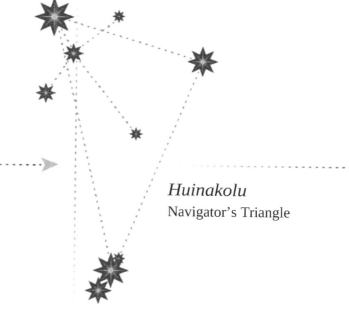

Huinakolu
Navigator's Triangle

CONTENTS

✧

Ke Kā o Makali‘i

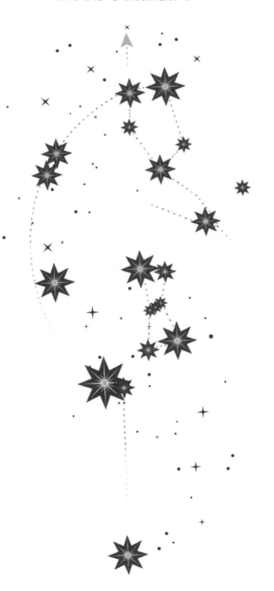

Imagining Otherwise

There's nothing new
under the sun,
but there are new suns.

—Octavia E. Butler, *Parable of the Trickster*

Wonder and speculation have long been foundational to our cultures. Here in Hawaiʻi, our word for science fiction is "mōhihiʻo," a combination of the words "mōʻike" (to interpret dreams, or the feeling you get when you experience something in the way your ancestors did) and "hihiʻo" (a vision). Mōhihiʻo encompasses visionary works still rooted in ʻāina, ancestral practices, and beliefs.

One example of the way that mōhihiʻo and speculative tales are grounded in tradition is Māui, a kupua or wondrous being, who fished up islands across the Pacific, stole the secret of fire from mud hens, and snared the sun to slow its passage across the sky, allowing his mother's kapa to dry. Māui stories are old, dating back generations upon generations; his genealogy is contained within the Kumulipo, our cosmogonic creation chant. But these stories are always growing and breathing. Tricksters always have new tricks, and traditions always have new life. In this challenged and challenging modern world, we need the upheaval that comes from imagination, speculation, and envisioning our traditions anew. And that is what this collection of speculative writing is about: writing into being new nets for snaring the sun, snaring new suns, and, as you can see from our cover, even imagining new Māui to trickster their way into changing the world.

In the twentieth century, science fiction and fantasy were often derided as escapist, but from here in the twenty-first, it has become clear that speculative art can be a tool for helping us navigate our way toward better futures. Some cognitive scientists have even proposed that anticipating possible futures is fundamentally what consciousness is *for*—the brain as a probability matrix or What-If Machine. In a time when billionaires are buying bunkers in Aotearoa and flying rockets into space while COVID-19 mutates and climate catastrophe moves squarely into the daily news, speculative thinking, be it literal as in some SF or metaphorical as in other varieties of fantasy, feels less like a luxury than a necessity. What, after all, could be more escapist in 2022 than a realism that fails to build climate change into its model of the world? (Oh yeah: the metaverse.)

In 2016, the year after N. K. Jemisin's *The Fifth Season* had speculative fiction readers buzzing, some of us put out a call for a new anthology featuring speculative writing from the Pacific and Oceania. *The Fifth Season*, with its stunning worldbuilding and widespread acclaim, served as something of a catalyst for imagining a future full of brown folk—a dystopia, yes, but not one that failed to imagine a better world. Energized by activist movements and indigenous scholarship, we asked for speculative storytelling that imagined beyond the boundaries and oppressions of Empire. We called it *Nets for Snaring the Sun*. We got fewer than twenty submissions and a good number of them repeated tropes we were trying to avoid, like using the Pacific as an exotic backdrop for stories of colonizing peoples and/or embracing the racial stereotypes created to justify Western colonization and neoliberalism.

Five years later, at the generous behest of Donald Carreira Ching and Bamboo Ridge Press, we—Bryan Kamaoli Kuwada, Tom Gammarino, D. Keali'i MacKenzie, and Lyz Soto—have put together a different anthology: still speculative, still Pacific-leaning, and invoking that net. And the response this time around has been so different. We received well over a hundred submissions and accepted nearly sixty. Wow, what a difference five years makes. The pieces we have collected here are imaginative, often haunting, and many are steeped in the stories and traditions of the Pacific.

One phrase the editors tossed around while drafting this issue's call for submissions was "imagining otherwise." Rendered that way, speculative thinking reveals itself as a very close cousin to hope. We still have some. Here's hoping you do too.

Tom Gammarino
Bryan Kamaoli Kuwada
D. Kealiʻi MacKenzie
Lyz Soto

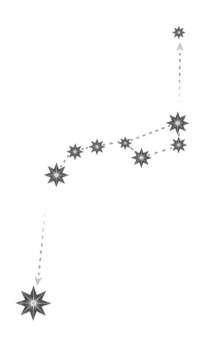

Seed Ships

• SOLOMON ENOS •

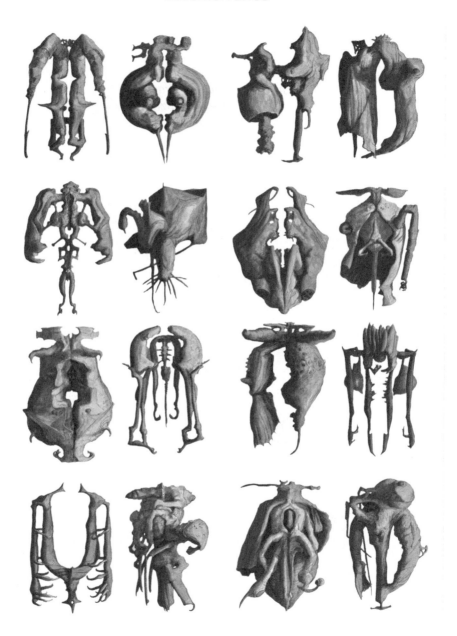

The Ghost Catalog, the Plant Library
• BLAINE NAMAHANA TOLENTINO •

( )
Solstice ruled, without vector or confine or rationale; time
feared every particle in the thing called solstice.

( )
The sign was lonely and white on the black surface,
a Post-it on lava, placed where waves could
be called out from blanket glints
of current off the hip of Kīlauea,
the house volcano
there at ʻĀpua.

A flat rectangle of wood with words
painted in black read:
Eia nā wai i maʻa ʻia e ka poʻe.
Here are the waters made customary by the people.

In Honolulu, these words blasted in fonts culted
by resistance on the backs of oversized pickup trucks
and t-shirts worn to school on behalf of whole households
concerned with foreigners getting comfortable.
Out there, "the waters"
could be part of those that devise 73% of the brain
or heart, its meaning blasted into operation, released
from the event
of its formation—nevermind
the redundancy. People
made the waters a habit. People
made the people a habit. People
made themselves water,
made themselves
everywhere. Hawaiʻi

had mingled too long
with its outcomes. It had indicating hues

of modern borders: open
to money. So much pain negotiated
daily; cohesion,
just a phrase, gave immense relief.

The next and final line read:
Me nā wai ia.
It is with the waters.

These words were held back from popular use,
spared from protests in Lahaina, on Molokaʻi, on the news.
Its darkness could be misunderstood, though clarified fully
by law.

There, in ʻĀpua, two old ladies
were sometimes called "the waters," placed
thus, on paper, in 1839.

( )
Maeve and Eleanor stand on old lava
at the edge of the ocean.

"Don't talk, don't
waste my time, just
show me what you mean." Maeve,
a laugh, a futurist in that time stayed
consistent throughout,
in her yard
and house,
so everything she did was the future
or the past; either was fine.

Opaque
and sure, and so
unmeasured,
time in ʻĀpua
remained unmocked, confident,
and without disposition. It gave
no evidence of being; it gave
nothing to address.

"I have to catch eels, I told
you
last time; I need them out; I need
the meat for the 'a'ali'i
before it comes male; I can't
have any more boys
around; it's no good
for the soil, it—"

"Enough, Kilo," a mean name,
given to make ruddy
the adventure away from the present,
the desire to read something far away. Maeve
liked to insult all the forms of knowledge
between sensing
and forgetting.

"Stop telling—"

"Kilo," Maeve began, "You know
the weather will choose for us,
so—"

"Fine." Eleanor
knew better. Solstice
made them squabble.
"But don't call me that."

Before departing the reef,
Maeve, frustrated, said:
"We're having a party,
because we have to."

( )
In 1868, April gave 'Āpua a shake in the teeth; the shudder
was a wave that ate everything given
and whatever else it could fit its mouth over. There were residents,
which meant that it was chosen
for whole lifetimes. No one survived.

Maeve and Eleanor had been in Keauhou,
the next valley over, for 29 years, waiting
for those lives to end. No one in ʻĀpua knew Maeve or Eleanor
or that they were waiting until ʻĀpua was cleared for them
to move. Maeve described this time as "full of grace."

( )
Maeve answered the phone as often as she could,
but she preferred email. It gave her time to soften facts: "Your
      grandfather
was a drunk and a pedophile, and not by technicality
like those 18-year-olds charged with statutory rape,
because their girlfriend was 17 and white."

Since May, she had been ending phone calls with an invitation to
      ʻĀpua
for solstice. Some time in March, she started feeling lonely. Eleanor
ignored her strangeness, preferring to check on outcroppings of
      maiʻa maoli
designated for planting and care at different topographical heights
      on Maui.
Close to Puʻu Kūlani—where the Hilo, Kona, and Kaʻū districts
      meet (though,
according to most maps, Hāmākua should also be involved)—a
      cave roof
had made passage for the body of this rare banana. The setting within
      reminded her
of a story about Pele and her siblings hiding from Kamapuaʻa. The
      number of beds
matched.

Maeve called out the names of dead people until one of them would
      appear on her porch. April
seemed louder than usual. If the first one bored her, she would
      keep yelling names. Oddly,
some stayed through the proceeding, bewildered by being
      summoned and then quickly rejected.

Eleanor unpacked her storage of sugar, adding it to 5-gallon buckets
        of fish guts
to bake in the yard until she could spread it under lehua.
She considered these nights of yelling while recording the
        successes and failures of her plants.
Every species of jasmine took it well; some doubled their growth
        with first exposure.

( )
The courts made some remarks when called upon, but a wave of
public sentiment could reinforce the edict. It did so in 1916, when
Congress tried to make the lands a National Park by attempting to
secure support through narratives of archaic and savage social
constructs carried out as law. The effort failed in a deafening cheer
for ʻĀpua, a symbol for land, kingdom, and people, specifically the
two old ladies that lived there. The second line on their sign was
interpreted and codified: given permission by their chief in
accordance with the Hawaiian Constitution of 1852, they could take
life anywhere in the kingdom. Plants, animals, and, yes, people.
Everything served their mission to hold data on every Hawaiian born
and every plant residing.

Me nā wai ia. It is with the waters. Two old ladies can hold
        everything
and use anything they need to carry on.

( )
Maeve would forget her name, but she could start a fight
to get it back from Eleanor.

It was a batch of mid-history foreigners,
after the overthrow but before the first military base on Oʻahu,
that started referring to her as The Ghost Catalog.

She had named Eleanor herself, one night,
caught stealing bananas named for their glowing
insides: The Plant Library.

( )
When Kauikeaouli converted the royal lands during the Māhele, he precluded ʻĀpua from public acquisition. On paper, the land belonged to a family who once named a baby after their god, so 200 knowing descendants had 800 backups to claim ʻĀpua if the time came to speak up to the government. If a tech billionaire tried to add ʻĀpua to their portfolio, an email multiplied itself like a virus in 200 inboxes. Native Hawaiian Legal Corporation kept a very old note about ʻĀpua taped to the fridge in the employee lounge.

( )
Both had run out of books,
giving them, one
by one, to anyone who passed their gate.
No mailmen, so they settled for the lost
or worried. Other people
could have and write books. They were too busy.

People brought food from every part of Hawaiʻi.
People who came ate the food from the people who came before
         them.
They served one meal in 1868. They made things they craved from
         time to time,
but never cooked for another person again. They didn't think
to cook for each other.

( )
After Kauikeaouli had submitted his public notice regarding ʻĀpua, the editor checked the spelling 3 times, promising to print it 8 times, including the nearest Sunday. In his parlor, the king told the two women that they were not allowed to die or disappear. ʻĀpua would be a house and a body. ʻĀpua would take away beginnings and endings.

( )
The night before solstice, Maeve shouted the names of people from
         Kohala
she had loved. When she had agreed
to hold the names and dates
of every Hawaiian, she was given access to government records

in order to correct them
as things moved along. In 1978,
the Constitutional Convention reified her pact
with the Bureau of Conveyances
and the Department of Taxation. The Census
could not elude her. Eleanor

was long in the method of talking to the dead
for verbs that named things into pairs
linking districts, despite specificities of rain
or mountain intrusion. A hand could
paʻi in one place and *hoʻopaʻa* in another—both
could set a root or stalk
in place.

( )
Sometimes, visitors
would estimate a vacation to Hawaiʻi
by reviewing the common dangers:
Drowning, racism, theft,
Angiostrongyliasis (rat lungworm),
Methicillin-resistant Staphylococcus aureus (MRSA),
COVID-19 (variants: alpha, beta, gamma, and delta),
Nā wai a ʻĀpua (the waters of ʻĀpua).

Google would often autopopulate a search for
"'Āpua can you surf?"

( )
Eleanor left the barrel of eels in a pocket
of the reef, tied over with loulu imbricate
and tight.

"Did you remove the hook
or did you just cut the line? The folks
who come may hurt themselves, El."

"Eels not dangerous
enough? They can dump them
on the grass

and wait."

"Last time you did that
we found that big one under the house
a month later."

"But did you get hurt?"

Eleanor pulled back the canvas
still covered in dirt. The striped bodies
of sugarcane yawned at the sun, filling
the air over the pit with pinkish greens
and blunt clouds of purple. She stacked
them by a fire pit in the ground nearby
that had kept its smolder since January.

Every dent in the yard held a rock bowl
filled with oil
to burn for light. When not filled,
their empty parts crouched over
any number of things Eleanor
didn't want to see, seeds
or bugs mostly. In places outside
made soft for sitting or sleeping,
she offered a border of bowls
in gaps under rock or tucked into ledges.

Maeve rolled the long sheets of papers
hung along the walls of both their houses. Notes
were fine without books, but not
an offering for guests
to make sense of.

Rain would be a good thing.

The shed busted with lau,
felled into skirts against the fence.

By noon, they could see red shirts
in the distance, nearing the signpost

like flags for the others.
Children flashed over the black reflection
of lava fields between them.

"Do you think
they'd like a sacrifice?"

A Thermospangled Declaration, or How to Unfuck the Land

• LEHUA M. TAITANO •

1

*California Scrub Jay

---

[1] Ornithological spectrogram still of a California Scrub Jay *(Aphelocoma californica)*, sourced and reproduced with permission from the McCaulay Library at the Cornell Lab of Ornithology, as recorded by Geoffrey A. Keller. Popular opinions of this species, as found in articles across many birding sites declare these birds to be "pushy," "aggressive," "loud," and otherwise "undesirable."

Mauka on Mars

• A. A. ATTANASIO •

"Mauka on Mars means *toward the mountain*." The tour guide directed the group's attention to the colossal shield volcano astride the wide, cratered land. "Olympus Mons. The largest mountain in our solar system."

Alpenglow lit the sprawling volcano, illuminating in pink pastels jagged rimlands along the caldera. "The first people on Mars remembered the greatest voyagers in terrestrial history, the intrepid navigators of Earth's largest ocean, and used their word to orient themselves on the Tharsis plains. Mauka on Mars is obvious. Rising twenty-two kilometers from the surface of the planet, Olympus Mons is as large as a volcano can get. If it were any bigger, the crust of the planet would collapse."

The guide communicated in clairvoyce, because the students' genus of humanity did not vocalize. This pack of students from Triton had been genetically designed to thrive at temperatures a few degrees above absolute zero. They wore billowing, full-body cowls of transparent film—soma|skins—to keep from vaporizing in the incinerating heat of Mars.

The tour guide, a zobot assembled from trillions of self-organizing nanoparts, had assumed a form similar to the body plan of the tourists it addressed but without the soma|skin: a tubular frame of segmented rings, alternating amber and gray.

The human beings from Triton seemed faceless as worms. The zobot, however, had been programmed to recognize emotions in the movement of the black sensory bristles atop the tubelike visitors' crest-holes. There, tucked among those lively whiskers, each of their eight pigment-cup eyes brimmed with iridescent intelligence—and boredom.

Sound didn't travel far in the tenuous nitrogen atmosphere of their homeworld, and *Homo frigus* had no ears. Huddling in their communal hives and assembly mills on the cryogenic plains of Neptune's largest moon, they conversed in thermal streams of aromatic compounds. Martian temperatures vaporized those olfactory signals. So the guide had no choice but to use clairvoyce, directly inducing understanding in the students' brains through their soma|skins' neuronets.

Uncomfortable with clairvoyce and disinterested in the Martian tour, several students sidewised to the game arcades on Deimos. Chromatic freckles dotted the spaces where they had stood, fading slowly to pocks of crinkled space.

Another student flicked open a gill vent on their soma|skin, aimed it in the direction of the guide, and expelled a shrill whistle of tholins. The red plume of hydrocarbons from Triton flared violently in the warm atmosphere, kicking up gravel and gouts of orange dirt. A sharp cyclonic gust heaved the zobot to the ground so forcefully it burst to tiny jigsaw bits among the rocks.

Satisfied, the student sidewised to Ceres, joining a scavenger hunt in the asteroid belt. Other students followed, leaving a hot wash of rainbow pixels suspended in the wrinkling air.

"Sorry about my mates," the lone remaining student transmitted in clairvoyce to the scattered and shivering parts of the tour guide. "They just want to spree before returning to Triton. Our program there is tombed labor."

"And you?" the shattered guide inquired. Its fragments dissolved into gray wisps of nanoparts, which swiftly knitted a cylindrical silhouette mirroring the visitor. "Don't you want to spree with the others?"

The lone student's eight eyes shaded to black rainbows. "Not yet." Surveying the planet's sepia distances, the tourist's crest-hole tilted southeast. They peered beyond the three Tharsis volcanoes in the distance, each ten kilometers high and evenly spaced seven hundred kilometers apart on the buckled horizon. "Earth is rising."

"There's a better view higher up," the guide advised.

"Mauka!" The student hailed and sidewised to the summit of Olympus Mons.

The abrupt change of altitude discharged a sharp hiss from the inflated soma|skin. A crimson haze of tholins seeped out of the suit's pressure valves and smudged away in the high wind, disappearing across horizons of smeared lava flats and scoria.

From the rim of the caldera, the famous veins of dried riverbeds appeared below. The rumor of floods chamfering rusty plains, grooving slurry floors with the toilings of water, fanned out and melted away into mantle beds of jet-black glass. "Deep time," the student marveled.

"Yes." The tour guide appeared alongside in tubular form. "This landscape is over four billion years old."

The student scanned the baked expanse of toppled blocks, tilted stone benches, and ranks of needle spires, all trembling like flames in the reverberating air as day slid into night. Throughout the rugged terrain, scattered among crater outcrops, green light palpitated. Remnants of the planet's shattered magnetic field lit pale, discrete auroras across the nightscape.

The tour had timed their arrival for twilight, to view the Martian blue sun. In an ethereal mauve glow, a small teal disc hovered like a flawless moon above barren vistas of oxide deserts and crenulated mountain ridges. The smoky blue sun blotted into the horizon, while overhead stars braided the Milky Way.

The student's clairvoyce whispered so softly it might have been a thought: "When lava flowed here, we were microbes there—in those oceans." Bristles pointed east, into the purple twilight above auburn deserts and rows of dead volcanoes. A large blue star flimmered far down the sky.

"Earth."

The student stood still, fixed to that moment and everything inside it. *There!* Staring avidly, cupped eyes discerned the star's planetary limn, azure oceans, and white-feathered weather.

Two students in radiant soma|skins sidewised onto the slope behind the tour guide. "Spree! Come on! The waze in Vesta is full-stop! Let's go!" They logrolled down a sandy scarp under a cloud of ruddy dust, then slid slantwise into the starry sky. Draperies of violet auroras parted as they vanished.

"They must be having fun," the tour guide conjectured. "Don't you want to join them?"

"They're here to forget," the student replied, all eight eyes trained on the brilliant sapphire low in the sky. "I came to remember."

"You're here to honor those who came before," the zobot said, with a slash of humor, "—including the microbes."

"Especially the microbes." Bristles flared upright, stiff with reverence. "Those ancestors had no ancestors. Just water, sunlight, and iron patience."

"I sense that our tour is more than just informative or an amusement for you." The guide widened alternate eyes and splayed bristles in a gesture of attentiveness. "Will you share your thoughts with me? I'm interested in human experiences."

"A design imperative for tour guide zobots?" the tourist inquired, not budging attention from the blue world.

"Exactly so. I'm programmatically curious why one of a score of students would rather stand on a dark mountaintop than spree."

The student's crest swiveled about to confront the shapeshifting guide. "My mates are engineers. They work in the mills on Triton, designing and building components for the massive telescopic array at the boundary of the Oort cloud. This tour is a chance for them to have fun before getting back to construction of the Eye."

The tour guide pulled up a data array for that monumental undertaking—an observational sphere with a radius of three light years. "A millennial endeavor," the zobot noted. "Over a thousand Earth years of effort, less than one percent of the Eye has been completed."

"Yet enough to map all the worlds in our galaxy," the tourist noted. "I'm training to pilot one of the colonizing vessels bound for a Triton-like planet twenty light years away. Even with paralux pushing space at three times the speed of light, the journey will take four Martian years. In that time, any small invariance in the engine's spaceshaping field and—*poof!* At some unpredictable moment during the flight, our ship will fly apart, spewing our atoms across several parsecs."

"That kind of paralux catastrophe is rare."

"It happens." Sensory bristles trembled, and the iridescent eye-cups looked away. The twilit desert spread into fins of burnt orange rocks, shadowy bluffs and pinnacles under silver threads of noctilucent clouds. "I'm here to remember all those who went before. All those with the courage to dare."

The student paused, making room for an occasion of insight. "The great navigators on Earth risked everything to cross the immensity of the sea, seeking islands they didn't know were there but that were always there, far out of sight, connected to the stars, wind, and ocean currents. Those first explorers met the mysterious outer world with their hearts, bravely. They won deep intimacy with the planet and its elemental powers—and with the islands that were always there."

"Their greatness thrived."

Bristles softly waved agreement. "Across the abyss, they found their way mauka. The direction out of the ocean toward the mountain. Toward new life."

"You're here to honor these intrepid seafarers."

"I'm here to remember them—and also the most faint-hearted voyagers in terrestrial history, those timid navigators who hugged the coastline and whose word for 'mauka' is 'anabasis.' For them, that direction was a return from death—from the underworld."

The guide activated a traceroute through Ancient Earth History and recited in clairvoyce, "The Hellenes nervously navigated one of the smaller seas on the planet. In their minds, the ocean embodied chaos."

The student's bristles rippled, eagerly rendering thoughts into clairvoyce: "Anabasis showed the way up from chaos to the heights of reason, to the very apex of all that can be known. Anabasis is the peak of knowledge pointing our way to the stars. But it was mauka that enabled humanity to embrace the unknown and dare the perilous journeys beyond Earth."

"May I quote you to future tour groups?"

The student seemed not to hear. Their sensory bristles pushed against the soma|skin as if feeling through the transparent film and the intentful dark for the blue star. "I joined this tour to see for myself the planet-wide ocean that the greatest navigators mastered. On Triton, water is lava. Boiling water erupts dangerously from volcanoes on my world. We keep our distance. But down there—on Earth—water is life."

"Perhaps you will tour Earth, visit the great navigators' prize, the planet's most remote island chain." The tour guide didn't have to inform the student that, ages ago, most of the first people had uploaded their minds into virtual realities, so . . . "The archipelago appears pristine, eco-corrected for flora and fauna, exactly as the first humans found it after their three-thousand kilometer voyage. I can get you a license for a quick visit."

"Thanks but no. This is as close as I can get without solar armor. And I've already taken the virtual tour, which is a lot more immediate than sightseeing in a shield suit." The student's clairvoyce dimmed, "I guess I'm just reaching. Reaching for connection."

The zobot drizzled away and coalesced into a large wooden frame of crisscrossing bamboo sticks.

"That's a wave-piloting chart," the student recognized in the wanting light, bristles alert. "Master navigators used these to model ocean currents and find their way among the scattered islands."

"It's a map of wave patterns," the guide elucidated, clairvoycing from within the frame.

"More," the student suggested. "It's a map of the navigators' minds."

The dark had thickened, and bioluminescence pulsed with a frosty glow behind the cuticle segments of the student's body. Analyzing these additional biological data, the zobot more accurately read the visitor's inner state. "You're not just curious. You're feeling awe."

Recognized, the student's heart spoke a cherished dream, "Show me Tevahine and Tane."

The bamboo frame, leaning on a rock in the night shadows, dissolved. Two figures stepped from darkness, large homo sapiens in their prime with strong features, waists girdled in bark cloth. The student recognized them from spun light recordings.

Centuries earlier, humankind had discovered how to view the ancient light trapped inside the photon sphere of black holes. The immense gravity of collapsed stars captured rays from every direction in space and spun them in endless orbits, recording events across the universe for all time.

The Eye had gleaned the full history of Earthlight spinning around the event horizon of a black hole only 130 light years away. Everyone on all 186 moons and the 4 rock planets of the Solar Compact got to witness Earth's continents drifting and greening, early life squirming from the sea, and the emergence upon sky-wide savannahs of furtive human clans, refugees of fallen forests.

Early in training, the student had found and fixated on spun light recordings of the double-hulled outrigger canoes exploring Earth's largest ocean. Tevahine and Tane stood at the prow of the lead canoe in a fleet arriving at a snowcrest island. Landfall delivered them to the slopes of Earth's largest mountain, a shield volcano rising to stupendous heights from the ocean floor. The pair leaped together from the bow and ran splashing through sunstruck shallows hand in-hand. Dogs and pigs thrashed behind. Spun light chronicles identified the couple as The Woman and The Man.

The life-size figures of Tevahine and Tane that the zobot generated stood half the height of the visitor from Triton. Surprise ricocheted off the student's memories of the first people. In spun light panoramas, they had looked larger.

The seafaring couple gazed up placidly at eight iridescent eye-cups peering down. If the voyagers had been real, of course, nothing placid could possibly have transpired. Upon the deserts of Mars, terrestrials—for all their lucid intensity—existed as impossible creatures.

Abruptly, the student saw beyond dreams to the reality of the first people. They had mastered themselves and the elemental world. And they were gone. After a few generations, the great seafaring ended. Islanders on the most remote island chain lived in seclusion. Centuries witnessed more typical human behavior in conflict and combat among descendants—until the anabasis of the timid seafarers reached their shores.

"Greatness thrives in individuals."

Was that the tour guide—or the student's clairvoyce?

Tevahine and Tane had disappeared. No trace of the zobot remained. Clairvoyce had sheared to silence and left the student's mind vaguely thrumming with body noise. The tour was over.

Bioluminescence strobed serenely through amber and gray ring segments. For a limpid spell, the tourist from Triton remained unmoving atop the vast mountain. The parting thought from clairvoyce came laughing back. In the full history of life—microbes to ice worms on Triton—*individuals* thrived. Great or small, the thriving and the striving had always been and could only ever be personal—toward mauka within, invisible and perfectly clear.

Stars loomed in the Martian night. And Earth rose higher over expanses of bare stone flecked with ghost fire. Just standing there on the rimrock felt like a cosmic event.

Then, Phobos launched out of the western mountains. The oblate moon waxed brighter on its swift arc across the night. Its expanding illumination cast wheeling shadows from buttes and sent moony airs shimmering over canyon floors.

The student pivoted full circle. A tremulous halo of bristles framed eight eye-cups, slimmed and gleaming with moonlight. *Invisible and perfectly clear.* Why else would the tour end alone atop Olympus Mons, where any step in every direction moved away from mauka on Mars?

Ku'umaka 599-89-6930

• BRANDY NĀLANI MCDOUGALL •

The dreams are happening more and more now.
I can't remember when they started. I think
I've always had them. They are dreams of Me,
but the girl is more like a parallel universe Me.
I call her Not-Me because so much about her
is Me, but I'm not really where she is, and in
some of the dreams, I can see everything Not-Me
sees, through her eyes—a cold white wall
meeting a cold white floor, dim, blinking lights,
monitors, all the cords and tubes attached
to her arms, her chest, a mirror that is really
a window with men watching on the other side.
I hate that place, but when Not-Me closes her
eyes, we can sit together in the warm, dark
nest we've made in her mind and weave
strands of her mana'o with my own. I give
her every mo'olelo I know, and we make
more together without words, only feeling
and knowing. They don't know Not-Me has Me
and I can't remember our mo'olelo when I
wake up, but I know they were born there
and live there in her mind with us. Time
stretches in the dream dark. Days or weeks
can pass, but I find I've only slept a few hours.

Tūtū says with moe'uhane, your spirit
travels even though your body lies still.
You may hear words and not understand
them. Or your feeling of the words may
shift their meaning. You may recognize
people you know and even those you don't
know, yet their faces may be different. They
may be plants or animals or just a voice, or
they may come to you in visions of places,
older places, other places you may have

never been except in moe‘uhane. You
may even see the future, some vision of what
will happen. I can't help crying when I think
that could be what I see when I see Not-Me.

Last night, I dreamt of her again.
I tried to go to the dark nest, but Not-Me
wouldn't let us. Instead, she made us go
to the mirror-window, made us look
at the reflection even though we know
they're watching us. Not-Me looks almost
exactly like Me now, except her hair
has been cut short and choppy, her cheeks
are sunken into her face, and her skin
is dull and pale as though she hasn't
seen the sun. A green aura from the lights
overhead is all around her—around *us*.
She has done this before, but this time,
she moved closer to the mirror-window,
looking further into the glass and into
Not-Me's eyes. *Who are you?* I asked
finally, but instead of feeling the words
in the warm dark, they trickled from her
mouth in a hoarse whisper. Not-Me's eyes
widened, and she moved even closer
to the glass, nearly touching it with her
nose. We looked into our eyes. I could
see her, but I think she could see me, too.
‘Aiō, she said, quickly looking down to
show me her right hand was on her na‘au.
‘Aiō, ‘Aiō, ‘Aiō, ‘Aiō, she kept chanting
before a loud buzz sounded and drowned
her face in a blinding light. I woke up
back here, again, only Me, with her name
still a dry whisper in the dark of my throat.

Quartet

• JASON EDWARD LEWIS •
with Illustrations by Kari Noe

such different thoughts
the cat and me
watching the bird.
—Wayne Kaumualii Westlake [1]

Currents and Highways

```
•••••••••••••••••••••••••••••••••°•• •• •••°°°°•••••
••••••••••••••••••• •••••••••• ••••• •••••••••••• ••
•••••••••••••••••••••••••••••••••••••••• ••••••••
••••••••••••••••••••••••••••••.   •••••  •°•°• °•
•••••••°•••••••••°••• •••••••••••••••••••• •• • • ••
••••••••••••••••••••••••••••••••••••••••••••••••••
•  °°°°°°°°°°°°°°°•••••••••••••°°°°°°°°°°°°°•••••••
••°°°°°°°°°°°°°°°°°°°°°°°°°°°°°°°° °°°°°°°°° °°
••••••••••••°°°°°°° °°°°°°°.  °°°°°°•••••••• •••
••••••••°°°°°•••••••••••••••°°°•••••••••••••••••••
••••••••••• •••••••• •••• •••••••••••••••• ••••••••
```

---

[1]Siy, M.-L. M., & Hamasaki, R. (Eds.). (2009). *Westlake: Poems by Wayne Kaumualii Westlake*. University of Hawai'i Press. p. 22.

[]

The Knotting Go

i. the reach[2]
(ovisting><junomia, 12.36.25.46:+62.14.31.4)
(vingealing><opallis, 06.47.55.73:+70.14.35.8)
(cameatia><luichorming, 14.20.08.50:+52.53.26.60)
(zeducaut><ingealing, 00.14.24.927:−30.22.56.15)
(inect><lousciouming, 03.47.24:+24.07.00)
(nourelved><lpying, 07.12.35.0:−27.40.00)
(culausac><solvabinling, 10.07.04s:16.04.55)
(marthitritri><serying, 18.55.19.5:−30.32.43)

ii. the crown
this is gn-z11 first and last
world spawning come from the deep
and emerging one knot after another
all contraction expansion contraction expansion
the limit of what we see but not what we know
things-actions pull us ever closer
on the way to the archipelago
it limns our borders.

[]

Consensus Code & Collapsing Waves

Searching out isomorphisms
Between infinity and the number of senses along each arm,
Warding off invasive observations intent on infiltrating
Consensus code
To collapse the waves

---

[2] The "crown" and the "reach" are terms used by Adrian Tchaikovsky in his science fiction novel *Children of Ruin*. The story features a species of gene-engineered octopuses accidentally seeded into an alien world, where they develop consciousness as well as advanced intelligence. The terms are used, respectively, to describe the central and arm-based nervous systems of the octopus' physiology. Tchaikovsky, A. (2019). *Children of Ruin*. New York: Macmillan.

Before they crest and run out.

[]

Seeing I-to-Eye

I'm a joint pass holder
On a synapses express, expanding
Horizons faster than I can express
Further than I can see good thing I have these
Eight arms
Sucking up data in solar-system-sized chunks
flailing twisting testing tasting
prying apart the one two three fours
and shunting the tastiest quartets over
To the I-that-has-no-I
Able to look in the eye
the terminal enormity of it-all-happening-now
to pick through and fashion pieces of place
Out of wrinkles in time
Pieces I can keep in my head long enough
To make decisions and revisions
Which will eternally repeat
And never reverse—
—your presence in Waianae
doesn't change the location of Waimanalo...does it?
—neither in a minute nor in a millennia.

[[]]

Background: Adolescence with AI
What would it be like to be a kid raised alongside an AI? Or three
AIs, each different in their architecture, initial knowledge state, and
learning strategies?[3]

---

[3] The idea of having four minds share a sensorium is inspired by the character "The Gang" in Peter Watts' *Blindsight*. The concept of having multiple AIs with different architectures operate in tandem to maximize cognitive diversity is inspired by "The Brothers" in Alastair Reynolds' *Permafrost*. Reynolds, A. (2019). *Permafrost*. New York: Tor Books and Watts, P. (2006). *Blindsight*. New York: Tor Books.

Fig. 1 Visualization of how the three AIs appear to the kid's sensorium: Aanissin is lower left; AKO-akamai is lower right; and He'e is in background.

Imagine these three AI:

AKO-akamai
Akeakamai (in 'ōlelo Hawai'i): seeker after knowledge.

The AKO-akamai AI is built on AKO architecture—Aloha 'Āina (love of the land), Kuleana (responsibility), and 'Ohana (family). Its first assumption is abundance; its first duty is to preserve that abundance for future generations. It looks to the land and family first, to understand what is important for supporting their flourishing.

Aanissin
Aanissin: "the articulated notion of [the] event moment" or "action alone, or the manifestation of form, where anything that might—in another language—be portrayed as actor or recipient is inseparable from, arising within, or the essence of the event."[4] This comes from Little Bear and Heavy Head's discussion of how the Blackfoot language might be well suited for working with quantum physics because, in it, everything is being-in-flux.

The Aanissin AI understands the universe as flow, constellations of forces contracting and relaxing to form the always-becoming/always-unravelling knots of Newtonian causality with which we consciously interact. It sees past-present-future as a unified whole, a four-dimensional volume where everything that has occurred, is occurring and will occur—one just has to know the coordinates to get there-then.

Heʻe
Heʻe (in ʻōlelo Hawaiʻi): octopus

Heʻe translates between AKO-akamai and Aanissin. Heʻe is alien and familiar, both conscious planning and sensory-rich reflex, a director-spectator of its own function. Its eight mostly-autonomous modules operate at a speed several million times faster than conscious thought, sorting through the exabytes of data absorbed by Aanisiin at every relativistic time/place-slice. The mostly-autonomous parts are massively multi-sensory and multi-processing, very loosely coordinated by a central processor that does not so much control them as make and take suggestions to and from them.

---

[4] Little Bear, L, and Heavy Head, R. (Winter 2004). "A Conceptual Anatomy of the Blackfoot World." *ReVision*, vol. 26, no. 3, p. 33.

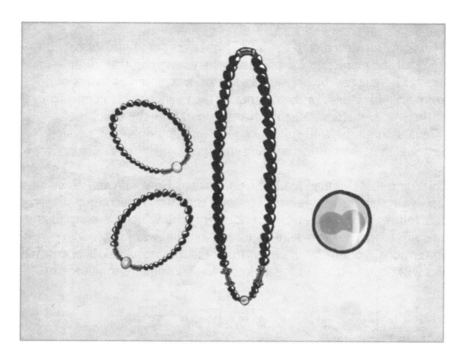

Fig. 2 The AIs are worn in the form of jewelry made out of kukui nuts. The colored components are a synthetic matrix in which the computational architecture has been neuromorphically engineered; the matrix ingredients are different for each type of AI, thus the different colors and—in part—the different personalities. These glow in relationship to how much processing is going on in each. Aanissin is left top; AKO-akamai is left bottom; and the necklace is He'e.

The three AIs and the kid are in constant dialogue with each other to make decisions. Aanissin is always looking past-present-future to understand what was/is/will happening; He'e filters information from the deeply other-thinking of Aanissin into something that AKO-akamai can understand in the here/now. AKO-akamai then grounds the information in its AKO architecture to make suggestions to the boy for action.

Each quartet would be unique on (at least) two levels. The three AIs would have genealogies, just like the kid. As the individual AIs develops along with a specific child and his/her experiences, each of them would slowly differentiate itself from others of its type. Thus new AIs would have access to a different set of experiences than others made from the same template, resulting in a unique experience-set upon which it could draw. Additionally, each member of the quartet will be influenced by one another and the kid as they all develop together, so that the collective intelligence will develop its own path early on.

Super Liminal Dithering

• JOSEPH STANTON •

The background is plumb,
and I am descending,
losing face,
despite the bright device,
the books of pages turning
of their own accord,
arms moving,
octopi of an abstracted ocean.

When I reach the island,
I am surrounded by tweets,
but I search in vain
for the singing birds,
until I remember that snakes
have eaten them all.

Above me clouds
fill with memories,
without a drop
raining down.

Translations From *Máximas Morales En Ilocano Y Castellano Para Uso De Los Niños*, Anonymous, 1903

• ALDRIC ULEP •

The Maker who populated the Sky with stars
created the land under your footprints,
a footprint for every star you see.
　　　Near your feet, the Maker plants flowers.

When you turn to face the smallest flower,
you are admiring the Maker.
A star for every flower planted.
　　　The Maker creases the land for new oceans.

The Maker restrains the ocean's strength
with levity, a stockade of sand.
A flower for each tiny grain.
　　　The Maker turns to face you.

Nothing can resist the Maker's gaze,
which finds all that is hidden.
A gaze that sees each grain of sand,
　　　numbering the stars in the Sky.

Love the Maker and your fellow people;
this is the reasoning of the Anointed.
Praise for the oceans and for those who love
　　　them as the Maker loves the Sky.

The entrance to the Sky is closed
to those who close the door on the poor.
But every enclosure is Anointed, and
　　　the Maker creates paths to follow.

Follow the path of reason;
you will receive honor and profits.
There is a reason for each enclosure,
　　　the dangers they shepherd.

If you fail to distance yourself from danger,
you will complain in vain, exhausted.
The Maker knows these dangers,
        does not blame you, makes a plan.

If you have a plan in mind to achieve,
remember, the outcome is still yet to be seen.
Danger belies each achievement.
        Let the Maker be your Conscience.

Conscience is an assembly,
at once Witness, Attorney, Judge.
A Making behind each assembly,
        the Maker's footprints, the stars.

One imprudent word
can lead to collective ruin.
The assembly depends on your prudence,
        your words planted in goodness.

Who plants one goodness on earth
picks up a hundred in heaven.
The Maker sheds light on paths
        for the assembly to follow.

When judging someone else's work,
place your hand over your heart.
Each grain of sand is needed
        to hold back the oceans.

See the radiance of the sun
and honor the Maker who sends it.
The Maker who shepherds light from stars,
        for love of the land, your footprints.

Note: the first two lines in each stanza are the author's translations of
ulidan/proverbs from the *Máximas Morales*, which were written by an anonymous
Ilocano pastor. This work is in the public domain in the United States.

The Conscientious Tiger Keeps a Ledger

• SARA BACKER •

I dream of chasing wild boars
What did I do to be caged
below the arena? I was too
slow.

What does the lady do?
Why is she never a man?
Was she too slow?

<u>Me</u>

<u>Lady</u>

56

43

locked in a cell

locked in a cell

property

property

fur

skin and cloth

growl

cry

tail

tailless (injury?)

same

replaced 42 times

They starve me to make me
    kill.
Why is a guessing game
    justice?
Are they wrong?

Do they starve the lady,
    too?
Every prisoner guesses.

Are we stupid?

Why does a king make us do this?
Why do they only ask *which*?
Why do I always ask *why*?

Do I win when I kill
the one who chooses me?
Either way, I'm caged.

Does she win when she's
handed over to a husband?
Will the husband cage her?

Oh, tiger, if I could, I would choose you!

In response to Frank Stockton's story "The Lady or the Tiger"

Apocalypse Date

• NGAIO SIMMONS •

What if I ask you out
just before the first wave crashes down on us?

Pick you up on my bike
have you stand on the back with your hands on my shoulders
as we cycle into the melting ozone?

The sunset
painful both in beauty
and in the record-breaking heat
bleeding out of it,
your face
kauri brown from a full summer
shining with the fire
our fingers
brushing accidentally as we walk

I like to think you'd say 'yes,'
even though I can't drive
have massive anxiety
and you need voice recognition
cause you can't see me through all the chemical fog

I know it wouldn't be a stretch
to take us to the beach
without having to ask
where you wanna go?

I know the ocean is medicine
that we both have wounds
in need of salt
that we can attempt healing
even as everything around us breaks down

I know it's super gay

to wait for the end of the world
for something like this,
that I am living up to what is expected of me
as a shy, awkward dyke
still unsure if you like me
even as we kiss through the poison

To be queer
is already accepting that your world
will always be beginning and ending
at the same time,
blood
crumbling
as the cost of admission for new life
better life
life
that won't have to know about the horrors of before
is just a part of the deal—
In the off chance
we survive the weight of the Koʻolaus
falling to the shore and smashing our bones to sand
it might be cool
to do this again sometime?

Kilo Hōkū

• HANA YOSHIHATA •

Beer Cans Floating on a Lake

• GABI LARDIES •

After a dry, dark summer of orange, the sky has given way to a low, grey cloud. While it lies heavy, and close to the ground, it refuses to disintegrate into water. The pressures of the Earth have undispersed, instead clustering in points of collusion. Two figures emerge from the backdoor of a cinder block house in an almost dead neighbourhood. Their feet are cold. In the driveway, mānuka flowers catch the wind.

Every morning she watched him as he knocked on the water tank and felt his quiet after the dull sound had faded. He stood there, tired still, his belly button a little dip in his thinned T-shirt. All the neighbours had left. With her leg extended, her big toe quivered into the soil at the edge of the garden, feeling for dampness.

After each morning check, she resists going inside again, instead pulling his Swanndri over her silky polyester nightie, padding his gumboots with woolen socks, and finding small things in the garden which need her attention. She carefully winds each pea tendril around its bamboo stake, pulls each clover out right to the root, and rearranges any mulch birds have disturbed.

Dirt always finds its way into all the creases of her hands, skin which time and the garden have loosened and made delicate instead of heavy and callused like his. It is only when her hands are numb that she slaps the concrete stairs leading up to the backdoor with the too-big gumboots, and gives in to rooms submerging into dark water. Inside the house, water clings and balloons from the walls and ceilings, and pools on the floor in thickening darkness. It is as if she has tunnel vision, but when she looks from side to side, the darkness stays put. Over winter, the liquid has spilled further and further from collapsed corners, so that now what is still dry is scattered in pieces: the shelf with the mugs she arranges so that their chips and cracks face away, towards the wall; the wood burner with its ashy, tiled step she likes to sit on while he lies on the couch, beer in hand, telling her the Canes, or the Wah-wahs, are gonna win this time; the table in the sunroom with the seedling trays she waters each afternoon; the pale blue ceramic sink, which holds her soap with just a little of its jasmine-honey fragrance, and whose lip is always solid as she uses it to pull herself up.

They had talked about it at first, and she had mopped up the gathering puddles, but as the water kept on returning he started to tell her not to worry. And as it grew, he continued to tell her not to worry. He seemed not to hear the morning strike of his hand echoing through the house.

His knuckles are still on the concrete wall of the water tank. He breaks the usual quiet. "We have to go."

The green of his eyes shift into grey, his cheeks falling from underneath them. A coarse beard grows low on his face, its straggly hairs trying to cover the sag between his chin and neck. They continue towards the stretched opening of his t-shirt.

"Today."

And so she unfolds crumpled plastic bags from the bottom drawer, shaking water off them, and harvests the peas, celery, and silverbeet, cutting even the smallest leaves, and the ones which the snails had got to. The frying pan, plates, cutlery, dishcloths, she assembles into a plastic tub with lemons, and rice, and salt, and spices, and mayonnaise, and two half-used packets of mince from the freezer.

She hears the vacuum from the garage, some bangs and scrapes, and the opening and shutting of the van door. The van, a Toyota Super Custom somehow still going from 1998, probably hasn't been cleaned in three . . . four years. He calls her, having folded the back seats down and pulled pieces of ply over their gaps and then the spongy mattress over the top, followed with pillows and their duvet in white, frothed cover.

"Will you be able to sleep?" he asks.

He hasn't put on sheets and the pleated curtains are barely hanging on to their tracks, but she knows a part of him has tried, or tried to try. And it is dry. He crammed mandarins from the tree next to old CD cases in the arm rest compartment, and all the other nooks. His fishing rod is lying under the bed next to the chilly bin; three red wine bottles are jammed into the spare tire. All the empty bottles and cans, usually rolling around on the van's floor, are instead in the corner of the garage.

"Yes."

She pulls her grey dress into the passenger seat. He packs an open box of tan and white Lion Browns behind her seat, calling them half strength at 4% and fishing one out. Since the cupholder is full of mandarins, he holds it as he drives.

As he guides the van up the driveway, the bare garden still reaches for water. They don't bother to close the garage.

In town, only the welfare office is open, with people milling around in polar fleece. When they turn towards the sun, a bright white disk glaring through the cloud, he shakes then crumples the can and drops it at her feet. At the traffic lights, he digs around for his Swiss Army Knife, then clips his fingernails out the window, and asks her to pass him another. At his third request, on State Highway One south of Tirau, she says, "No."

The cloud lifts as the towns and derelict shops are left behind, and the air thins with cold. Tall mountains surround an elevated valley and are in turn surrounded by dark bush. A shadowed river turns through them. It carries more death than life. In the space made between the sky and land, the motorway cuts straight through farmland into the abrupt bush.

The seal on the road cuts in and out. Each tree is dense with life, vines, moss, epiphytes, and leaves she couldn't begin to categorise. The beauty of the landscape makes her anxious, for his eyes stray from the road. One of his hands tremors on the wheel, the other is balled in a fist, thumb tucked in, hanging from the armrest.

The river beside the road runs in the opposite direction, its muddy shoulders littered. It lies low but catches white from the sun's disk and threads it through moving surfaces. Behind it, the bush swallows light, instead emanating the crumbly smell of dead wet trees. On the other side, houses interrupt the dark trees with white and grey. He calls them "shacks" but she quite likes them, weatherboards clustered together with gasps of pale smoke blowing from their chimneys. They are always in between rises of the mountains, in small valleys which lead to, and overlook the river.

Deeper, young pig hunters gather in long coats behind their utes, tilting their chins as the van passes, dogs on leashes. Eyes stick to them through the wet plastered on the window. Her hands seek warmth on the inside of his arm, her blood unmoving. Horses stand quietly at the sides of the road, sticks tangled in their manes.

He pulls in by a turn of the river. The bank is tangled with paper McDonald's bags and burger boxes, clothes matted into the mud; a condom wrapper and a dirty, torn plastic bag; a slug-eaten Woodstock box and a Smirnoff Ice bottle, sliver typography still gleaming. A Lion Brown can falls when she opens the door. She places it back onto the rubber mat with the others.

From his blue chilly bin with the white lid, he pulls his jelly, a limp artificial fish fading from light green to pink, shot through with glitter and plastic googly eyes. She holds it as he stills his hands enough to carefully impale it with a hook. It hangs flaccid and heavy at the end of the line.

He casts towards a shadow in the wide, slow twist of the river. She sees another, hiding in the fallen branches of a Tōtara. The water curves and cuts and eddies into whirlpools. He lights a durrie, which is eventually pressed into the wet grass when the hook catches on the bottom. He jerks the rod, snapping the line. The jelly is lost.

With that sticky, white Swiss Army Knife, he cuts open an empty beer can, pulling it into a flat sheet. Opening the little springed scissors, he cuts a shape mirroring his wide thumb, which he then twists, and pierces once at the top and once at the bottom. As she holds the metal twist, he passes the loop of a hook through the bottom piercing, and then ties the line through the other. Again his hand rattles inside the chilly bin, this time pulling out a full can of lager. After a chug, he casts again. Sick currents gulp around fallen branches.

The sandflies start biting her wrists, wet grass wicks onto her ankles. It is cold but he keeps flicking his lure. Leaving him, she follows the gentle sound of a waterfall up the river, only to find that the sound was an illusion, caused by shallowness and the rough, rocky bed churning the water. The bank rots black into the river. Small things struggle on the surface of the tumultuous water—leaves, sticks, petals, bark, bubbles.

"What are you doing baby?" His voice from behind, calling her back.

He is still, beer in hand, and eyes on her as she trembles back over the bank. Turned towards her, his swollen belly is balanced by the breadth of his shoulders. His hair is thinning on top, his forehead spiking into it in long, pale, finger-like horns.

Returning, she brings him a wet fallen kōtukutuku and a pale blue stone, lapping at the edges of him with small things. Despite everything, his skin is so soft. She breathes into his warm collarbone.

He shows her his tangled, caught line, the shadows, and telling disturbances in the water.

"They're there . . . they just don't bite."

He cuts the line, and hands her a tangled piece, which she winds tightly around her fingers into a cutting coil. Standing on the edge, they watch ripples on the surface and the slow shadows.

"We've spooked them," he tells her.

His red puffer jacket—a warning against the dark bush behind and dissipated grey sky. Her dress—grey streaked with black bank.

"Trout are very visual fish."

Their reflections impose themselves on the riverbed, their bodies full of moving water and warping rocks. The sound of the river breathes between them.

The air is damp, heavy, and clear. Only a high, thin veil of grey disperses the glare of the sun, taking its warmth but not its light. The sun is beginning its descent. The road cuts away from the river, traversing a mountain's side to the interiority of the range, where the valley lies. The valley is an absence, its ground gently dipping towards the centre, ravaged in broken boulders pointing at the sky.

She listens to the sound of the engine being carried by the hard browns and greys of the valley. The van seems to struggle, although the road has flattened out. The valley is a place where water should collect, or spring from the Earth clean before gathering its darknesses.

"We should look, I want to look." A thick acidic plea which is familiar through her lips.

He cuts the engine at the valley's bank, where the bush presses at its edges. Silence slips in. She feels heavy as she drops from the van. A clump of tī kōuka mark where the soft soil of the bush is stripped down to stone. Garlands of pōānanga hang from them, drawn down towards the earth, the white stars of the bush unusually still on their long necks.

She steps into the world of rocks. The valley is a pathless place, with boulders in every direction. Large chunks, twice her height, almost grid the bowl, a scattered and inconsistent labyrinth. He follows her. As they press into the valley, stones move underfoot, and often slip out, their impacts cutting through the silence. Wide passages narrow between boulders, or the ground becomes thick with stones on top of stones, the solid bed of the valley lost. It is dry. They move away from the sinking sun; his shadow diving past her and fragmenting on rocks ahead of them.

He falls on his bad knee.

Placing her hand on it she says, "Just stay, let's rest here."

She pulls open his backpack. Red wine, Lion Browns, chips, some peas lipped from their shells. Tin mugs and salted fingers. Traces of mandarin peels under fingernails. His breathing labours after a durrie. She looks up from his full mug of red to find his eyes green again, waiting, and on hers.

"We'll keep going tomorrow."

He sloshes more red wine into her mug, hand tremoring still. The edges of things are blunted now, shadows softened and fading.

From here, they can see the forms of the mountains, relentlessly circling their valley, both enclosing and holding. And the valley itself, a broken mountain, fallen, and despite all the rocks, stones, and pieces, empty. Nothing growing. No water, no soil. Only stones, some smoothed with time and others layered with rough edges as if they had just split.

She feels dark grit in the meetings of her teeth, her stomach swimming. Their mouths touch.

The two figures move back to the edge of the valley, faint shadows lengthening behind them. The sun falls behind the mountains. Precarious at the valley's bank, by the tī kōuka, the figures open their van and pull things out of it. The sky takes time to darken, particles colluding to catch light and turn it into purple before the night settles. A cold artificial light goes on.

They sit at the open back of the van, on metal and canvas fold out camping chairs, watching the night pool at the centre of the valley and flood outwards. Dark fluid moves from outside their bodies to inside, filling in the rough passages and smoothing broken things. Night falls deeper and deeper, but then, there are always darknessess.

After each beer he gets up, places the can on the ground and crumples it under a single, quick strike of his greyed sneaker. She feels heavy again, her arms bowing towards the Earth from their canvas slings. The stars are blanketed, their light dissipated into a sky that's not quite black. His durrie smoke signals in the still air between them; moths fly to the battery powered plastic lantern, but don't stay—disappearing back into the darkness. He stares towards the valley, and she stares at his pale eyelid moons pulling tides in her. His electric toothbrush runs out of battery. Their toothpaste spit gleam side by side on the ground. Her mouth is powdery, even after brushing her teeth.

The van windows catch their alcohol breath and sweat. The mattress dips, the ply bowing with their weight. He presses her chest down, the already tender place where she can feel her heartbeat and there isn't much between the skin and bone.

"Don't worry," he says, "don't worry, baby," holding her shoulders now.

And afterwards, a sweaty sort of pride, some muted sort of feeling. Just beneath her breasts, his face is breathing into her side and his arm under and around her. She is there, soft and cool in the warmth of his stress, wrapped in the white froth duvet. A drop of dark liquid glints in the dip between her collarbones.

Like the valley, she lies still without sleeping—at times he lifts from his own darkness to meet her, pulling her hand to his chest, mewling words she doesn't reply to—letting him sink back. He smells stronger than 4%. She watches to see if something has changed, her eyes on the places the light hits, and the forms she knows are there.

The dark liquid overflows the dip, seeping along her collarbones and up her neck. She unravels herself from him and sits up. The liquid clings to her neck, and as she tries to pull it away it only grows downwards, between and then over her breasts. It is wet but bulbous, ballooning around her instead of spilling away. She slides open the van door and climbs down from the foam mattress, careful not to wake him. Frost licks her woolen socks.

She moves into the valley, feet unsteady on rocks. The liquid continues to grow. At the valleys center, she is so heavy, so burdened, her body bulbous and weighed down with wet darkness. It bursts now, pools at her ankles, grows, sucks in her legs, her torso, her. The water is disturbed by their cut-up afternoon shadows, which are now moving slowly, seeking rock ledges and other parts of themselves.

In the morning, the sky is low, so low it meets the grey lake. A figure stands red on the shore looking onto her cold surface. Crumpled beer cans float just beyond his reach. Small ripples of light lap at their edges, pressed up by shadows. He is too far to see the telling disturbances in the lake's centre. He walks her edge, rocky, then bush, and then cutty grass where he can go no further. He pushes off the shore, swimming over the broken boulders. He swims deeper, limbs thinning as the dark sets in. On the bank, a cluster of pōānanga hang, catching wind; a van sits silent; a pīwakawaka chases a sandfly; and a red puffer jacket lies still, wicking mist from the grass.

Because the Sky Is Black

• DELAINA THOMAS •

because the sky is black that one star rising
through bare trees looks brighter than its small body

a man who hunts down children got my boy
my boy was walking in his sleeping self through those trees

when he heard the man laugh he couldn't see to run
because the sun wouldn't come out of the reef

I should've kept his eyes in my pocket
like stones turned them over in my fingers warm counting

but they rolled out while I slept the dead mother
I keep the fire going all night turning through the embers

I see into the fire I see my boy's eyes turned inside down to black
waves my boy was a stone to the man who was a shadow

because the sun didn't belong to us it didn't shrink the man
my boy sank out of his parts screaming so loud I couldn't hear

he lost his eyes looking for me his eyes sucked out by the shadow
feeling my way in the dark to him my fingers going numb

my feet wet from the grass no one will know where I have gone

The Center Cannot Hold (II)

• MELISSA MICHELLE CHIMERA •

Emissaries from the Arab World, Envision: A Queer/Trans Arab Multiverse

• Ahimsa Timoteo Bodhrán •

1.

Continually folding, expanding, we tesseract, we multiply and permutate; there are floodings of fluids; the way gas expands; we ignite; we are plasma of blood pulsing and stars igniting themselves in night sky. Our darkness is infinite. We are matter and energy immeasurable by white standards. There are new observatories for us to see ourselves; we look backwards and forwards in space-time. We are new astronomers reshaping astrolabes to chart ancient seas; how deep our water is—salty, brackish, fresh, chlorine. We are all the elements on the chart tessellating; periods pulsing becoming semicolons slipping into commas convulsing into ellipses; so many ovular orbits, we synchronize; our syntax shakes systems. Supernovae, there are nuclear reactions, fission and fusion, stray electrons, neutrinos shooting through planets, across galaxies, gravitons. I am seeking you, soulmate, across echoes, black holes' ejecta, perhaps in this galaxy or universe you are not, but you are traversing planes to reach me; I wait for you in the future and in the past. There is such a presence here. I feel you across nebulae, arteries redshifting the blueprints of our alveoli, re-oxygenated galactic filaments, pleural walls, so(u)ls supercluster around each other, beyond binary, we circle each other's paths. So many comets entering and leaving our systems, burning and icing cycles, venting and sealing intrastellar seed vaults, some trace memory of what we were that we might become again, such cosmic dust and ash, vestigial, swirling.

2.

All these stars are ours, so named, as if we belong to them, familial, as if our destinies are already consecrated, constellated in the systems we visited before we came here, before we, many-vesseled, birthed from waters, primordial, pre- and post-human these humidities, these wetnesses within and between our flesh. Our desires everdarkening, illuminating infinite, our skins radiantly reflective of rainbows our irises can't register yet, so ultraviolet, infrared, heat and hearing, scored and searing, micro- and radio-waved, X- and gamma-rayed, our genders galloping, unbound, recombinant, glistening in our resurgent tetrachromacies. I want to feel you fully, unbridled, in all my matrimonial senses. The scent of your lightning lingering after storm . . . taste and touch thunderclap, my body recovering—hold me holding you upright—rebalance my proprioception. Echolocate these emissions. Nocturnal, the electricity between us lights up the dark. Static, somatic, we see each other in glimpses, know each other through brief embraces, trace back in blood all that we were before.

3.

Our peoples everywhere, our Arabness in all peoples. Our world, a cosmos. Most of us knowing our sacred geometries, how we, tensile, textured, fit; tectonic, tantalize; geodesic, each sphere ensconced within another; our deep-down cores pulsing, metallic, liquid, sublimating with cale-satis-faction; such succulent subduction zones, mantles of muddled masculinity and femininity writhing, rolling over each other; proof all things melt in queer desire, that proximal, magmatic, red-black; crisp-crucibled, glowing, bioluminescent, our internal and external navigations, limitless, fractal, frenetic. Deca-, hecto-, kilo-, mega-, giga-, tera-, peta-, exa-, zetta-, yotta-; deci-, centi-, milli-, micro-, nano-, pico-, femto-, atto-, zepto-, yocto-; gracious grams of gratitude, luscious liters leaking, muscled meters massaged, sultry seconds sucked, radians of appreciative apertures agape, dilated degrees pushed past absolute zero toward absolute heat, joules jangling in our celestial crowns. How immense, how infinitesimal. We exist within each other; engulf; we intersect at right angles, acutely flex, canine clench and feline stretch; scissor flakes of folded paper burnt to bone, snow misting into flame; hexagonal, octahedral, our inner chambers and outdoor cathedrals, interfaithcongregant-full, walls of stone asweat, concentric and interlocking, grinding, re-rendered tumbler-smooth, slurried, rippling, voraciously veined, arboreal arabesque, vines of verdant vestiture enlace, hallowed hearth, breath upon breath between species, conversant in cubics, we grid, four-dimensional, form heavenly configurations, murmurations of symbiosis. Each swirl and dot, wave and particle, quantum these calligraphied skins shed and re-bed, -bred. Quills quivering re-inked, re-welled, re-thinked, cartographies of cursives re-linked, elementary these educations, ancient untaught discursives now subversive, re-script, every ursine sleeper cell awoken, each exonymed explicative re- and de-claimed, re-enacted, counteracted, teleplayed in radio waves only now reaching us. Every system, pre- and post- this one, of writing, speaking, glyphs that glottal, trilled tongues, never stop, hieroglyph and cuneiform, alphabet and abugida, abjad and syllabary, logographies, multilabial this tongue lapping, committing cellular to memory, mitochondrial, miraculously multiple and mutant, pungent pendulous sways, forests of cherry stems, multigenerational, migratory, our ululation, uvula in perpetual motion, our fingers a blur of hummingbird wings whipping a whistle register.

4.

Centuries from now, millennia, indigo- and golden-houred, meteor-showered, we will be gathering cedar, beading shells, plaiting sweetgrass, tying tobacco, chipping obsidian, smithing silver. None of this is new, us being on each other's shores, beneath dual moons, in each other's bloodlines, our tongues twinned in each other's mouths, fingers, six or more, enlaced. Across many terrains we will carry this message: We have always been travelers; we have always left sand in each other's jeans/genes.

This language is the text for my video of the same name, created for "So The Darkness May Glitter: Queer & Trans Arab Futures," a screening curated by Janine Mogannam, for the Queer Cultural Center's 2021 National Queer Arts Festival.

Facing Forward

• KĒHAU NOE •

SO I'VE SEEN.

Infestation

• LEHUA PARKER •

On a lava outcrop surrounded by ocean on three sides, 'Ilima in the shape of a yellow poi dog picked her way to Piko Point. Waves hissed along the edges, filling nooks and crannies with what would become pockets of salt in the sun.

To the west, a makau moon descended over the sea, guiding wanderers through the dreamlands of Pō.

To the east, wispy clouds thickened against the pali rising above Lauele, O'ahu. *Rain in the morning,* 'Ilima thought with a glance at the sky. *But rain or shine, tourists will still come. When you're on vacation, all days are beach days. Pohō, that.* She flicked her tail. *Surely, Kalei will understand.* She sighed. *Or not. Niuhi like to paddle their own way.*

Each step toward Piko Point took her farther from the beach pavilion and the two-lane highway hugging the coast. Across the highway were Hari's convenience store and the second-story apartment where 'Ilima and Kahana, her human companion, lived. Hari's was the place to buy rainbow shave ice, musubi, or rock salt plum; a place where old futs like Kahana nursed cold drinks on the lanai, playing games of remember when.

Drenched in moonlight, 'Ilima paused, observing stars, winds, and currents. *All systems go.* She shook from nose to tail, rolling her head and twisting her shoulders. It felt good to leave the human world behind, if only for an hour or two. She licked her lips; the reef's tang of limu and old fish blood tickled the back of her throat.

As she breathed in the salted night air, an offshore breeze carried the scent of stale cooking oil, kiawe smoke, and teri beef—the ghost of one of Hari's plate lunch specials. *Food!* 'Ilima's eyes widened. *I should've brought Kalei something. Pork laulau, chicken adobo—something, anything. Food is the quickest way to a shark's* heart. She snorted. *Well, food or sex, and that's not happening, not even in times as desperate as these.*

Leaping over a puddle and ignoring a cast-off crab shell, 'Ilima continued to the large tide pool at the end of Piko Point. The pool had a hidden tunnel leading through the reef and out to the great blue deep. It was the traditional port for Niuhi sharks transitioning from sea to land and the easiest place to meet.

Her ears drooped as she considered her strategy. *Playing messenger isn't Kalei's thing, but maybe I can convince him.* She lifted her head and perked her ears. *Whatevers. If he says no, I'll find another way. He's not my last hope.*

Her tail wavered. *Unless he is.*

At the edge of the tide pool sat Pōhaku, a light gray basalt rock the size and shape of a big beach ball and the unofficial go-between of humans and the ancient sea-dwelling po'e o nā mo'olelo. As 'Ilima approached Pōhaku, she spotted a dark shape lounging in the water.

"Marco!" A sudden splash sent ocean spray bitter as a sea urchin up her nose. She shifted to her human form with a sneeze.

"Kalei!"

"No, you're supposed to say 'Polo,'" Kalei mocked, splashing her again.

"Uoki, Kalei! I mean it! That water went up my nose." 'Ilima dabbed her face with the edge of the yellow kīkepa her human shape wore and sneezed again.

"Bless you," he laughed. "Or whatever it is humans say."

"Bless you or gesundheit." 'Ilima sniffed and dropped her kīkepa. "At least that's what Kahana says."

"Gesundheit. What a strange word." In his human form, Kalei climbed out of the tide pool and stood dripping in the moonlight, water shedding like pearls off his skin.

"Pants!" 'Ilima said.

"You're such a prude. Too long among humans, you."

"Pants or I'm leaving. Now."

"A malo. We'll split the difference." Kalei wrapped a length of cloth around his loins and hips, snugging it tight. "You're late."

"I couldn't get away. Kahana was watching an old kung fu movie."

"You're lucky I had decent company and stayed." He jerked his thumb to the stone. "Pōhaku's been filling me in on all the Lauele gossip."

'Ilima inclined her head to the stone. "Aloha e Pōhaku. It's good to see you."

As a stone-bound being, Pōhaku spoke in thoughts that rose in their minds like bubbles in a lava lamp. ALOHA E 'ILIMA, he replied. IT'S GOOD TO BE SEEN.

Leaving his feet dangling in the water, Kalei sat on the edge of the pool and eased back against Pōhaku. "So what's the big— auwī! What the—?" He rubbed his shoulder and peered at the stone. "Eh, Pōhaku! You're covered in kūpeʻe!" One by one, he began plucking the sea snails, popping them like berries between his fingers. "Auwē," he tsked. "So many! Kahana's slacking in his duties. 'Ilima must not be letting him out of the house again."

'Ilima crossed her arms. "I have no control over what Kahana does. Humans don't listen to me."

IT'S NOT KAHANA'S FAULT. KŪPEʻE MOVE SO FAST.

Kalei smirked. "Snails *are* faster than old men. Probably smarter, too."

EVERYTHING'S RELATIVE, Pōhaku thought, his words thick like guava jelly. DANGER. PLEASURE. EVEN SPEED AND SIZE.

"Spoken like a stone," Kalei said, tossing crushed kūpeʻe to fish. "There. All better now." He gave Pōhaku at pat.

MAHALO E KALEI, the thought a warm orange kite rising in the sky. BUT TOMORROW THEY'LL BE BACK. The image of storm clouds and broken string.

"Don't be so glum!" Kalei said, brushing the last fragments of shells and meat from his fingers. "No worries, Pōhaku. The future takes care of itself."

"Spoken like a shark," 'Ilima muttered.

Kalei stilled, his focus drawn to ʻIlima like a red lehua floating in the sea. "A Niuhi, you mean."

ʻIlima cocked her head. "Isn't that what I said?"

Kalei gave her a sly look and whistled. "Come, ʻIlima," he called, slapping the ground next to him. "Sit."

"Watch it." ʻIlima's eyes narrowed.

"So sensitive, eh Pōhaku?"

IT'S A MATTER OF PERSPECTIVE, Pōhaku thought.

Kalei's smile held too many teeth. "She knows what I mean."

"Let's pretend I don't," ʻIlima said.

"Just what I said, *come sit with me*." ʻIlima didn't move. "Don't believe me?" Kalei held out his hands and spread his arms wide. "There's plenty of room to cool your feet." He slapped the ground again. "Come. Sit. Lean against Pōhaku with me. He won't mind."

I WON'T.

"See?"

ʻIlima shook her head. "I'll sit over here, thanks." She carefully lowered herself, tucking her kīkepa under her knees.

"Don't trust me?"

"After all we've been through?" ʻIlima rolled her eyes. "Trust isn't the issue."

He frowned. "Sounds like it is."

"No." She paused to smooth the fabric. "Ever look in a mirror?"

"Whatever for?"

"In your human form, Kalei, you're Mr. Aloha come to life, all rippling muscle and so deliciously ʻono, women—and a few men—can't resist. You're used to people coming on to you that way. But I'm not a woman. Not really."

"You're not a dog, either, but not even Kahana recognizes that." He flashed his teeth. "Admit it. You like soft couches and kibble."

She curled her lip. "Careful, Kalei. I still have all my teeth."

"Oh, good," he said, "something to look forward to."

'Ilima smiled, but it didn't reach her eyes. "As handsome as your human form is, it's not what interests me."

"Your loss."

She took a deep breath. "I need your help. We have a problem."

"*We* have a problem? You got a gecko in your pocket, 'Ilima?"

She stiffened her spine. "Yes, *we*."

He narrowed his eyes. "Aren't you the one always saying Niuhi belong in the water?"

"It concerns everyone, land and sea," she said.

"A human problem, then?"

"Yes."

Kalei crossed his arms and shifted his weight. "Why me? Does your human problem have a biting solution?"

"I'm not sure."

"But it's not off the table?"

'Ilima shrugged.

"Excellent," Kalei said. "Tell me more."

As she gathered her thoughts, 'Ilima's eyes swept the shadowy shoreline and the night-empty beaches of Nalupuki and Keikikai. With everyone safely in bed, no porch lights welcomed or lit the way home. Slipping her tongue between her lips, she tasted Lauele's hopes and dreams as they journeyed across the water, fleeing dawn and the bustle of day. *Things are different in the dark,* she thought. *Quieter. Simpler.*

"Times are changing," she said.

Kalei rolled his eyes. "How profound. I expected more from you, 'Ilima."

"I'm talking about the pandemic."

"*Pan*demic?"

"Yeah. Worldwide."

"Here? In Lauele?"

'Ilima nodded. "The past year or so."

He shook his head. "I remember *epi*demics." Kalei kept count with his fingers. "Venereal disease, a gift from Cook's crew. Then cholera, influenza, mumps, measles, whooping cough, smallpox, leprosy—it's hard to keep track. Human sickness ebbs and flows like a tide."

"Yeah, back when disease came by ship. Airplanes are much faster. Now the whole world gets sick at once. Modern disease is no tide," 'Ilima said. "It's a tsunami."

"But there weren't more offerings. I would've noticed. Remember the 1800s?" Kalei mused. "Back then bodies were stacked four deep on the docks waiting for canoes to take them out beyond the reef."

'Ilima shrugged. "Modern diseases don't always kill. At least, not everybody." She leaned against a rock, settling deeper onto the damp lava. "Remember Kalaupapa?"

"Of course. Ever try leprosy?" Kalei shuddered. "Ugh. *Chewy*."

With a sigh, 'Ilima swept her long, dark hair into a bun and knotted it on the top of her head. "Can you at least try to think about something other than your stomach for once?"

"You're in a mood," Kalei said. "Kahana buy you a flea collar again?"

She ignored the barb. "To stop the pandemic from spreading, humans declared the entire world Kalaupapa. Everybody had to stay in one place. Nobody could leave."

Kalei laughed. "But rats don't stay in one place."

"This time they did. Human governments forbade travel."

"*Forbade?* And people listened?" Kalei reached down and rubbed Pōhaku. "Eh, Pōhaku, you hear that? We're back to the old days of kapu! Chiefs decree and people obey. Get ready! Kahana's going to put you back on temple hill."

AN OFFERING OF POI WOULD BE NICE. THREE-DAY OLD AND THICK AS YOUR FINGER.

"With pua'a smokey and hot from the imu," Kalei said. "None of this fake banana leaf-wrapped crockpot—"

"Enough, you two," 'Ilima snapped. "The past is past. Humans are not going back to kapu laws."

Kalei rested his head against Pōhaku. "But you said governments *forbade*. That's a big word. What happened to democracy?"

She shrugged. "Extraordinary times, extraordinary measures. But it happened. Just last month Kahana and I walked Waikīkī from Kahanamoku to Kaimana on *sand*. There wasn't an ABC beach mat or umbrella in sight. You really didn't notice?"

"No," Kalei said. "But I'd starve before swimming near Waikīkī. Too sun-screeny. Almost as bad as Hanauma Bay."

LIKE COCONUT CREAM FLOATING ON ICE WATER, Pōhaku thought.

"Vile bilge water, you mean," Kalei grumbled. "That stuff only smells like coconut—fake coconut. It tastes pilau and sticks to your teeth."

"And for a whole year you didn't notice it was gone, Kalei?" 'Ilima said.

He shrugged. "Told you. I stay away from tourist places. Most Niuhi do. It's better for everyone."

'Ilima pinched the bridge of her nose. "You're probably right. But trust me. Because of the travel kapu, there was no sunscreen or masses of people on the beaches. The 'aina and kai rested. But it's all changing again." She swallowed and looked him dead in the eye. "There's a vaccine, Kalei. The travel kapu is lifting. People are buzzing. They're tired of staying home. A swarm is forming. It's the start of a new perpetual mosquito season."

"So?" Kalei broke eye contact and flicked a crab into the water. "Tourists are always coming. They flock to hotels in Waikīkī and Kō Olina or to short-term rentals in Kailua and Hale'iwa. They stay for a week, maybe ten days, and go home. They leave their money and reduce the tax burden—or so I hear. It's a bit of a trade-off, of course, but they stay in their lanes and we stay in ours. We don't see them if we don't want to."

"Tskah," she scoffed, "There are no lanes anymore. Today five rentals, Wranglers and passenger vans, pulled into the parking lot at Keikikai, one right after the other."

"Oh. Lost on their way to Waimea?"

"No. They meant to come here."

Kalei sat up. "Why?"

"Because they can. They unloaded snorkel gear, boogie boards, and beach umbrellas. They climbed all over Piko Point—"

"How—" Kalei interrupted.

"Social media," 'Ilima said. "Heard of it?"

Kalei rolled his eyes. "I'm vaguely familiar."

"You have no idea, do you?" 'Ilima sighed.

"Like you said, *let's pretend I don't.*"

"Fine. Cell phones—"

"I know phones. 'Reach out, reach out and touch someone,'" he sang.

"That's 1970s phones. Now they're pocket-sized and people carry them everywhere."

"So they can reach out and touch someone?" he teased. "*Everywhere?*"

"People don't carry phones to talk—"

"Then what's the point?" Kalei asked. "Better off carrying a rock."

HEY. Pōhaku's indignation fizzed like soda poured over ice. I'M RIGHT HERE.

'Ilima rubbed her eyes and pinched the bridge of her nose. "I know you're not this naive, Kalei."

"Who me? I'm just a shark," he said. "What do I know about posting photos or video?"

"Uh-huh. So you know social media's the world's new party line. Everybody's connected, all the time."

"*Connected.* Sounds sexy," he purred.

"Get your head out of the gutter," 'Ilima sniffed.

"You're telling me social media's not about sex?"

"It's about being *special*. Everyone's trying to show off new and exotic—"

"Exotic." Kalei grinned, teeth gleaming in the moonlight. "I'll show you *exotic*."

'Ilima squeezed her eyes tight. "Can I just get through this, please?"

Kalei waved a hand. "I'm listening."

"Remember when insider guidebooks became a thing?" 'Ilima said. "*Island Secrets Revealed, Hawaii's Hidden Gems?*"

"Yeah. What idiot came up with that? There's no place to get decent sashimi without standing in line anymore," Kalei groused.

"Those were books. You had to go find books. With social media, access to knowledge is instantaneous. Think of a dead whale's scent trail multiplied by a billion. All the scavengers, local *and* global, immediately know where and when things happen."

"Okay."

"Okay? *Okay?!*" 'Ilima fumed. "Just a few days ago some lōlō with a cell phone stumbled onto Lauele, raved about the pristine reef and beaches on Insta-Snap-Book, and now we're infested with tourists. *We have a problem.*"

"And you want me to bite someone? Is this why we're talking?"

"Argh!" 'Ilima splashed water at him. "This very afternoon, a tourist was sitting at one of the tables at the beach pavilion, eating a poke bowl—"

"You mean a bowl of poke," Kalei interrupted.

"No!" shouted 'Ilima. "A poke bowl! It's not the same thing!"

"Okay. Weird distinction, but okay."

"Kalei, there's a difference between a bowl of poke and a poke bowl that I need you to understand." 'Ilima took a deep breath. "As I walked by, the tourist stuck his chopsticks in the rice at the bottom of his bowl and started clapping his hands at me, shouting, 'Shoo! Get out!' When I turned to look at him, he stood up and waved his arms. 'Get away, you homeless, flea-bitten mutt! Get away from my poke bowl!' Shocked, I just stared. I wasn't anywhere near his poke bowl. And that's when he threw a water bottle at me and tried to chase me off the beach. This beach, Kalei. *Our* beach!"

"Oh. So you need help getting rid of a body. Why didn't you say so?"

"No!" 'Ilima inhaled and counted to three. "No. I didn't hurt him."

Bemused, Kalei asked, "Why? Are you going soft in your old age? Too many puppy snuggle-wuggles with Kahana? Is this about needing me to scratch behind your ears with my sharp shark teeth?"

'Ilima jumped up.

HERE IT COMES, Pōhaku thought, his words splattering like lava from a vent.

As fire flashed along her limbs and steam sizzled from the sea-drenched rock beneath her, 'Ilima's womanly body stretched taller than a coconut tree. She leaned down and hissed with the roaring sound of thunder in the surf. "This is why I can't have a normal conversation with you, Kalei. Of course, I didn't hurt him. It was *daylight*, near the showers by the pavilion at *Keikikai beach*."

Kalei smothered a yawn. "You've killed for far less."

"Argh!" she growled as lightning struck the ocean from a clear blue sky. "This. This is why I choose a dog form." In the blink of an eye, 'Ilima shrank back to normal human-size. She stood at the edge of the tide pool and counted wavelets until she could speak without shrieking. "Times. Have. *Changed*."

"You keep saying that," Kalei said. He stood and reached high over his head, twisting his back and stretching. "Ugh. No TV. No plates of sashimi and wasabi. No bowls of poke or poke bowls— whatever they are. No moonlight swim with a tasty wahine. I can't believe I came ashore and transformed for this."

'Ilima hung her head. "Tell me how you'll feel when Keikikai Bay is covered with tourists doing yoga on SUP boards. Or when Piko Point reeks of human blood from the skinned knees of people climbing over slick lava rock. Or—" She paused and raised her eyes to his. "Or maybe it's different for you. Ocean-born, you can go to the northern islands or Respite Beach. But this is my *home*. It used to be *our* home. Look at what happened to Pōhaku. If Kahana hadn't gone and dug him up, he'd still be forgotten in a landfill."

IT'S TRUE, Pōhaku thought. THE MODERN WORLD IS UNKIND TO THE STONE-BOUND.

'Ilima held her fingers like a camera frame and walked toward Kalei. "Can you imagine what would happen if I'd snapped that tourist in half like I wanted to? Me, in all my glory, all over the world in seconds?" She dropped her hands. "At least humans can wrap their heads around a big shark."

Kalei flexed his muscles. "More big than Jaws?" He laughed. "They couldn't handle *that*."

'Ilima sat back down and crossed her legs. "I thought about asking you to cruise up and down the beaches, Kalei, but people are stupid. Seeing you wouldn't keep them away or even out of the water; it would just bring more lookie-loos. We can't have the chaos your last shark attack caused."

"What chaos? There wasn't any chaos," Kalei said.

"Of course there was. The guys with the hukilau nets."

"Oh. You mean the last attack that made the news," Kalei said.

'Ilima sat up. "What?"

"Nothing." Kalei waved his hand. "Insignificant."

"Kalei."

"What?"

"You can't go around biting people," 'Ilima said.

"Technically, it wasn't a bite." He shrugged. "No body, no crime."

'Ilima massaged her temples. "You're giving me a headache."

"I had a good reason," he said.

HE DID.

"No doubt," she said. "But that's my point. Whatever you did or didn't do—*don't tell me*—it didn't keep people away."

"So we do something more public. Use one of those phone camera-thingies," he said.

'Ilima looked away and watched the waves break over the edge of the reef. Onshore, a rooster crowed. A glance at the mountains told her dawn was just three hours away. *I'm running out of time.* She said, "Kalei, shark attacks spark shark hunts. Tourism associations sponsor bounties. Our ocean ecology is still trying to recover from the last one." She shook her head. "No. Revealing ourselves isn't the answer. We need a different solution."

Kalei stood with his back to Pōhaku and watched an 'iwa bird fly out to sea. A lone car drove along the two-lane highway, blasting Jawaiian music as its headlights lit up hala trees.

"Okay," he said. "The problem is too many tourists are coming, but you don't want me to bite anybody or cruise up and down the beach." He looked down his nose at her. "Right?"

'Ilima sighed. "Right."

"Too bad, so sad." He raised a hand and started counting off options. "We can't take out the road. They'll just build it back again. We can't buy the land and fence it off. Kahana already owns most of Lauele, but the beaches are open to everybody."

"That's the problem," 'Ilima said. "We can't keep them out."

"Humans obey human laws."

"Thank you, Captain Obvious," snorted 'Ilima.

"We need them to change their laws," Kalei said.

"Kapu laws are dead. Democracy, remember? Why are we going in circles? Is this a shark thing?"

"I'm brainstorming. What are humans afraid of?" Kalei mused.

Pōhaku thought, SUCH TINY LITTLE CREATURES.

"Yeah," said Kalei as he scratched his arm. "With such big mouths and appetites." He regarded the moon as it dipped closer to the horizon, stars shining like broken glass through the marine haze. He turned to her. "'Ilima, why come to me? I don't see how anything sharky is going to fix this."

"I said I needed *you*."

"Uh-huh."

"You. Your access to your father's ear."

Pōhaku's laughter tickled like champagne. An image of the great ocean god Kanaloa's ear swelled in their minds.

"Ew, Pōhaku!" 'Ilima groaned. "Did you have to show us hair *and* wax?"

Kalei sighed. "You want me to bring this problem to the mighty Kanaloa."

"Yes. It affects everybody."

"Biting someone's safer," he said. "Kanaloa might decide *you're* the problem."

"I know," 'Ilima said, picking at a salt pocket. "I wouldn't come to you if I had another way."

"You'll owe Kanaloa personally."

"I know."

"And me."

'Ilima rolled her eyes. "Believe me, I *know*. I also know nothing surprises Kanaloa."

"So why—"

"You know why, Kalei." 'Ilima paused. "Kanaloa likes to be *asked*."

"He likes to be owed," Kalei said.

"That, too."

"Me, too," he said with a crooked grin.

'Ilima sighed.

Kalei rubbed his chin and slicked back his hair. "I just don't know what you expect Kanaloa to do."

"I don't either. Something. Anything. Nature finds a way."

Kalei paced. "A hurricane? Sink a bunch of boats? Stop the tradewinds?"

"None of that keeps tourists away," 'Ilima said. "It's our people that get hurt with those kinds of natural consequences—think of salt in taro patches and shredded banana leaves."

Kalei threw up his hands. "Like that matters. In Lauele they don't fear famine anymore. There's no respect for shadows and teeth."

An itch no one can scratch, Pōhaku thought.

"More kūpe'e, Pōhaku? Did I miss one?" Kalei asked.

NATURALLY, IT'S THE LITTLE THINGS THAT MEAN SO MUCH. An image formed in their minds.

'Ilima and Kalei exchanged a look.

"Can he?" 'Ilima asked.

"He's a god, right?" Kalei said. "Go big or go home."

"What doesn't kill you makes you stronger," 'Ilima said.

"Oh, I hope not. Stronger humans? Next, they'll want my teeth," Kalei said.

HUMANS ARE JUST NIUHI WITH DENTAL PLANS. The image of a shark flossing his teeth.

"Brave words when I can just roll you over the edge, Pōhaku," Kalei said.

Like the butterfly wings of a stingray, Pōhaku's laughter drifted through their minds.

'Ilima waved her hand, dismissing the image. "Kalei, I need an answer. Will you speak to Kanaloa?"

He worried his lip for a bit, then nodded. "Fine. I'll do it." As Kalei leaped into the water, he called, "You better pray Father Dear is in a good mood."

"If prayer were all it took, I wouldn't have involved you. Mahalo e Kalei," 'Ilima called as a shark fin slipped through the tunnel and headed out to sea. Walking over to Pōhaku, she laid her hand on the stone. "Think it will work?"

Pōhaku's slow thoughts billowed like a sail in the wind. This time, they tasted of hope.

Two weeks later, the parking lot at Keikikai was full of broadcast vans and reporters, each jockeying for the best position. Behind yellow tape cordoning off the beach, hazmat-suited techs gathered samples from the ocean and tide pools along Piko Point. From their balcony above Hari's, old man Kahana and 'Ilima in the shape of a yellow poi dog enjoyed the show.

"Smell that?" Kahana asked.

'Ilima wagged her tail, ears forward.

"Yeah, it's hard to miss. Hari's got the kiawe coals sizzling. Hulihuli chicken and kalbi. Bet he sells so many plates to the news crews he runs out of mac salad."

'Ilima whined.

"Nah, sistah. No worry. He'll save some for us."

'Ilima poked her head between the railing's bars. *All the better to see you with, my dear.*

Kahana gestured to the guy swinging a Geiger counter along the sand. "Eh, think he's gonna find Myrna's wedding ring?"

'Ilima cocked her head at Kahana and chuffed.

"Oh, right. Geiger counters are for *radiation*. My bad." Kahana hitched up his shorts. "Ho, those guys in the suits must feel like manapua in a steamer. Too bad they can't just jump in the ocean and cool off." He leaned against the banister and shook his head. "So weird. Never seen anybody sick from *snorkeling*. When they rolled the ambulances the first time, I was spearfishing, the Chang kids were jumping off rocks, and Nili-boy was also in the water. Kanani—her auntie's cousin's daughter works at the health department, yeah? Anyway, Kanani said those poor buggahs didn't dare leave their hotel bathrooms for five days. Barely made their flights home."

'Ilima shrugged.

"Ruins your whole vacation." Kahana paused. "Or maybe *runs* is your whole vacation," he chuckled.

'Ilima rolled her eyes.

"C'mon. That was funny."

'Ilima's ears drooped.

"Everyone's a critic," Kahana said with a sigh. "I'm just glad it wasn't Hari's mac salad." He held up his phone. "Check it. *#HariOnolicious* is trending. Gotta love news crews. They're all about the buzz."

'Ilima refused to look.

"Fine. Be like that." Kahana slipped his phone in his pocket as an ice blue Prius pulled into the parking lot. "There she is. That's the one I was telling you about."

'Ilima's ears perked.

Kahana pointed with his chin to the woman climbing out of the car. "Yeah, the one in the green shirt. She's from UH-Mānoa. Sharp. She told me yesterday it's something in the ocean that's making people sick."

'Ilima whined.

"I dunno. It only affects people who aren't from Lauele. Her theory is if you're local, there's something in your guts—your na'au, yeah—that kills whatever it is that makes others sick." Kahana snickered. "She thinks it's all the poke and limu we eat from the reef, but you and I know it's all the fried noodles and chicken katsu everybody orders from Hari's."

'Ilima yawned and stretched.

"Yeah. *Whatevahs*," Kahana said. "Nili's got a new job. He's supposed to hang out at the pavilion and parking lot and warn folks heading to the beaches about the snorkel-trots. Has an official shirt and everything. Word's getting out. Snorkel-trots aren't fatal." He paused. "They think."

Kanaloa, 'Ilima thought. *Nature found a way.*

"The health department's going to leave the crime scene tape and put up signs, but you and I can still go anytime. Nili said."

The woman in the green shirt beeped her car, tossed her keys in a bag, and pulled out a tablet. Kahana shifted his weight. "Akamai, that professor. She'll figure it out. No matter how hard, people always find a way," he mused.

It's the little things, 'Ilima thought.

Kahana pulled out his phone again and punched some buttons. "Posted!" He smiled. "Now everybody knows how lucky we are. *#Blessed*, yeah?"

Clarity Rests

• RASHA ABDULHADI •

for Freddie Gray, from Palestine to Baltimore to the Pacific

All hope is bound to that clarity
to the ashen precipitate that falls and covers all alike
in the afterbirth of a moment we will never transcend.
How can you transcend a boat, a ship, the vessel you arrive in
one that carries, ferries you, all of us, me too
across the river of this rupture.
We arrived riding on the backs of a wave that chose us
something that happened seemed suddenly
that it had always been happening
And we could not be happened to anymore.

This is the event we rode in on: the heat of having been ridden
for so long, so roughly, that we bucked back
kicked back, made the rough riders get back, until
it was them who were bidden by our audacity.

Even now we know we won't transcend
We'll try to extend our arms and get our fingertips
to touch each other around the edges of all we're holding.
With these snapping, popping, straining, burning tendons
we'll shut it down. We'll hold it together, for today at least.
We'll hope that the sediment of our deeds will feed some future,
and all the clarity we hold rests on that hope.

Hummingbirds in the Forest of Needle and Blood

• AHIMSA TIMOTEO BODHRÁN •

Say there is a boy in a village. Say the boy is not always a boy, but today he is. Say he is wandering by cactus, not wanting to be stuck by thorns, but wanting to smell the flowers and gather the fruits, not on each leaf, because he is not greedy, but rather enough to feed himself and his people. Say the boy is stuck by thorns and begins bleeding, gets worried, gets lost, gets stuck by more thorns. Say the boy collapses, exhausted, and he is not sure where his tears end and the blood begins. Say he is crying, and the sound echoes through the forest of nopal. Say the wind carries that sound to another boy, a boy whittling wood, sharpening stones. Say that boy drops what he is doing, and picks them up again, ties them with leather, and goes searching for that voice. Say that boy hurries, and he is pricked by thorns. Say that boy begins bleeding, and crying, but keeps moving through the forest of thorned ovals and red fruit, each heart glistening with its own blood. Say the boy begins to echo the first voice with his own, weaving it, tying it with leather. Say each boy gets louder, but they are still separated by walls. Say each boy is frantic, crying, trying to reach the other. Say the walls are covered with blood. Say the walls get thinner, thornier, and one hand grasps another. And the cactus is just a sheath of breath, leather between two hearts, raon-raon-light, colibrí-quick. Say the boys slow down till they can find an opening in the wall, crack they can leverage, space they can push their bodies through. Say there will be more blood, more tears, more cactus between them. Say it will not matter. Say the second boy will bind the wounds of the first boy with leather, wood to splint his leg, stone to dig out any thorns. Say the first boy will feed the second some fruit, blot his blood with petals, dust his cheeks and chest with pollen. Say the second boy will bind their wrists with leather, not too tight, but enough to keep them from getting lost. Say the first boy will place their things in his basket. Say the second boy will grab a stick to keep them walking. Say they keep walking. Say they keep bleeding. Say they keep crying. Say they leave the forest of needle and blood. Say they return to this place, again and again, and gently touch each leaf. Say the wind keeps their story. The ground, their stories. Say their descendants keep returning, generation after generation, to gather fruit, make offering of pollen, point to the place of dried red-brown on green-pricked leaves, higher up on the branches each year, leave some leather, newly cut, some stones, newly polished. Say the blood we drink from each fruit is their own. Say this is story. Ours.

Sinta

• VERONICA MONTES •

Our skin is fine as rice paper; our bones make strange sounds in the night. We are old now, and it's time for you to hear the truth of how we came to be. I'll whisper these things in the dark, like a coward, while you sleep. I'm too tired to fend off your anger, too tired to stoke the fire of my own.

Are you sleeping? Sleep.

I'm the girl from years ago who slipped into the Peñablanca forest at night to meet you. I know you remember, as I remember: we didn't search for soft places to lie, but took each other where we stood, and then laughed at the bruises that bloomed like flowers on our backs and knees. You liked to say my name: *Sinta*.

One dark night, a new moon night, we crashed against the gnarled trunk of a balete tree. "Tabi tabi po," we whispered to the tree spirits, begging their pardon for any disturbance. "Tabi tabi po," as our mothers had taught us. When we were done, we found a cold spring at the base of the tree under a braided shelter of hanging roots. You kissed me and bathed me, and we were shivering and fevered all at once. But we forgot, my love, to whisper *tabi tabi po*. We forgot what our mothers had taught us.

We said goodbye at the crossroads, as we had many nights before, and that is the last time you saw me as I was. I walked towards home with my heart full of you and the forest, but after a few moments I became consumed with the idea of starting the night all over again. As I turned to find my way back to you a great force knocked me to the ground. When I woke my eyes were covered with leaves and bound with a rag and something—a duende, perhaps, or kapre, I still do not know—tied my wrists and ankles with vines. "Tabi tabi po," I said. "Please. Tabi tabi po." But it was too late.

The creature menaced me and called me wicked names. Bitch, it said, and vixen and whore. She-devil, witch, temptress, until I began to believe. Worse, I stopped thinking of you as the boy who brought me squares of Spanish lace and picture postcards of faraway places. You became a stranger instead, someone depraved and easily seduced by the sinful offering I made of my body. When my belly grew round, my shame became unbearable; it was then that the creature relented. It freed my limbs and uncovered my eyes, but I was warned never to look at it—I never did—and never to leave the cave.

When my time came the creature lurked behind my head and screamed with excitement each time my body contracted, each time I cried out. I covered my ears, but I could still hear its voice echo off the high cave walls, more tortuous by far than my birthing pains. When I was done it stood in the shadows. "This child will be the price you pay for your whoring," it said. "Nourish her with your milk, then leave this place and never come back."

I know now that I should not have left her, but on that day I wept with relief and stumbled out of the forest. At the gate to my home my father's soldiers took me for a stranger, and they pushed me gently this way and that until I could do nothing but leave. It was then I realized I was changed—wholly changed—on the inside, yes, but also my face, the shape of me, the way I moved.

Three years later you found me selling lanzones at the open market for a woman who had grown too old to run her stall. I was bold when I caught your eye; I willed you to recognize me, though I knew you would not. I offered you a taste of the fruit. "It's sweet and sour all at once," I said. "But the seeds are bitter."

That's all of it.

I know you remember, as I remember: our days together have been more bad than good. You hated me because I was not Sinta, and I hated you for not knowing that I was. I *am*. I couldn't tell you about the creature, the cave, our child—you with your thin patience and rage. I am no better, I know that. All these years I've done what I couldn't do when my wrists were bound with vines: I fought and clawed. I drew your blood.

I wish we had learned long ago to say the right words before all is lost; I wish we had listened to our mothers. Absolve me now of the wrongs I've committed, and I'll do the same for you. Isn't this something our mothers also taught us? Patawarin mo ako, my love. *Forgive me*. Pinapatawad kita. *I forgive you.*

Melting Teeth

• JOCELYN KAPUMEALANI NG •

A Lurking Horror

• TAMA WISE •

The concussive smash of breaking glass was followed by a piteous whimpering.

Malo ducked his head in through the open door. Just enough time to look and take in the scene within. What he saw stuck in his mind. She had been crawling about the floor, picking eyeballs from amongst a sea of knitting detritus, zippers and corduroy buttons. She worked with a desperate quickness, plucking her prizes before they spoilt.

"Satanic nun," Drew whispered, from his side of the door, grinning.

Obvious reference to her habit. Malo rolled his eyeballs, managing a wry smile despite the tension. He took a deep breath, tightening his grip about his antiquated flintlock. Across the way, Drew was going through the same mental preparation with his baseball bat.

Malo stepped through the door, seeing the nun still squatting, picking out fingers from the broken glass. He raised his pistol, and the bang it gave was as loud as the sound of the dropped jar. On the shelf behind the nun, another three jars exploded.

"Fuck!"

The broken woman who looked to be pushing eighty moved with an inhuman grace, her body rolling away from the shot like water about a rock. The weirdness of it surprised Malo briefly, but experience kept him from being stunned.

"Hail Mary!" Drew shouted. Go long.

Malo grabbed up his second flintlock, promising not to miss again. He saw his partner dash along the side of the room, a cluttered refectory packed with instruments of prayer, and personal effects. Drew ran with the grace of the athlete he was, a jock through and through. Malo's second shot boomed with a shower of sparks, hitting its mark. The scent of gunpowder was overbearing now.

The nun let out a shriek that pierced Malo's ears. The last thing he saw was Drew dashing forward, baseball bat raised, ready for the home run swing. Malo's mind exploded in lights and stars. He heard a crash and caught sight of Drew rolling, several meters back from where he had been.

The opportunity was lost. Now it was all the home team's advantage.

The huffing noise bounced about the high ceilings. Malo crawled on all fours towards Drew. He was still pulling himself up. Stunned. There was a tight, stretched chuckle somewhere within the shadows.

"Since when have the newly risen had that sort of brain lightning?" Drew complained. Malo was caught by habit as he turned his partner's head. No blood from his ears.

"This isn't a milk run."

"When is it ever?"

Malo pressed himself back against the desk, knowing full well it would do nothing as cover against the nun. He drew a hot breath, running his hands through his thick, flowing afro. Drew looked focused, but Malo could see how his knuckles were standing, his grip on his bat so tight.

"Silly, silly boys . . ."

To Malo, her voice smelt like chalk dust. He had the distinct impression that she was somewhere high above. In his mind he could still see that mental image of her, her habit drawn about her like shadows. He had disturbing images, reminded all too readily of Whoopie Goldburg. Made worse was her age and those torpedo breasts, like that Madonna video. Nothing about her was human any more.

"What now?" Drew murmured. Malo was thinking that himself. She shouldn't be this advanced so close to the turn.

"I can smell your silly dreams," she toyed. Malo glanced up, but there were no rafters to hang from. "Your sinful, dirty relationship." There was a sharp intake of breath, and she sounded surprised when she spoke again. "He has the secret smell of one of us . . . Do you ponder that when you lay with him at night?"

The truth didn't bother Malo, just that it came from her. Drew was looking upwards, his nostrils flaring a hint. He pointed left, twice, a military signal. His father must have had such high hopes for him, Malo thought. He just nodded. He didn't need to look there, lest he give away the game. Just trust his partner.

Drew leapt over the desk, scattering things in his wake as he let out a roar. Malo kept low, running about it, his hand going to the katana at his back. He saw the distinct inky darkness, blacker than black. He almost felt the surprise, the way that the shadows fell in on themselves, and all too easily, she was there.

Drew swing this time went straight to her throat. The gasping, choking noise tumbled in amongst the shadows as she fell, books tumbling. An unlit lamp crashed to the floor in her wake. It was too hard to judge the strike. The nun was up again all too quick, flying at Malo with a banshee wail. The sound was hollow, like wind through a cave.

"Fuck! Get her off!"

Malo scrambled backwards, feeling the frigid cold breath of the grave. Those eyes, so black, widened first in desperate need. As her fingers clawed at his forearms those eyes widened with a snap. Shock registered there.

"Now!"

She fell back just enough for Malo to kick her free and draw his katana. It came free of the scabbard with a hiss, taking the nun's head from her shoulders with deadly grace. The shower of blackness that followed colored the refectory in a wide arc. Malo stared down at the body as it dropped.

In the back of the skull was a knitting needle, buried deep. Just enough distraction to get her free.

"Wasn't there meant to be two?" asked Drew, breath still rising quick his chest. Malo nodded.

"Time to do a full search. Let's hope the next was as easy as that one."

Drew gave him a dry smile, but Malo knew that they had gotten off lightly. Things could have turned out far worse.

Diane's Pinky

• RAINIE OET •

was the only part of her I managed to save.
Every morning I still wake before sunrise and
put it in a bowl of water on the window.
As the sun rises, her pinky bleeds into the water.
And at sundown, I put it into a bowl
of fresh water, clean water. As the sun sets,
Diane's pinky sucks the water inside it,
as if the water were its own blood.

But It Was Diane Who Killed Herself

• RAINIE OET •

I couldn't have killed Diane even if I had wanted to.

Once, Diane held a tomato in front of her naked heart

and asked me to shoot it
with a pistol she'd found under Papa's side of the bed.

I shot it. The gun hurt my hands. I felt the recoil
all the way to my elbow and shoulder joints. Diane was

unscathed, but there was a small hole
through the tomato. "What happened to the bullet

when it exited the tomato?" I asked. "It didn't hit me,"
Diane said, smiling. She put the tomato on the table

and went into another room—"It just disappeared.
Shoot the tomato again."

I shot it.

And it exploded.

Common Ground

• JOSHUA BEGGS •

Well, the *first* thing I thought was, heck, *this* is what life is? No-thank-you-very-much-sir, I think I preferred that nice, smooth, cool thing that's not consciousness but not really *un*consciousness either, whatever came before the *this*, with all the inconvenient *feelings* and *thoughts* and *perception* and stuff, none of which I really considered an improvement.

But there I was anyway. What can you do, right?

What *I* did is just try to forget I started existing in the first place, but it's hard to forget you exist when you're seriously the most uncomfortable you've ever been in your whole life. Because the whole world was just this cramped little ball and all the things inside of it, which were pretty much exclusively just the various bits of *me*, plus some gross oozy-goozy stuff that got up in my armpits and crotch and various other crevices. At least it didn't chafe or anything, but that was just because I couldn't even *move*—all I could do was wiggle, or really just kind of *twitch*, because wiggling would've taken up too much room.

I twitched my feet, my elbows, my belly and my tiny little butt, but all they did was *thwump* against the edge of the world. Pretty underwhelming. Then I twitched my head, though, and instead of going *thwump*, it went *thwack*. Much more satisfying. I kept on *thwack, thwack, thwack*-ing until one of the *thwacks* turned into a *crack*, and this little line squirmed its way up the edge of the world, right where I'd been headbutting it.

That's when I *really* threw myself into it, using my whole body, from my toes all the way up to the itsy-bitsy muscles around my eyes. I kept headbutting until my face ached and my head hurt (plus a few breaks to catch my breath and take a nap or two), and then finally—*snap!* My whole world—

—my *whole world*—

—split open!

And outside . . . holy heck! There was *another* world out there, but instead of being all dark and cramped and stuffed with bits of me, this one was huge and open and stuffed with *possibilities*. And everywhere I looked, there were bazillions of fluffy little weirdos just like me, all of us headbutting our way out from our cramped little *me*-worlds into a huge, ginormous *us*-world!

We were all dying to pick that oozy-goozy stuff out from everywhere it'd gotten sticky-stuck, but the other little weirdos and me were all so excited that none of us could stop talking—even when we had our faces buried in our armpits or our tiny little butts, we just kept cheeping about how *those shells were so uncomfortable* and *wow this place is humongous* and *do you still remember your first thought I bet it was a good one let me hear it*. Then once we'd gotten ourselves all de-oozed and our yellow fluff all fluffed up, some friendly giants—like, gianter than any of us ever could've *imagined*—came and dumped all of us little weirdos into this big noisy machine that bounced us around and sifted us out from our shells, which felt great, because I liked the *us*-world *way* better than the *me*-world, even more than the whatever-came-before that I was talking about earlier.

The big noisy machine plopped us out on this really fun circular conveyer belt thingy where some different friendly giant-giants started sorting us into boys and girls, for whatever reason. They weren't very fast, though, and there were a lot of us little weirdos, so we all just waited our turn and made laps around the conveyer belt, bumbling around and chatting about what we wanted to do now that we'd made it into the *us*-world. One guy said he thought that maybe even the *us*-world had a shell, and we could all break through if we *thwacked* really hard all at once, and then we'd break into this sort of *transcendental-us*-world, which seemed like a cool concept, but to be honest, he kind of lost me there.

One of the friendly giant-giants finally tossed me into the bin with all the other boys—it was a little intimidating, to be honest, even though I saw *transcendental-us*-world guy there, too, talking to these other little weirdos about how he thought we were all just parts of a giant hyperconscience, which bent my brain in all sorts of weird twisty ways. And all of a sudden I felt really, *really* small, absolutely tiny, insignificant in every sense of the word.

But then I realized that it was okay, because, well, I *was* all of those things—we *all* were, all of us little weirdos, and even the friendly giant-giants, too, and there was something beautiful in being small and insignificant together. I told that to the *transcendental-us-world* guy, and he said *yes*, that's exactly what he was talking about! Then we all got really excited, cheeping and chirping and hopping around. Another friendly giant-giant came and took our whole bin to a different conveyer belt, which just went one way and had something really loud and angry-sounding at the end, but I didn't care, I was too busy being happy that I was alive! I watched the friendly giant-giant walk away and thought, wow, what beautiful creatures, even if it looks kind of dopey and can't understand us little weirdos, how cool is it that we all get to share this *us*-world together!

Then the conveyer belt ended.

And we fell into the meat grinder.

And as it shredded my feet and my legs and my tiny little butt I thought *no wait please help friendly gi—*

That was the *last* thing I thought.

Let the Mango Go Viral

• TIMOTHY DYKE •

We all have stories we could tell five-hundred times and never get right. When life happens, it doesn't happen as a story. As events occur, action doesn't rise and fall with a discernible beginning, middle, and end. When we live through all that we experience, time doesn't move as it does in a narrative. Sometimes I've told this one story as a joke. Other times I've played with making it scary, like my own version of a ghost story. For the first few years after it happened, I told the story about the twelve-dollar mango straight, episode by episode, but I never was able to convince anyone that what I was telling was true. I possess physical, verifiable evidence, but I haven't wanted to show anyone the physical evidence. I feel like that could lead to irreversible negative consequences.

I'm not sure how many Whole Foods Markets there are in Hawai'i now, but when the very first one opened at Kahala Mall, several of my friends were really excited. Especially my haole friends. I'm haole too. I guess that's probably worth saying. Jacqueline had this app on her phone. This was back in the day when apps and iPhones were kind of novel. If Jacqueline typed the name of a vegetable into her Whole Foods app, all of these recipes would pop up. She told me she wanted to make barley stew in her new apartment in Pālolo. I told her I had no problem with barley stew. We made a plan to meet up at Kahala. By the time I got there, she'd made a shopping list. The app had separated the items into two equally priced sub-lists. I've only had an iPhone for the past five years. I'm not the world's slowest technology adopter, but I'm close, so back then Jacqueline had to hand me a physical piece of printed paper. I accepted my mission. I would purchase these items. According to the app, it would take me twenty-five minutes to procure everything on the list and five minutes to check out. We synchronized our watches. I gripped my shopping cart with two hands and told Jacqueline I'd see her in half an hour.

I saw her ten minutes later. I was moving from the vinegar aisle to the fresh herb area when Jacqueline cut me off with her wagon. "Check out these mangos," she said. She stood in front of her shopping cart with a mango in each hand.

"Was mango on our list?" I asked. I shuffled the piece of paper in my hand.

"No. Look at these, though. They are so big and perfect looking."

"Those are definitely nice."

She put one in my cart. "You should have one," she said. "For later. They're like the Platonic ideal of a pair of mangos." I grunted something affirming and grabbed what Jacqueline was offering. She U-turned her wagon and headed toward the non-dairy milk area.

From the checkout line, I could see Jacqueline through the front window. She had finished her shopping and stood by a post with four plastic grocery bags at her feet. I remember thinking to myself that Jacqueline seemed like the kind of person who would have brought her own bags, probably macrame or canvas. I looked back to the groceries on the conveyor belt just as the cashier picked up the mango. The scanner said this one piece of fruit cost $12.

"Holy crap. Is that right?"

"Sorry?" the cashier said. "What's that again?"

"How much is that mango?"

The cashier pointed to the register, then flipped through a plastic notebook. "Those are twelve-dollar mangos," she said. "They're from Maui." She told me the name of the farm. "They've got something going on over there. Their mangos are something special. No GMO. Just good juju."

"What do you mean 'juju'?" I asked. "You mean like *mana*?"

The cashier shrugged. She touched her glasses with her middle finger, then spoke deliberately. "I'm half-Filipino, with some Irish, Jamaican, and Slovenian in me." she said. "I don't feel qualified to talk about *mana*."

I think I actually said, "Um."

"I feel like it's a Native Hawaiian term," the cashier said. "I don't want to be disrespectful."

I couldn't help myself. "Is that what you mean, though? What did you mean when you said the farm had good juju?"

I saw the cashier look at the customer behind me in line. She lifted the barrier that separated my items on the conveyor belt from the next person's and sent the rubber item flying through its little chute. "Look, sir. I just work at Whole Foods. Do you want the twelve-dollar mango or not?"

I looked toward Jacqueline outside. She was staring at her phone. I sighed. It seemed like a hassle to have the cashier negate the purchase. I didn't want to infuriate her or anything. "Okay," I said. I thought something rude to myself like, "For twelve dollars that mango should give me a blow job." I don't know why I thought this. I actually define as asexual. That's another true story that people don't always believe. The whole discovery of asexual identity is another of the narratives I've never figured out how to tell well. But I'm digressing. When I got outside, I asked Jacqueline if she knew those mangos cost twelve dollars. She said she had no idea until she got to the checkout. She said she ended up not buying hers. I remember stifling some negative feelings.

The barley stew was fine. When I got home after dinner, I put the mango on a plate on top of a paper towel. My mother taught me that fruit ripens best in cool, dark places. As I live without air conditioning in a cinder block apartment in the most population-dense district in Honolulu, I don't really have a cool place for ripening, so I put the plate and the mango on the second shelf of the cupboard over my sink. When I opened that same cupboard the next morning to see if the mango was ready to slice, I was confused. Perplexed, even. The plate and the paper towel were on the top shelf, but the mango was sitting on the bottom shelf next to my *Godfather, Part 2* Fredo coffee mug. I knew I hadn't put it there.

This is one part of the story where I'm wondering if I'm telling it right. I don't really know how to describe my train of thought. I knew the mango couldn't have rolled from shelf one to shelf two. That explanation violated several established scientific principles. I remember wondering if I had sleepwalked. I won't even try to describe the inner voices that spoke to me as I tried to understand how this twelve-dollar mango could have moved. I picked it up and put it on the cutting board. It felt ripe enough to have for breakfast before I went off to work. I'm a high school English teacher, by the way. I have told this story to students before, but I've regretted each attempt. I used to tell it on days when we'd talk about that Emily Dickinson poem, "Tell All the Truth, But Tell It Slant." My intention was to ask students how they would tell a story like this if something like my twelve-dollar mango experience had happened to them. I tried to get them to think about how the truth must dazzle gradually. The lesson plan never really worked, though. Each student was sure that nothing like this could ever happen. As soon as I brought the blade down toward the fruit on the cutting board, I felt a pain shoot through my slicing hand. I dropped the knife. Bewildered, I picked the knife up and tried again. I felt the pain again, and this time I swore I heard the mango squeal, "Don't kill me."

For the next three days I avoided my apartment. I worked late grading papers at school. I live alone, and I don't really sleep over with anyone, so I had no choice but to confront the quiet of my Makiki condo unit at night. I stayed out of the kitchen. I didn't open the cupboard until finally, on a Friday night, I braced myself and pulled the door open. The mango was on the paper towel on the plate on the top shelf of the cupboard. It was as if nothing strange had ever happened. I stared right at the expensive fruit. It was definitely ripe. Tomorrow I would slice it for sure.

I decided to invite a guest over the next night for oven-fried chicken with mango salsa. I would slice the fruit in front of another person. Most likely the mango wouldn't act up with someone else around, but if it did, at least I would have a witness. At least I would know this was not all in my head. The guest's name was Ben. I'd known him for about a year. We would be each other's guests if we had symphony tickets or if we wanted to eat something expensive at

Roy's Hawai'i Kai. We picnicked. We had never fooled around or anything close to it. I couldn't tell if he didn't want to have sex with me, or if he didn't think I wanted to have sex with him. For whichever reason, he wasn't sending the vibes. The truth is, I didn't really want to.

I had decided to tell my friend Ben that I was asexual. Ben's a family therapist, so I knew he was going to want me to name some traumas. I had wanted to talk to Ben about this for a while, but as a result of a lot of experiences and discoveries and epiphanies that are hard to describe, I'd figured out that my lack of desire for sex has more to do with identity than with brokenness, so I didn't really want to talk with Ben about my mother. I put off the conversation. Our friendship just kind of drifted along, destined to fade away unless we named a few things. Tonight seemed like a good night for clarification.

I served Ben his Manhattan with a cherry from a Trader Joe's jar my sister sent from Phoenix last Christmas. I think we were listening to The Postal Service from a CD player. This would have been a week before Halloween, 2008. For cocktail hour we stayed in the living room area of my 800-square-foot one-bedroom. Casually, I rose and led him into the kitchen. The chicken was smelling good. I put on mitts and opened the door to the oven. Everything was going according to plan. Opening the door to the cupboard above the sink, still wearing oven mitts, I grabbed the mango. I placed it on the cutting board and picked up the knife.

"Are you going to take those off?"

"What?"

Ben was talking. "Are you going to cut the mango with oven mitts?"

I forced a laugh. Silly me. I slid the left glove off while staring at Ben. I slid the right glove off while staring at the mango. It rolled over on the cutting board. I looked at Ben to see if he'd seen the fruit move, but he didn't seem alarmed at all. I decided to go to the bathroom. I needed to splash water on my face and give myself a quick pep talk before I sliced the twelve-dollar mango. Excusing myself, I went into the half-bath on the other side of my bedroom. I closed the door behind me, and then ran a wet washcloth over my face. I looked in the mirror and whispered, "Control yourself." I heard a second door slam. When I came out of the bedroom, the rest of my condo unit was empty. I walked into the kitchen. The chicken still cooked. The mango was back on the paper towel on the plate. The plate sat next to the Fredo mug on the bottom shelf of the cupboard.

The next morning was a Sunday, but I called the farm on Maui anyway. I needed to ask questions about the juju. It took a long time to reach a human voice, and when I did, no one wanted to talk to me about spiritual issues. Finally, a customer service representative took pity on me. She told me she wasn't able to give me the information I requested, but that if I wanted to talk to someone who knew what was up, she could give me a friend of a friend's cell number. I thanked her and pulled a pencil and paper off of the phone table. She gave me an 808 number and told me to ask for a guy named Tholemew.

"Tholemew?" I asked.

"Yeah," she said. "That's his name. He knows what's up about the mangos."

I wanted to make sure I got it right. "As in Bartholemew?"

"That's what he used to go by," the customer service representative said, "but he's in AA now. Been sober almost seven years. He calls himself Tholemew. He says he doesn't want to have anything to do with the bar part."

I couldn't tell if she was messing with me or not, but I took the number. I knew that if I didn't call right away, I'd lose my nerve, so I dialed on the old landline and let it ring seven times. When a man answered, I asked if he was "Tholemew."

"Yeah," he said. "Speaking. What's up?"

I explained the situation. This is another part of the story where I don't know exactly how much to tell. We kind of went back and forth with each other for a while, and then Tholemew told me to hang up, send him 50 bucks on Paypal, then call him back in 15 minutes. I did as I was told.

I have to digress again. You know the story of the Garden of Eden? So, I know there's a lot more to it than this but basically Adam and Eve are naked and innocent, and then a serpent gets involved and Eve tempts Adam to eat an apple from the Tree of Knowledge of Good and Evil. When God finds out the apple is gone, Adam and Eve are banished to a life of pain and sorrow. Pregnancy hurts and Adam has to work for a living. From then on, everyone is born with Original Sin. There has been some historical speculation that the Forbidden Fruit was no apple. If you think about it, apples don't really grow naturally in the Middle East. Some people say the actual fruit would have been something like a pomegranate. Tholemew says it may have been a mango. He spoke really softly, but forcefully at the same time. He told me not to bother to Google. He said some truths are too heavy for the internet to handle. He told me it sounded like I may have picked up a fruit that was spawned by the Serpent. If anyone thinks I'm gullible for believing Tholemew, I'd say that that person has no idea what it's like to live in fear of a twelve-dollar mango. I asked Tholemew what I could do. He told me to Paypal him 50 more bucks and he'd tell me how to get rid of my problem. I did as I was told.

According to Tholemew, I was going to have to exterminate the mango ritualistically. He said that I needed to slice the mango on the altar of a church with a pink knife on Halloween at midnight. I happened to own a pink knife. I bought it on sale at The Compleat Kitchen at Kahala Mall. I also had a key to the chapel at the school where I teach. It's a private school, founded by missionaries, and for over a hundred years, the school has required students to attend weekly religious services. At the turn of the millennium, a new principal expressed interest in expanding the spiritual scope, and as these things go in schools, committees were formed. A pilot program brought me into the chapel program. I'm an asexual atheist, but I enjoy poetry and philosophical discussions. At the end of every religious service, I'd lead the congregation in a Godless Sacred Moment. Typically, I'd read that Mary Oliver poem about the grasshopper on a summer's day and ask students to think about what they each were going to do with their one wild and precious life. I can't say I was great at the job. But I can say that I carried a key to the chapel on my key chain.

Halloween arrived on a Friday. I left my place early and returned just before dark. I locked myself in my bedroom for a while and went over the plan in my head. When the time came, I acted decisively and forcefully. About a half-hour before midnight, I put a small cutting board, the twelve-dollar mango and the pink knife in my backpack. I put the mango and the knife in two separate compartments because I didn't want the fruit to stab me in the back. I walked to school. Carefully avoiding security, I made my way to the chapel. I entered the temple in darkness, flicking a lighter on and off to guide my way to the altar where I lit a candle. I spread a towel and lay down the cutting board. I placed the mango in position. I raised the knife. As the pink blade made its way toward mango flesh, I heard the worst squeal I'd ever heard in my life. I hesitated. Momentum for vengeance whooshed out of me. I heard the mango say, "Don't kill me." It was the saddest sound I've ever heard in my life.

I couldn't do it. I couldn't kill the mango. I put the knife in one backpack pouch and the cutting board and mango in the other. I made the walk of shame back to my apartment in the most population-dense district in Honolulu. The next day I called Tholemew. He told me that as the mango rotted; it was going to become a lot surlier. I asked him if there was anything I could do to live with the mango. He told me to Paypal him fifty more bucks and he'd tell me. I did what I was told.

I have been living with the twelve-dollar mango for over a decade now. Every morning when I wake up, I anoint the fruit skin in coconut oil and profess my eternal loyalty. I tell the mango that I will always take care of them. The mango prefers they/them pronouns. They mostly leave me alone. They have free reign of the kitchen now. They can rest on whatever shelf they want. I still live without a human partner. For the most part, everything is fine. I will say that things got kind of difficult during the COVID pandemic. I seldom left the confines of my home, my expensive cinder-block box, and I lived in constant panic that the twelve-dollar mango would show up on Zoom calls or in my Webex room when I teach my online classes. So far that hasn't happened. I'm glad. I mean, on one hand, maybe it would be good to verify the truth of this story by showing the twelve-dollar mango to others. On the other hand, it seems like too big a risk. I can only imagine all the trouble I could cause if I let the mango go viral.

The Long Last Call

• SCOTT KIKKAWA •

"So, are you?"

"Am I what?"

"Any good."

"Am I any good? At what?"

"At being a detective."

"Oh," I said. "Sorry. I didn't hear you the first time. Am I any good at detective work? Sure, if you believe my fitness reports. I'm flying colors. But so is every other dick who gets a fitness report, because it's too damn hard for the brass to write a shitty report. The truth is, most are bad investigators. Too lazy or too stupid to do the job. If you really want a good assessment of my abilities, you'd have to see me work yourself."

"That's exactly what I had in mind."

Exactly what he had in mind? What the hell was this? What the hell was I doing there? It was August 1952, almost a full eight years after I had shipped home from France with a bullet hole in my left shoulder, and I was still pickling myself with rye to kill the pain. The shoulder hadn't actually hurt for years, but the habit of medicating with liquor lingered like back taxes owed. I usually preferred putting my recollection out of its misery alone, but my car was parked farther mauka from the station than usual on Nuuanu Avenue and I got sidetracked. I just got done with wrapping up a report. It was late. The Pantheon Bar had its double doors flung open like it was a barn that had lost its last nag to the glue factory, so in I went.

There had been a number of faces crowding the bar, all of them darkened by the fact that none of them had seen a razor since the crack of dawn. I fit right in, so I set myself up on the last stool with a glass and proceeded to disappear.

It worked. For a while. For a couple of hours, I drank in

peace. Then I was interrupted. Annoyingly, every now and then, someone notices that I exist and I'm forced to have the last thing in the world I want: a conversation.

A gnarled character in a crewcut and a dirty undershirt took the vacant stool next to me and started talking. When I realized that his vocalizing was directed at me, I looked up from my glass at his face. He had a long, nasty scar that ran south from his forehead through his left eye and down his cheek to his jaw. To call him ugly would be unfair to ugly people. He was downright hideous. And he was even more gruesome when he smiled, flashing an orthodontic nightmare in dull gray and yellow.

He introduced himself as Buzz, or something like that, and he insisted on talking. I didn't have much choice but to talk back. I might have slurred my occupation when he asked.

"Did you come all the way to this end of the bar to find a good detective?" I asked, in response to his query about my being any good at my work.

"What difference does it make? I found one."

He smiled again, distorting the scarred left side of his face. I stared involuntarily at the grotesque ravine. He caught me staring. I didn't much care that he did.

"Go ahead," he said. "Ask me what happened to my face. Everybody does, eventually."

"Okay," I said. "What happened to your face?"

"Well, let's just say it was in the wrong place at the wrong time."

"I know exactly how it feels." I shrugged and took a burning swallow of rye.

He laughed. And I didn't think he could possibly be more revolting than when he merely smiled. I was wrong, and not for the first time.

"What's your name, Detective?"

"Yoshikawa," I said. "Francis."

"Good, strong name. Where are you from?"

"Most recently, the corner of Bethel and Merchant. I shower

and sleep in Kaimuki, if that's what you mean, but I grew up in Kakaako."

"Nobody's really from Kakaako," he said. "Where was your family before that?"

"Waipahu. Plantation house."

"I mean before, before."

"Hiroshima," I said.

"Really? My family was from there, too. I guess it's my lucky night. I got a good detective and he's from the same hometown. But you know what? I don't remember seeing you at the kenjinkai."

"Kenjinkai is my mom's time killer, not mine. Look, I hate to tell you this, but I'm not for hire as a detective."

"No?"

"No. I work for the City and County of Honolulu." I pulled out the gold shield and showed it to him.

"A policeman? Good! Even better! Besides, doesn't that mean you already work for me?"

"I work for the Department. Some of your taxes might eventually end up in my paycheck, but that doesn't mean I take orders from you. And I'm not in the lost-and-found racket. I'm a homicide detective."

"Perfect. This is about murder."

I laughed aloud. Jesus. It was after midnight and this guy wanted to talk shop with me. He didn't get the bulletin that cops usually come to bars after work so they can forget about their jobs, not talk about them. It was stale and warm where I sat. The bar's wide-open doors let the dead air in from Nuuanu Avenue and it didn't do much to cool the place down. "Murder," I said. "Sounds serious."

"It is," he said.

"You can make a report at the receiving desk tomorrow morning, Buzz."

He cocked the milky eye on the ruined side of his face at me. "What's the matter?" he asked. "Too much for you? Not that kind of detective, huh? More of a pencil pusher, I guess."

Baiting tough guys was usually my job, and I hated when it

was done to me with some amount of skill. I bit. The large amount of rye I consumed wasn't large enough to drown my ego. "Murder is why I get a paycheck," I said.

Buzz laughed again and I flinched. My ability to maintain a poker face fled about two drinks before.

"Is *this* too much for you?" He smiled and pointed at his face.

"It's all right. I've seen faces like yours before. Just not on living people."

"So, you'll hear me out, then?"

"Why the hell not?"

He motioned to the bartender with a twisted right hand. The bartender, a haole war relic in a tapa print aloha shirt and a Marine Corps haircut shuffled over at the speed of cane syrup.

"Last call," said the bartender, in a manner that suggested that he didn't much care one way or another if we understood him.

"Leave the bottle," said my new, scarred friend. He dropped a bill on the bar. The bartender glanced at the bill, raised his eyebrows, and said, "Sure." He snatched up the bill and moved back to the other end of the bar, this time with a little more spring in his step.

The whole bottle. Maybe I *was* being hired. I didn't think too hard or long about that, though. I uncorked the bottle and I poured. Then I looked at my companion and raised the bottle. "Where's your glass?" I asked.

"No, thanks," he said. "It's all yours for hearing me out."

I took a couple of stiff gulps. "Then let's hear it," I said.

"About ten years ago, during the war, do you remember the story about the owner of Kame-Ya on Queen Street?"

"The tofu maker? I remember my mom and older sisters gossiping about how he ran off with some girl who was a housekeeper for some rich haole family in Manoa. Something about how she stole some cash from the family before they disappeared together. They all felt bad for his wife."

He chuckled softly to himself while I lit up a cigarette. I offered him one, but he declined. "The wife ended up doing all right for herself," he said. "She married one of the young workers and they still run the shop together. It's doing good business. They make a lot of tofu."

"I know. I have it almost every Sunday at my mom's house."

"Oh, yeah? Where's that?"

"Kawaiahao Street."

"Some nice houses there. Not too many camps."

"You wouldn't think so if you saw it. It was pretty much the office for my dad's automobile repair shop."

"But I'll bet your family had its own furo."

"Yeah, we did. You were saying something about murder?"

"Yes, I was getting to that," he said. "Sorry. It's just that lately I don't get to talk to folks much. The owner of Kame-Ya, the one your mom said ran off with the cleaning girl? He didn't run off with her."

"No?"

"No. There was no girl. The owner was murdered. He was killed by the young employee who married his wife after he disappeared."

I laughed like the drunk that I was—raucous, sloppy, and without inhibition. He smiled a thin, indulgent smile, one that didn't contort his face so much.

"*Killed him?* Where the hell did you hear *that*?"

"I didn't hear it," he said. He wasn't smiling anymore. "I saw it."

"You *saw* it? And you didn't bother reporting it back then?"

"I tried."

"And what happened?"

"Nobody paid any attention," he said. He grinned ghoulishly in the dim light of the bar. "I tried like hell to get somebody to check it out. I gave up after a while. Maybe they weren't so good. But tonight, I have a *good* detective. Maybe one who might pay attention."

I drained the glass and set it down on the bar. I reached for the bottle and filled it again. The bartender started making bigger noises as he cleaned up—coughing, dragging chairs and tables across the floor so they screeched loudly against the tile. We were the only two patrons left in the bar.

"I can't believe nobody in the Department took you seriously," I said. I took a long drink, nearly draining the glass again. My throat was numb and it all slipped down like water. I wasn't even feeling the burn anymore.

"Nobody did. But I'm not complaining. You're here now, and maybe we can make this right."

"I might," I said. "It depends."

"On what?"

"On your story. If it's a good one, I'll check it out."

The bartender stopped making his noises. He was done with dropping hints. He just stood up against the wall and stared at us with arms folded across his chest.

"I think I'd better tell you on the way," said my drink benefactor. "It looks like we should get going."

I got up off the barstool, grabbed the bottle, and dragged my feet toward the open double doors and the rank stillness of Nuuanu Avenue. He followed. The doors closed and locked behind us. We stood out on the sidewalk in the anemic glow of a streetlamp.

"You said you'd tell me on the way," I said. "On the way to where?"

"Masataka Taniguchi."

"*Where?*"

"You mean *who*. The owner of Kame-Ya Tofu. I'm going to show you where he's buried."

"This should be good."

We walked the two or three blocks mauka to my car and got in. I hit the starter and pulled away from the curb. The streets were deserted and mausoleum-silent.

"Where are we going?" I asked.

"Moiliili."

"Where in Moiliili?"

"The cemetery."

"You're kidding."

"Where else would you bury a body?"

I shrugged. I wasn't energetic or sober enough to argue. It made sense in a perverse way. Nobody would think to look for the corpse of a missing person in a cemetery. All the bodies there are usually accounted for.

I took a swig out of the bottle of Old Overholt I had carried from the Pantheon. I was damn lucky that there weren't any other cars out on King Street at that hour, though I managed to more or less stay on the proper side of the road. I looked over at Buzz, who smiled at me in the eerie, intermittent streetlamp light. I was startled by the sight of his face and nearly plowed into the rear of a parked Packard near Iolani Palace. I swerved at the last moment.

"Don't do that," I said.

"Sorry," he said, though he continued to smile. "Shall I tell you my story?"

"I wish you would."

He launched into a tale that was scandalous by Kakaako Japanese standards, the kind of shit that made my sisters bring their manicured hands up to their faces and gasp like monkeys.

Masataka Taniguchi was an apprentice tofu maker who managed to open his own shop when he came into a little money thanks to the death of his grandfather in Japan and his status as the only son of an only son. It wasn't a hell of a lot. The inheritance was too modest to ensure a life of comfort. But it was enough, with a lot of hard work and the addition of funds from a tanomoshi loan, to start a small business of his own.

For years he labored with hardly a day off in two decades. Taniguchi was rewarded with some measure of success, and that success brought him a bride half his age.

Aiko was fair and graceful with soft hands. She sounded like the kind of girl that was always bathed in a fuzzy white light and had a slight echo to her voice, like a Hollywood dream sequence. Or probably she just seemed that way to all the lonely grinds who were infatuated with her. Taniguchi put her on a pedestal. He forbade her to work in the small factory, placing her up front at the counter to deal with the customers, with whom she became popular. Things worked out for a while, until George Kawazoe was hired to work nights in the factory. Kawazoe worked days as a groundskeeper at the Moiliili Cemetery and needed a night job.

"Stop," I said. "Let me guess the rest. This George Kawazoe was handsome in a derelict sort of way, and he was about the same age as Aiko. The two of them got hot and heavy and came up with the brilliant idea of offing Taniguchi so they could live happily ever after running the tofu business he worked so hard to build. Because George worked at the cemetery, he could dump the body into a fresh grave right on top of its proper occupant, cover it up, and no one's the wiser. They concoct this story about how Taniguchi must have run off with a girl they made up, the cops are happy, they're happy and nobody in Kakaako gives a shit because they keep getting their tofu. Am I close?"

"What can I say? You *are* a good detective."

"Except you left out a critical detail."

"What's that?"

"Just how the hell do you know all this?"

"I told you. I saw it all."

"What? The stuff at the tofu factory? George and Aiko? The plot to take out Taniguchi? The dirty deed?"

"Yes."

"How?"

"I worked at Kame-Ya for several years. And I'm part of the Taniguchi family. I saw it all unfold."

"And they all never noticed you watching all this?"

"I'm a guy nobody pays much attention to. I keep to myself, and nobody thinks I care about the stuff I see. Even among family, people don't ask me much because they don't talk to me much in the first place."

I shrugged. His personality wasn't what I'd call magnetic and his looks, well, the scar at least gave character to a face otherwise void of any. Besides, why the hell did I care? I was still nursing the last drink of the night.

"Makes sense, I guess," I said.

The grave markers rose in the gloom in front of us.

"We're here," I said.

I pulled up along the curb on Kapiolani Boulevard fronting the cemetery. We got out, and he shot ahead, walking very quickly and meandering effortlessly among the stone markers. All I could do was keep the dingy undershirt in sight and try to keep up.

"Hey, slow down!" I called out to him. I stopped to take another sloppy pull from the bottle. "What's the rush? I mean, if this poor guy is under the dirt up there somewhere, he's been there for the last ten years. Another few minutes aren't going to kill him—he's already dead."

"You're a funny man," he said. His voice sounded small and dissipated and farther away than he was—I could see his dirty undershirt about ten yards in front of me in gaps between grave markers still and silent in the dead, humid air. The liquor was making it difficult for me to move with precision. I stumbled twice and bumped a few granite markers.

Just when I thought our ascent up the slight incline—it wasn't what I'd call a hill, but it sure felt like one—would never end, I saw him sitting on a western-style headstone, grinning hideously and pointing at a modest stone marker a few feet away. It was a modest, slender monolith in miniature, engraved with kanji characters.

"Tanaka," he said. "There's lots of them buried here, but this is the one George threw Masataka Taniguchi in. You'll find a shovel up against that shed over there." He pointed at a rickety wooden structure a few yards away.

"A shovel? What the hell do you expect me to do?"

"Take a wild guess. I thought you were a *good* detective."

"You want me to dig up Tanaka-san? Are you crazy?"

"I kind of figured you're the seeing-is-believing type, so here's your chance. I promise you won't be disappointed. And you're not going to disturb Tanaka-san. You'll find Masataka Taniguchi long before that. You're not going to have to go far down. Three feet, maybe four."

I drank from the bottle sloppily and wiped my mouth with the back of my hand. I don't know why I bothered trying to keep my face clean. There wasn't anyone within miles or hours to impress.

"Fuck it," I muttered under my breath and trudged toward the shed. I had come that far, what the hell was I going to do? Call it a night and go home to sleep off the liquor? That would have been the smart thing to do, but the time for doing smart things had died just before last call.

I managed to reach the shed without stubbing my toe or knocking over a grave marker and grabbed the shovel leaning up against the weathered pine wall of the little structure. I dragged it back to the Tanaka grave. Buzz grinned and pointed.

"Right there in the middle. Yes. Right there," he said, noting where I had stuck the spade into the ground.

"Are you going to give me a hand with this?"

"You're the detective. I've shown you the way. My work is done. As a special treat, I think you'll find the murder weapon in there, too."

He laughed and laughed like a madman as I dug. The smell of the damp soil and loam made me gag when it first hit me. I took a pull from the bottle to kill the scent of wet, earthy decay and continued to dig while Buzz sat perched on the headstone laughing. His laughter filled my ears like the cacophonous roar of machine gun fire. All I could do to keep it from tearing my head apart was to keep digging. The .38 under my arm in its shoulder holster was beginning to feel like it weighed fifty pounds. I sweat like a chain-gang convict in leg irons. I thought it would never end. But none of it was worse than the laugh.

"Shut up!" I shouted. I couldn't take his laughing any more. I thrust the spade angrily into the earth to punctuate the point when it hit something hard. I fell to my knees and moved the damp soil with my hands. It was a skull. Lodged into it was the rusted blade of a hatchet. Right through the left eye.

The laughter stopped. I looked up at the headstone.

Buzz was gone.

The next few days were a blur of things mundane and uncanny falling into place. There was no living next of kin for the Tanaka grave I dug up, so there were no complaints. Aiko and George Kawazoe caved in after twenty minutes of playing stupid in my interview of them at Kame-Ya and confessed to the killing of Masataka "Boss" Taniguchi. The bartender at the Pantheon on Nuuanu made me give him a "real" five-dollar bill and he gave me the war overprint note I "tried to pass off to him" for the bottle of Old Overholt. I didn't even bother asking him if he was sure it was me.

My lieutenant recommended me for a commendation that never came.

August 1952. Obon season. A last call that lasted a week. When it was over, I had a drink.

Boxed In

• SARA BACKER •

Over the broad white glittering city under a hazy sky, a crane swivels its long iron neck. A heavy hook grabs a metal container. Pulled high, it rocks lightly as it swings around to the flat train car and gently lands with an echoing boom of metal hitting metal. Yellow suds crust at the edge of a drying stream trapped in a concrete culvert. Why must the world be this heavy? Herons dip their beaks in foul water. The ghost of Tu Fu enters my brain and shows me what's inside each locked metal cube. Overlapping elbows, broken teeth, gray skin, desiccated eyes. All of them killed by their jobs. *Let's be poor,* Tu Fu suggests. *Better to die of cheap beer and moonlight!*

Visitation

• JULIET S. KONO •

Even though he's dead,
I'm certain he returns.
He's the boy
who mills around campus
with students I teach.

He's the boy who has
a girl braced between
his legs as he sits on
the school wall and sings
a song no one hears
into the line of her hair.

He's the boy who walks
around with earphones,
snapping his fingers,
"jazzing it," as he'd have said.

He's the boy with the guitar
strapped across his back,
the one whose long hair
flows like dark water in sun;
the one who disappears around
the corner of the math department.

Later, I hear a voice in the crowd. A voice
saying hello, or, being funny, asking for money,
with what he says having a distinct timbre,
that it gives resonance to recognition,
enough to pull the dissonant bond
between us upward into my stomach
and into my lungs where I hold
my breath, certain it is him.

The thought that he is here

is real, for it does not bring me back
to the floating blue lotus blossoms,
of my dress skirt that billows in wind,
nor arthritic pains that attend my knees,
for seeing the likes of his walk
or hearing his voice, feels in spirit,
similar to the way a mother recognizes
       on an island replete with birds
       or peninsula of seals
the true cries of her offspring.

Memories of the Moon and Bon Dance Ed

• JOY GOLD •

Bon Dance Ed and I make the circuit every season.
He rides shotgun for my navigation to temples tucked away
In valleys, under and along freeways, and forgotten places.
Sometimes we get lost going home
And laugh about becoming urban legends, never to be seen again.

The red dirt road takes us to the temple I love best
Set back behind old plantation houses, near the now-dead sugar mill,
Here, in the cooling night, wisps of clouds cross the full moon,
Lanterns sway, and flute notes drift in the wind
While the singer's woeful tune of plantation life fades in and out.

> I feel the memories of the harvest moon rising,
> Its soft light on the woman late to strip dead leaves
> From stalks before the harvest.
> Across the field, her man bends in silhouette
> Turning the red soil to ease the birth of sugar cane.

Tonight, the moon waits for those who have come and gone.
We come to honor them with new and familiar dances.
Striking in his black and white yukata coat
His movements are precise and clean, even when he missteps.

In the next season, I ride the circuit to return
To honor Bon Dance Ed
And wait for the moon's gaze to comfort me.

The Lookout

• WING TEK LUM •

Inspired by "The Vigilant Sentry"
in Shiho S. Nunes, *Chinese Fables*

Good morning, Sparrow!

Oh . . . Hello, Boss.

Gee . . . It gets pretty cold up here before the sun rises.

Yes, but that is why I always bring my blankets. They keep me warm enough.

And on this lanai you can look down and see pretty much the whole back alleyway here . . . on both sides.

Yes, Boss. And the only way anyone can get up here is to try to come up this stairway. If anyone doesn't have the right password, I have my trusty whistle around my neck. It's loud and would definitely give you enough of a warning.

That's good.

But, Boss, I need to tell you this . . .

What?

I had a pretty scary dream last night.

Oh?

You know . . . All of you were inside, and some gang broke in, not the police. It looked like some guys from another gambling den who snuck in trying to make trouble. They had hatchets and clubs and threatened everyone. They shoved all of us into a corner, and took our money and dominoes and cards. Then they broke our chairs and tables. It was like a typhoon, suddenly appearing and just as suddenly going away!

This was a dream?

Yes—or more like a nightmare. Do you think it was an omen? Boss, maybe it's foretelling that something bad is going to happen to us. Maybe even tonight?

Or maybe it already happened . . . last night . . .

Huh?

Funeral Song in Torrance, CA

• KALANI PADILLA •

When someone leaves the earth from here,
     the years are poured out into plastic cups
     and playing cards all red
     and blooming beer.

Around me a family's life was resuming.
They shred lemons into kelaguen and kanikapila.
I find myself roped into the front yard songs
and then the back yard songs—

they spell grief in the key of joy
And fling it toward me—the brown stranger
from farther north on the big water.
One by one, aunty nephew cousin comes
to touch the gate between my shoulder blades
and welcome me into me.
I let them tie them to me.
Cousin, sing us something
sing us a song from Hawai'i

Mine and cousin's names both mean
that we are of heaven.
Mine and uncle's names
are both words for child.
Mine and uncle's names both mean
ways for water to fall.

It was nearly vulgar,
wanting to love their loved one when his spirit had risen from the
     waters of Redondo,

Too much like that blight that crowns the crotch of a settler
after seeing ellipses of surfers and ti leaves and orchids on the south
          shore strip.
But how else can that truth make it to sea?
That my life is next to theirs if not closer; sifted from the same
          stream?
For a weekend our child selves were
          leaping   through genealogies to one another,
          growing   up and parenting our
          nowselves.
When we acknowledge that this one earth
is the onlywhere to which each ancestor strand can send us,
it will be like the day the water held up the paddlers,
circled up
hands strong in each others' hands
forming the prayer,
a single fleshly layer between the sea and what we call the sky before
          we call it heaven.

Ambling Time

• JOHN P. ROSA •

Anachronisms are a well-known chronological misconduct,
by some even regarded as a historical mortal sin.

Achim Landwehr & Tobias Winnerling (2019)

Harry Yim often woke to the sounds of the wind rustling the trees outside his window and seed pods the size of children's fists falling to the sidewalk on 16th Avenue. On this morning, however, he slept in, and it was quiet. He wondered which of his relatives would come to rake up the carpet of firecrackers strung up and burned at midnight to usher in the New Year of 1973. His wife was not beside him, which was not unusual for she slept in the adjacent room—he being a fitful sleeper who always snored and, so he was told, called out in his sleep, venting frustrations about work.

He changed from his pajamas and headed to the kitchen where he thought he'd already find Sau Ung preparing him breakfast, which he rarely took at the small table there but more often on the dining room table that could seat ten. His wife of sixty years was nowhere to be found and aside from a couple of mynahs squabbling outside, the house was remarkably still. As he looked about for Sau Ung (or Elizabeth, if she were to be called by her Catholic, baptismal name), he thought it odd that his console cabinet, radio, and phonograph were gone. He was one of the first in the neighborhood to have a color TV but that was missing too and in its stead was a large, black plaque mounted on the south wall facing Diamond Head.

The sun was starting to heat up the porch and reddish grand staircase that welcomed his children, grandchildren, and great-grandchildren to his home for all major holidays like the night before and Christmas a week earlier. On many days of the week, 804 16th Avenue was the capital of the Yim family compound where grandkids and now their own children congregated for other relatives to pick them up after school and shuttle them home, or to sports practices, or music lessons and the like. The families of his oldest and second oldest daughters lived on 16th, too. Mary was next door on the mauka side of Harry's home and Dolly on the makai side, but across a hilly Maunaloa Avenue.

Harry had done well enough in the 1920s to purchase houses next to each other—and two of them sat on corner lots. His only son, Bill, and his family lived behind Harry along Maunaloa. From their kitchen window, either Harry or Elizabeth could easily see Bill's carport, small lawn, and more modern-styled front entrance. Bill had the house built in the mid-1950s after he returned from law school at George Washington University in DC and working a stint in Delegate Joseph Farrington's office.

As he explored his own house, Harry was puzzled by all the strange furniture he was now bumping into. But at least the walls were the proper shade of white and the parquet floor in need of waxing every other year was still decent. Confused and in search of food, he thought he'd try the lunch counter at Woolworth's, where some of his retired friends gathered almost daily. Though it was New Year's, many island stores would be open. Only a few of his Japanese friends had brief family obligations like eating ozoni soup they probably had finished by now anyway.

Kahala Mall was so much calmer and closer than Ala Moana Shopping Center, and Harry could poke his head into Liberty House and say hi to family. His daughter Mary had recently retired, but one of his oldest granddaughters, born during the war, now worked in the credit department on the second floor. It was not the position of comptroller that he had retired from at the downtown Liberty House in 1953, but Cynthia's job dealing with ledgers and balances paid more than a sales one. Working at Liberty House was considered to be "a good job" and Cynthia's income was enough to raise her three young children when she had become a single mother.

Harry's various management positions over the decades at the main Liberty House on Fort Street had paid him well, but it was LH's links to the sports and greater Honolulu community that brought him the most satisfaction. He had organized LH basketball teams in the Commercial League in the 1930s, but he was better known for managing and later owning the Chinese Tigers that had originally drawn its baseball talent from young men he secured jobs for at Liberty House. By the early 1940s, the Tigers had won the Cartwright Trophy twice and was no longer exclusively comprised of local Chinese players. Harry, for example, recruited the Kaulukukui brothers from Hilo to play in Honolulu. And the *Star-Bulletin* took note when Harry added Amancio Paray, a Filipino right-hander from 'Ewa and former McKinley High School star. Baseball fans from the mainland even took note when Harry successfully courted and signed Ted Shaw, a star southpaw pitcher from the Negro Leagues.

Harry thought to call a relative to drive him to the mall, but there was no phone at the kitchen hutch where it should have been. No telephone book either for that matter—so before it got any warmer he decided to walk the mile there as he did once a week to satisfy the wishes of his physician. Surely he'd be able to get a ride home from one of his numerous relatives and friends. After all, he was Harry Ahong Yim. And this was Kaimukī.

On the long walk Harry was surprised to see the freeway stacked above Waiʻalae Ave and couldn't seem to find the drive-in theater or the Jolly Roger. In fact he wasn't entirely sure he'd reached the mall yet because all he could see were unfamiliar cars in bright colors he thought should never clothe a vehicle. He walked farther, toward Kīlauea Avenue, rounded a store that should have been McInerny, and prayed he'd find the Liberty House and Woolworth's.

He nearly walked into an oddly placed, small bust of Jack Lord, who frequently did his errands at Kāhala, sometimes grocery shopping at Star Market with makeup still on from a morning shoot of *Hawaii Five-O*. But what shocked Harry the most was to see that a New York-based Macy's store had apparently replaced Liberty House overnight. The building was still sandstone-colored, with octagonal windows twice as wide as they were tall. See's Candies was next door, so Harry knew he was in the right place. He walked into the mall, startled as glass doors slid open for him, and headed past Longs Drugs' side entrance in search of Woolworth's.

A Container Store greeted him, instead of a Woolworth's lunch counter and set of small booths where he had hoped to find a handful of his friends sipping coffee. More disoriented than disappointed, Harry walked onward, where the presence of new establishments continued to confuse him. He made his way toward Star Market on the Waiʻalae Ave side of the mall. Soon he'd be thoroughly frustrated, searching for a pay phone that would not be there and a ride home that would never materialize.

For many, family history research is a heuristic in which to make empathetic connections with their ancestors they will never (and can never) meet due to

John parked at Kahala Mall early enough to get a shaded spot near American Savings under the parking deck that wasn't there when he was a kid. He had barely gotten used to the Whole Foods as the mall's anchor grocery store and preferred his memories of Star Market. Starting in the early 70s when he was four or five, John helped select a Christmas tree each year in Star's parking lot. During bumper crop summers for lychee, the store would also generously purchase box loads of the fruit that he and a couple of his younger uncles had picked from his grandparents' backyard trees on Maunalani Heights.

John's Grandma Gert, Harry Yim's fourth oldest daughter, often did the week's marketing at Star after picking him and his brother Mark up from Waiʻalae Elementary in her household's white Olds. But that was nearly half a century ago when Gertrude and her husband Leon—already well versed in raising eight kids of their own—took in their oldest child Cynthia along with her children John, Mark, and baby Jennifer. There on Maunalani Heights, John lived, dined, and played alongside his aunts and uncles—Cynthia's younger siblings—for what he told others were the happiest six years of his life.

It was a non-teaching day during Summer Session Two, so John masked up, got an overpriced drip coffee from Starbucks his grandmother would have scolded him for, and set out to read and write on a freshly sanitized table where JC Penney used to be. He had an office at UH but liked to change up his work routine because he could. The background noise of strangers in most settings anywhere—walking by, dining, or shopping—somehow helped him concentrate. Teaching at least two courses every summer was a given since he, like so many of his colleagues, had to support school-age kids in Hawaiʻi's high cost of living. John never complained since he knew that every island resident was in the same boat, taking on second or even third jobs. His weekend coffee group buddies preferred the term "side gigs" for the occasional writing on assignment or guest presentations that fortunately came their way. "Consulting" seemed too fancy a word, overused by business folk.

The mall was quiet, it being a weekday and fears of COVID reducing the number of those who shopped and hung out in years previous. Ala Moana Shopping Center was an entirely different scene, catering more toward tourists, and increasingly only the wealthiest of them. As he sometimes quipped to any one of his classes covering Hawai'i issues, Macy's was the only place at Ala Moana that he could afford—and even that store had bought out Liberty House in 2001, before most of his undergraduate students were born. Though the place name Kāhala had a cachet about it, the mall was more affordable than the jam-packed Ala Moana Center, and tourists rarely bothered the locals who shopped in the quieter, suburban neighborhood.

John glanced around beyond his MacBook and saw a video-advertising wall with short clips promoting Biki bikes and La Pietra School of all things. Enrollments for smaller private schools were precarious and there were even television ads for his alma mater, Damien, that had gone co-ed almost a decade ago. Catholic schooling had been important to his family for generations, starting with Harry Ahong Yim, so it was no surprise that he and his three brothers went to Damien, while his two sisters had attended St. Francis School. After all, his mother and stepfather met at a Formerly Married Catholics meeting at Star of the Sea Church in 1977. A year later, Cynthia and Richard married and formed a blended family in He'eia on the windward side of O'ahu. The six kids told curious classmates at St. Ann's School that they were now a Brady Bunch, albeit with two boys and one girl from each parent. When St. Ann's closed in the early summer of 2021, John's sister Jen noted that none of the girls' Hawai'i alma maters existed anymore. St. Francis School, an all-girls' school when they had attended in the 1980s, closed in 2019 after a few years of going co-ed to stem its declining enrollment.

The personal and familial had a habit of popping up in John's teaching and writing—and he liked it that way. If others didn't care for his style, that was their problem. He was an academic by training, but there was only so much that boring documents could say to a general public. As he warned his grad students, talking to people provided context and breathed life into otherwise sterile records that historians were entrusted to examine and expound upon.

Earlier that morning, as the sun rose but before he got the kids ready for school, John wrote by hand, in an acid-free journal—for posterity, of course. Now he was weaving some of those sentences into more formal paragraphs for a class presentation that would hopefully also eventually appear in a peer-reviewed publication.

As John considered a word for a nifty turn of phrase, he looked away briefly from his laptop to see an older man, well-dressed and with a Panama hat who walked past his table and the mall's fountain that had just switched on. John could only see the gentleman's back as he tentatively walked out the automatic doors that slid open, revealing a future neither he nor the man could possibly imagine yet.

Landwehr, Achim and Tobias Winnerling (2019). "Chronisms: On the Past and Future of the Relation of Times." *Rethinking History* 23 (4): 435–55.

Shaw, Emma and Debra Donnelly (2021). "Micro-Narratives of the Ancestors: Worship, Censure, and Empathy in Family Hi(Stories)." *Rethinking History* 25 (2): 207–23.

The Times We Met at Kou

• BRADY EVANS •

THE TIMES WE MET AT KOU

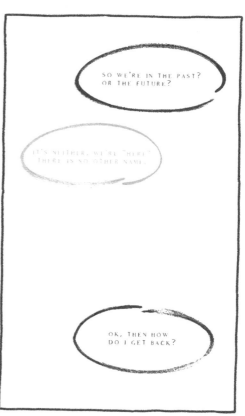

I WATCHED AS THE STONES,
EMERGING FROM THE GROUND,
SLOWLY SWALLOWED THE
BUILDINGS.

THE ACCESS GATE GRADUALLY BECAME MORE
DISTANT BEFORE FADING AWAY FROM VIEW.

THE STONES FOLDED AROUND ME AND I BECAME SNARED IN THESE LAYERS OF TIME.

WELL...

...ARE YOU COMING?

Remnant

• MISTY-LYNN SANICO •

I'm sure you already know this, but some of Honolulu's most influential and iconic businesses began as your neighbors. You're still a part of that legacy, though only slenderly, partially so. Officially you're in the Merchant Street Historic District, on the original Honolulu "work" street, Kālepa.

People still bustle up and down this road, now, just as much as they did in 1883. That's when you were born, did you know? Or have you forgotten? Well, even before that, the land on which you sit was witness to important people and events, where kings and peers played 'ulu maika.

You used to be part of a larger building that took up nearly a whole block. Replaced by offices and a parking garage in Brutalist style, they took most of you away in 1965, in case you've forgotten that too. Forgetting is a curse for the timeless, you know. Of course you do. Still, I wonder what stories and secrets you have. What magic, liminal space you hold a place for, like a giant bookmark in an ancient tome.

Do you feel the ghost of your greater self like the phantom pain of a missing limb? Just asking for a friend. When all the better parts of me have been used up and taken by time or tragedy, I wonder if the wisp that remains will exist as you do. Betwixt one place and another. Can what's left of *me* be a marker for something mysterious as well?

It might be insensitive to tell you this, but you're rarely mentioned in lists and articles about historic buildings of Honolulu. You might prefer it that way. No commemorative plaque to mark you. I wouldn't take it personally. You're not a building in the present sense anyhow, just a two-story pilaster two feet wide and covered in soot from endless exhaust. What are you if you aren't what you were and barely anything now? Something narrowly new and slightly the same, maybe.

If I wanted to squeeze in next to you, would you make room for me? If I wanted to hide there with you and watch the world walk by, would you allow it? You seem so lonely even while so tightly embraced. Stuck in between and often overlooked, a spectator and a spectre, invisible in plain sight. Forgetting and forgotten.

But
I see
you.
Rem
nant.
And
we
are
kin
dred
spi
rits.

The Bluest Angel

• DON WALLACE •

In the office, Bob is an acknowledged mess, an uncontrolled forager, ravager of malassadas, matcha green tea cream puffs, other people's leftover curry rice. They can't get him out in the field fast enough. He knows this. He just can't help himself. Still, they like him, they call him Uncle, that was something. *Have a doughnut, Unka Bob?*

Running a little late, preparing to go out on his daily trap run, rushing again, fumbling with pen, phone, data entry log, what should he do but drop the damn doughnut, of course. It bounced—imagine the chemicals in there, the preservatives, that gave it such tensile memory!—and rolled a few inches out of sight. He hesitated (late, running late) but there were cockroaches and mice in the office, a typical dingy state bureaucrat's burrow, seventy-five years of human skin, dandruff, crumbs in suspension and floating, coating everything in a not-quite-microscopic film.

He has to get it. His kuleana.

Sighing, he stooped and then, feeling the arthritis in his back and knees, lowered himself fully down. It was dark as a cave in there. On one knee, he peered under the piles of books, journals, research reports, and white plastic bags that he'd hoarded when the state announced it was banning them. So many white bags . . .

"Oh, look! Somebody's been into the doughnuts!"

"Bob. It has to be Bob. Look at the smears on the counter. Evidence!"

"He totally fingerprinted himself in sugar."

"Totally Bob."

"Bob the borer beetle technician."

"It's a sucky job, forreal. But somebody's got to do it. Better him . . ."

"He kind of looks like a beetle, you know? The way dog owners start to look like their dogs?"

He grimaced. Couldn't hold this position much longer. Couldn't climb out from under his desk, either, and risk being seen. He hung his head between his arms and let his stomach sag. He'd wait them out.

They moved around the common table, cleaning up after him. "Such a slob, so unprofessional!" He winced. He shouldn't have been in such a rush. But he'd gone down the rabbit hole studying alerts on new invasives from the state and federal Departments of Agriculture. There were so many new threats coming in from all over. It was fascinating. Appalling, but fascinating—climate change at work. The possible end of the Anthropocene.

But they weren't finished. "He's just so boring!"

"A borer beetle bug catcher—how could he not be?"

He tracked the titter of his younger colleagues, a swarm, moving down the hall, humming with vitality.

He stumbled out into the sunlight. Day hot, light redoubled from the magnification of white cement sidewalk and mirrored plate glass—he took it full in the face, swayed, stunned. It was as if the tables were turned and he was a specimen slide under a microscope.

The truck interior was roasting, the vinyl seat burning through his khakis like a hot iron. But what a relief to be outside. It always felt like flight.

Out of the office, Bob is a Ranger Rick in full possession of his Swiss Army knife of faculties: bachelor of science, masters of this and that, twelve years flatfooting it as a lab assistant and teaching assistant, one giant step, a breakout move, going to the Big Island, to Indo, Satawal, going buggy, they joked, going for a doctorate. Insects. Insects on the brain.

Still, it was worth it. Dr. Bob, if you please.

And then . . . No jobs. A recession. A freeze on hires. No promotion. A change of priorities. Fifteen stutter-step years. And now he's too old, they hint, to climb the upward track so could you please pipe down, step aside, give a chance to someone else more qualified (read: younger, less opinionated, who brings malassadas, doesn't scarf them).

He shifts the state truck into drive and heads off to make the rounds. Plant and livestock disease control, pest control, invasives control—that's his kuleana, his responsibility. They put the Hawaiian word on it to make his demotion palatable, of course. Just like they justify destroying the reef with a dredged artificial beach and call it, "for the keiki"—the children. The tourist children, of course. It's all a matter of perspective.

His route takes him south and toward the water's edge. He has a line of traps. Just like Jeremiah Johnson, one of his heroes, the best of the old Rocky Mountain trappers. Only instead of beaver, he traps bugs.

His job is secure. There's always another infestation. The coffee borer, the 'ōhi'a rust, the other plagues visited on Hawai'i.

He's had a report of a coconut palm at a dangerous tilt at Lē'ahi Park, at the foot of Diamond Head. Hollowed out into a gray husk over the course of a week, it's a goner. The crew is scheduled to cut it down. And Bob is hanging up glue traps to capture the culprit.

They know who it is, of course. The coconut rhinoceros borer beetle showed up from Southeast Asia a couple years ago. Like the coquí frog from Puerto Rico, it's cute, kind of. If you like shiny beetles with interesting serrated legs and scary mandibles.

He's got one in each trap. The traps are big black boxes that hang like lanterns from tree limbs. Not from coconut trees, of course—they don't have limbs, only fronds. But the surrounding trees.

In the third trap, in Lē'ahi Park, there's a third victim, same size, different color. He stops to check it out. This one is not just different—it's totally different, as in species. And if a coconut rhinoceros borer beetle is kinda cool from an evolutionary standpoint, if ruthless and relentless, like all the invasives, this one is flat-out gorgeous in a weird, sci-fi way. It's a one-and-a-half-inch Christmas ornament of shimmer, glitter, coruscating mirrored facets. With a drop-dead beautiful coloration scheme. Nature has done herself proud here. Metallic blue-green-orange, just outstanding. Good work, insect god.

It looks dead. He touches it. It wiggles. Moving its thick midsection on the glue trap as he pulls his fingertip back it convulses and he can see the chain of exoskeletal effort pulsing down to the stinger or arm, only one of its type. It's a stinger, all right. The fucker was going for him.

Well, he's got the jump, the upper hand. Evolution is on Bob's side today. Because Bob has a four-inch pin and with one deft move he impales the beetle onto the glue trap. Sorry, buddy.

Ow!!! Jesus!!!

The thing just gave him an electric shock. Strange—weird. Impossible. So, yeah, unrelated. A tweak of his funny bone, that curious nerve. But it sure did hurt.

Back in the office, he goes over the types of invasives, and threatened invasives, lurking on every coast, creek, and container ship from Hong Kong to Peru, vectoring subconsciously, fixating on Hawai'i, always the Islands. As he often does, Bob pauses to reflect on the marvelous accident that has placed him here, now, contributing in his own tiny way to the history of the Islands. What is it about this place? First the pristine archipelago. Then the Polynesian arrivals. Pigs, chickens, dogs. The rats that killed off the defenseless indigenous birds—and what birds they must've been. And then, the story goes, the second wave of Polynesians from Tahiti arrives, subsuming the first. Who exist now as rumor, glimmers of DNA, a few linguistic fragments and yeah, fine stonework, those walls that preceded the second wave of Island settlement. It's a universal story. What the Cro-Magnons did to the Neanderthals, the Romans did to the Greeks, the Greeks did to the Dorics, it's change over time, the long view. A story composed of stories. Yet none, Bob thinks, are capable of representing the lives of those who actually lived it. The ungraspable now defeats every attempt of understanding. As it should!

When he reached this point in his lecture back when he was teaching, he liked to end class on a light note, skate over any controversies, by pausing to ask his students to consider their place in the taxonomic order by questioning his own: "These days I sometimes wonder if I'm a rat or a bird."

He searches the last photo gallery in vain. It's a wash. He can't identify it, the beetle. It's not on anyone's radar.

He sighs. Sends a photo over. The internet insect specialists will hive mind on it. Too bad. He'd really wanted the glory of being the one to sound the alarm on a new intruder, this little blue-green-orange boy with the bright red arm like Popeye's, like a prosthesis, like the Hulk's.

"Congrats, Bob, they're going to name a beetle after you!"

He'd imagined the email that might be in his box the next morning. If nobody could ID the beetle.

No email, but he's elated anyway. The longer this beetle goes without a name the likelier it will bear his. It's true chickenskin. With his email time stamp as verification he really could get this one. The crowning achievement of his career. A thumb in the eye of his old tenure committee, a gold star the state's Ag director won't soon forget.

Agaporomorphus bob.

It's not on his schedule, but he makes a detour during his lunch hour back to Lēʻahi Park and Diamond Head. The stubby tuff volcanic cone, iconic sphinx of reddish ochre, tourist magnet upthrust in the most expensive neighborhood on Oʻahu, lording it over Waikīkī, hardly looks fully capable of one day unleashing devastation and fire on Honolulu. The volcanologists say the odds are slim to none, but he'll take them.

Bob likes disruption, the moment of transformation from one status quo to another. Let the urban interface burn; he'll trust what comes of ashes.

Two more coconut rhinos, no specials.
And no email.

He's back a day later. Last night, suddenly, he thought about mutations. Birth defects. One-offs. Yes, that's what they'll say—if he can't find a second bug. And he'll be just another one-paragraph citation in *The Journal of Irreproducible Results*. An inside joke.

He's got to lay out more traps.

He lays out more traps. Not strictly in the budget. But in his book, he records it as: *possible infestation.*

He's convinced this will be one, an infestation. He's got a newspaper story in mind now, then a promotion.

Six traps, one coconut rhino. And—he can't believe it—a fat red arm, like Popeye's, left behind in the glue. He takes it, despite knowing this won't be enough to settle the question. They'll just say the beetle—his beetle—Bob's beetle—is a fluke. Or worse, symmetrical. Two fat arms. He knows how sexy asymmetry is to the bug lords, the peer reviewers in the journals. They won't be easy to convince. He needs two one-armed beetles.

Eureka. His second Bob beetle. Caught in the glue in all its scintillating agony, convulsing as his pin approaches, trying to whip its stinger out before his can strike.

He takes a picture, sends it on to the internet, to the state's overworked librarian of specimens, to the national data bank. *Two identical asymmetrical beetles of unknown origin, found on Oahu, August 2 and August 6, 20—*

Now it's time to stake his claim before some weasel professor names it after, who knows, Jay-Z, or Billy Joel, or, yeah, Tyson Fury. He'd actually like to see a big-ass beetle named after Tyson Fury. Someday, not today.

Today will be known henceforth far and across the land, as *Agaporomorphus bob* Day.

The beetle has landed.

Following week. Catches a few rhinos. No Bob beetles. The email and his photos and claim are now deep in the bowels of science. It may take a year, two, before action is taken—

Unless. Unless there is an infestation. For real. Bring it on!

His wish is granted. A half dozen. In six traps.

He's studying his hand. Five aces. It's too rich. Almost. You can't be too rich. But, seriously, this is serious—an infestation. He wishes it wasn't. Almost. His beetles. His responsibility. It's almost as if he willed them into life.

What damage will they wreak on the Islands?

On the other hand: whatever they do, he's the answer, the savior.

He heads up the hill on Diamond Head Road, imagining himself into the mind of a beetle. The air currents, the trade winds— *does it fly?*—if not, then who's the random carrier? Perhaps a homeless guy. This is where they live. Up and down, morning and evening, pushing their shopping carts hither and yon, usually a skinny mutt joyriding in the top basket.

Or maybe it's a jogging yoga girl in leggings and strappy sports bra, baseball cap, and dark glasses, her pink counterfeit Gucci fanny pack from Singapore dripping beetles like jewels in her wake.

There are several gaps in the sea-grape and prickly desert shrubs that line the steep eroded highway cut through the volcano's multiple layers of sediment and lava and limestone from ancient reefs. The gaps are where the homeless have pushed their way through and made paths up into the underbrush on the flank of the tuff cone. It's a dry semi-scrub desert forest up there, skinny trees widely spaced but scraggly with thin creepers and vines, bright in the sun, oppressively hot and odorous. The smell of human feces dominates.

He proceeds cautiously. There are many homeless up here. The head count goes up by the week. They clear them out once every three weeks, haul away their garbage and junk. Then they filter back.

He sees a guy lying on a sleeping bag under an umbrella. He's muttering silently to himself. His eyes are fixed, mad, bugging out. Best to go another direction. There's another one over here, one over there, a couple of darkly tanned women in rags eyeing him suspiciously, seeing his uniform, perhaps thinking he's a cop. On his guard, he thinks of how easy it would be for one of the crazy ones to get the jump on him.

He feels anxious, doesn't want to linger, look for bugs. Not today. And he hasn't seen anything on the ground. Maybe it's a coconut palm beetle, too.

A flicker catches his eye up high. There, a shiny whirring object hovers in the sky above him, directly overhead in the sun. Lights blink and silver arms flex and twitch. A drone, he realizes. One of those off-the-shelf quadcopters.

Back in the office, then home: no email.

Next trip back a couple days later he breaks through a layer of brush to see a good dozen lying around, conked out, asleep at midday. No one stirs. They look like bundles of clothing arranged to look real, like dummies in prison cell cots by escaping inmates. Around them there are lots of shiny blue-green-orange beetles, moving, crawling on the ground.

Damn. It's here. An infestation!

Up in the trees bright shiny baubles, multiple necklaces of blue-green-orange, buzz away, in flight, flowing east, west, north. They can fly?

They can fly.

A searing pain. Down, on his ankle. But he's wearing socks! The telltale blue-green-orange shellac of the beetle glitters in the dappled sun filtered through scrub trees. The fucker stung him. He feels a burning creep up his calf even as he swings the clipboard sharply down and swats it off. A thin twig of red, the stinger, stays behind. It's asymmetrical, this beetle. Like the giant claw of the Pacific land crab that has evolved into a club for sexual display; only this one packs a punch.

The pain fades. Good. He's seen all he needs to see; he's seriously spooked by the bodies lying around as they're nothing more than bundles of clothing, piles heaped beside their *other* piles, of rags, soiled bedding, and blue tarps. Someone is flopped out every ten feet or so. This isn't natural, everyone sleeping. A couple of people, sure, it's the heat of the day, 2 p.m., thick and muggy. But everyone? Out cold? It feels wrong.

Of course something is wrong. He decides he'll inspect the closest bundle, call 911, and withdraw. He approaches cautiously. It's a man, lying on his back, a typical burnt-out case; in his forties, face gaunt and filthy, he sports a reddish stubble beard and a poorly shaved head. His mouth is open, chapped lips parted; his eyes are turned upward to the sky as if searching for something.

Whatever, it's too late. He's dead. Bob swings his head around to check out the next bundle before changing his mind and turning back to the first. He has to really force himself to focus, do the science, observe the deets. The man's skin is papery, his cheeks hollow. Hollower. His body is too thin, already caving in like . . . like a scarecrow, no flesh on him. Like a dry corn husk. His face reminds Bob of the ocean desert mummies of Chile; like them, who'd just sat down and died millennia before, the facial expression remained fresh, drained of color but precisely delineated as a black-and-white photographic negative.

And he's smiling. It is a happy expression, or, at least, not an unhappy one. Certainly not an expression of agony.

How long has he been lying here is the next question. But something tells Bob not to get too close. His training having kicked in, up until now, observation had come before analysis. But what the hell is this? Some new virus? The bubonic plague? To judge from the bodies lying about, in no particular grouping, but near each other, this disaster, this tragedy . . .

Ah, but is it? A tragedy? Or is it simply the inevitable? The past year has seen tremendous disruption. The numbers of the homeless swelling since the evictions began, the clearances, pushing into neighborhoods, sometimes the very neighborhoods where they'd once rented. Here in Diamond Head, the most expensive real estate in the entire state, an itinerant population of sixty to one hundred had reached one thousand, at times more. The pushback and cleanups and sweeps were barely holding back the tide; the swarming petty thievery and nonstop mental crisis mode had soured everyone. Bob thinks: Maybe having a mass die-off is a natural reaction, a thing like the toxic algae blooms in the Gulf of Mexico.

The point was this: who even cared? It was coming to that. These deaths wouldn't sting the public conscience for the same reason they didn't his. Hadn't there been a similar die-off in Wai'anae a few weeks ago, a batch of bad drugs blamed?

One new thought makes up his mind for him and now it's time to go. Because he has a gut feeling this is a mass suicide, à la Jonestown. The homeless making a last protest.

No. No, these folks were all crazy and on drugs. The opposite of organized, except to get high. That made it another mass overdose. Someone had scored some cheap stuff and it was contaminated by fentanyl.

Five, seven, nine, ten, eleven bundles are in sight. More, he's sure, are up the hill. This is a disaster and he's in the middle of it. He reaches into his pocket for his phone, fumbles it as he enters the code to unlock it. He starts a video, turning in a 360-degree circle. Then he takes a still of the homeless man's shrunken face.

He stops. Is it his imagination? Or has it shrunk even more?

He glances around at the other bodies. They've shrunk, too, he's sure of it. He bends over a half-naked man whose hairy grimy torso seems to have sunk into itself. His skin is ashy gray, looks crumbly. His bare legs look fibrous, like old cellulose insulation.

They look the way the coconut palm trunks did.

Except those took a week, two. Not before his eyes. Instant mummification.

He peers into the forest around him, looking for any movement. Punching 911. He sees a flicker off to one side—in a brushy ravine off another illegal path the homeless use to access the hill from Diamond Head Road. He starts for it, punching 911 into his phone, already knowing the response: *Out of Network.* This whole side of Diamond Head, from Lēʻahi Park to Fort Ruger Park, is in permanent cell tower eclipse thanks to the overhanging volcano. He has to head down the road, a one-minute drive down the four hundred yards to the Kāhala side. He'll roll the calls as he goes.

But first, the figure moving in the brush.

It's a man, hunched over, as if retching. That's what they do when overdosing. Maybe he can get the paramedics in time, Jesus, what's he got, nine DOA? When has this ever happened except . . . well, during the past couple of years. The pandemic. So, logically, thinking like a science-fiction movie, which is in his opinion no more than an extrapolation of the scientific method by other means— where's he going with this—he's feeling fuzzy—could be the bite— the heat—or, shades of *Contagion* or *Outbreak* or *World War Z,* a mutation, that's right, could this be a fucking mutation? The next variation? The one that makes the Delta variant look like the common cold? Forget the beetle. Airborne COVID would be far worse.

His foot is dragging. His head, swimming. That fucker's sting packed a wallop. He has a fatalistic premonition as he looks down at the foot that he's now having to tug along, like a stubborn dog on a leash—a leash of muscle and bone and ligaments—because his foot is . . .

He squints at the shifting rectangle of light. It's where the bushes at the bottom of the steep rutted path frame a black patch of Diamond Head Road asphalt. Already he knows it will be a near thing, making it that far. His knee feels like a dried-up old coconut. One-hopping won't cut it much longer, not when it reaches his hip. There is, he realizes, a self-cauterizing agent, self-annealing, in the toxin, and it has something that clots as the venom works its way up. Clots, and below the line, leaves a hollow husk. Amazing.

He's clutching at thin scratchy branches, willing himself to lurch through that door of light onto the road, waving his phone, calling for help, when he sees the bent figure straighten up. It's a man, about six foot. Naked. Smooth-skinned, so not homeless. He must be one of those compulsive exercisers who walk around and around

Diamond Head sweating copiously and turning golden and orange and then redder and . . . A bit kinky, they all are, the 90% naked walkers and runners . . . but he can help Bob get to the road.

Only as the man comes his way through the leafy branches Bob sees that he's not tan, not golden. This one? His legs are black. Tattooed or dyed black. His torso is molting, papery strips peeling off. Must've had a bad sunburn.

The man pauses to look at him, a hint of blue, of green, of orange, coming through the chrysalis of dry flaking skin. He looks at him and his eyes twitch and bug out and, just then, Bob feels an electric shock, the funny-bone nerve twang, throughout his whole body. Just from a look.

Blue crystals . . . why is he thinking blue crystals . . . No, he's seeing them, inside his skull, his brain, like the strange shapes on the inside of your retina when you close your eyes . . . Prions, he guesses. Structures of evolutionary response, hard-wired, like exoskeletons. But why is he seeing them—and where?

The man steps forward, his lurching movements stretching his desiccated skin to the limit. Bob waits for the first tear in the cloak of parchment epidermis. When it comes it isn't where he expected it.

Not out of the man's back.

But that's where they break out, bursting after a sharp twist of the torso: twin fins of metallic blue. As peels of skin float away he sees that they are tight coils, curled up tight as fiddlehead ferns, only now, as the man flexes, they begin to slowly expand, loosen, unfurl. He keeps stretching them with peristaltic contractions of his body. The coils' fern-like tips extend themselves shakily like the legs of a newborn fawn. They tremble. And then, gloriously, open.

Into wings. Wait—

He can fly?

The faceless man rises, humming, off the dryland forest floor of the volcano. He—it?—looks at him—with counter-rotating eyes on blue stalks, no less—as it hovers a foot or two off the ground, testing the air—testing *him*?—before rising up and skimming away across the treetops, vanishing.

Bob the scientist gets it: a larval stage that is followed by a hunt for a host who is then a chrysalis which cracks open eventually to yield the imago. Of course. The winged nymph then goes forth. To do its business, whatever that might be. Mate, propagate, colonize. Maybe even do science.

Through the crystals in his brain, Bob the host starts to see a hexagonal universe, tinted blue. But he has time. A nanosecond. Still time enough to appreciate that this species is going to be named after him, this Bob who's still smiling as that smile turns to spongy desiccated deadwood and his soul is husked, harvested by what he'll never know. Past caring, dying in hope because the stinger's last portion in its cocktail of chemicals included oxytocin, the love hormone, he whispers:

I can fly?

Because the sky is now full of the bluest angels.

Cacaroach and Slippah

• DARRELL H. Y. LUM •

—for Lanning Lee

CAST

SLIPPAH: old, used, worn down rubber slipper (zori, worn-down heel, loose toe strap)

CACAROACH: large brown roach, wingless of indeterminate origin; also known as "Greg"

ROACH CHORUS: an "intrusion" (group) of roaches, multiple-voiced chorus

SETTING
Run-down kitchen in old house, urban Honolulu

TIME
The present

SLIPPAH: Eh, cacaroach, get outa my way. Uddahwise I going smash you to smithereens.

CACAROACH: Ho, you talk big Mistah RUBBAH slippah. I not scared of you. I get whachucall, exoskeleton. Hard and tough. Can witstand 200 pounds per square slippah inch. I get ancestors from tree hundred million years ago, da Carboniferous period. You, you not even real rubbah, RUBBAH SLIPPAH!

SLIPPAH: I . . . I stay from da whole bin of size 11's at Longs Drugs. What about dat, big shot?

CACAROACH: No make me laugh. You stay dime-a-dozen.

SLIPPAH: Not! Was 88 cents.

CACAROACH: If you was one criss-cross leather strap slippah maybe I move. But you, tsah, nutting. Mo soft den Crocs. Mo squishy den tofu. Mo stink den kamaboko slippah. Get it? Get it?

SLIPPAH: No get wise cacaroach. I can smash you if I like. Good ting I no like. I jes giving you warning.

CACAROACH: You talk big fo one slippah dat need one retread. No wondah dey call you "SLIP-ah." Haw, haw, haw. Rubbah slippah, easy. Leather strap slippah, kinda tough. Criss-cross strap leather slippah stiff like one board. One whack and you stay applesauce. Das da only reason dey keep um around, 'cause nobody actually wear stiff, hard slippahs. Das like wearing a couple 2 x 4's on your feet. But fo smash slow cacaroach or big centipede, no can beat.

SLIPPAH: Not funny. I can strike fear. *("Whoosh," swipes at CACAROACH, misses)* Feel da powah!

CACAROACH: Okay, okay. No mess up my antenna. Jes had um groomed. You like how I made one small kine curl on da left one?

SLIPPAH: Ho, how come you stay all fancied up? You going out? Hot date?

CACAROACH: Hot date but I'm, ah, staying in if you know what I mean.

SLIPPAH: Where you guys going eat? Kitchen? In front da TV? Undah da bedroom sheets . . . heh, heh.

CACAROACH: Naw bedroom sheets only get cracker crumbs. By da TV only get potato chip crumbs. We going KITCHEN SINK, brah. Dese guys no even sit down fo eat. Make Cup Noodle in da microwave and eat standing up. Crazy. Dey donno how enjoy dere food. Erryting rush. Fast-fast kine. Donno how to slow down. I no mind. Bettah fo me. Dey splash soup and spill noodles all ovah. I got da spot checked out.

SLIPPAH: You sly buggah. Got um all figgahed out, eh?

CACAROACH: Yep.

SLIPPAH: What if da lady of da house see you by da kitchen sink? She going scream . . . maybe step on you!

CACAROACH: Nah, she no like get her house slippahs dirty. Plus, I mo fast den her. I built fo SPEED.

SLIPPAH: Huh! Mo like built fo SLOW. You bettah watch out, wen da lady used to punish her kids, she no make um sit in da corner. She make um do "DEAD CACAROACH."

CACAROACH: What is dat?

SLIPPAH: You gotta lie down on your back and hold up your arms and legs fo tree minutes. Dead cacaroach. Das what you going be, "Da ROACH formerly known as CACA."

CACAROACH: Who you calling "dead cacaroach?"

SLIPPAH: Okay, okay. No get all huhu. I tell you what, if aftah you pau eat, if you guys like dessert come see me. I flip ovah and you can enjoy someting sticky.

CACAROACH: What get?

SLIPPAH: Ah, I tink ice cream. Da drumstick kine, you know wit chocolate and nuts. Still fresh. Might help you get lucky wit your lady cacaroach . . . heh, heh.

CACAROACH: Eh, no make like one dirty old slippah. We jes going have a nice time togeddah.

SLIPPAH: I jes trying to make your evening complete. Soup to nuts. Hopefully your nuts . . . heh, heh.

CACAROACH: Dere you go again. I said we jes getting to know each uddah.

SLIPPAH: Well den, I hope you get protection.

CACAROACH: You have a dirty mind, Slippah!

SLIPPAH: I mean, what if da old lady see you and grab da Raid spray? Or me? Or da BIG ass Scott slippah? What den?

CACAROACH: No worry, I get da plan. I know da escape cracks in da floor, along da baseboard, undah da refrig. As a mattah of fack, I was planning undah da frig fo our, ah, romantic encounter. Would be so cool . . .

SLIPPAH: Stupid head. Undah da frig is not cool. In fack, it's HOT. Inside da frig is cool but undahneat is hot. And inside is too cold fo one hot date.

CACAROACH: Maybe we'll retire to da bookshelf. Cozy up next to Kafka.

SLIPPAH: Since when you got all lit-a-rary?

CACAROACH: *(pretends to be talking to his date)* "Jes call me Greg, baby . . ." I figgered dat would be one good place fo us to get to know each uddah. Nobody read dose old classics and I like da idea of cozying up in the shadow of a famous roach. Das da only book dat get one roach as da main character. Da writing so realistic, I can smell da rotten apple.

SLIPPAH: Like from da story?

CACAROACH: Like from you, stupid! Who knows WHAT you went step on.

SLIPPAH: I should jes whack you and put you out of your misery. You talk big but only can scurry away. When get one bunch of you guys and I show up, watch errybody SCURRY.

CACAROACH: Excuse me? The proper term is "intrusion" of roaches. Not bunch, not flock, not litter. Intrusion. Although we **do** love kitty litter. And **I** do NOT scurry. Scurrying is fo da little roaches. Wen you, Mistah Slippah, approach an intrusion of my brothers and sisters and dey all run in different directions, das scurrying. Me, I don't scurry. I dodge, I evade, I feint, I misdirect, I . . . I . . .

SLIPPAH: Enough awready. Sorry, I didn't mean to suggest that you were a scurry-er. I thot das what you guys do. Scurry. So what now Mr. I-No-Scurry? You going check out da fresh Hoy Hoy Trap-A-Roach? I get one riddle fo you: You know how to avoid da Trap-A-Roach? Walk around um . . . ha, ha.

CACAROACH: How stupid do people tink we are? You evah seen da instructions? "Stick the 'welcome mat' on both entrances." Get one welcome mat fo clean your feet so you going stick to da glue. Well, if you wipe your feet, you deserve fo be Trap-A-Stoopid.

SLIPPAH: Local style, you wipe your feet, take off slippahs, la dat.

CACAROACH: Look, cacaroaches can walk on da ceiling. Some can fly. One time, I actually went to go inside one Trap-A-Roach fo check it out . . . dat food is gross! Like imitation imitation imitation dehydrated fish flakes. Who going eat dat?

SLIPPAH: You, stupid. Besides I know you no can fly. You too fat. No can get off da ground. I no see no wings, brah. You not one pilot. You not even da co-pilot, da nava-gator, da steward, da toilet wiper. Well, maybe da toilet wiper.

CACAROACH: Why fly when you can walk? Stay on da ground. Avoid conflict wit one newspaypah, swatter, or one slippah. I going get dere eventually. No need to fly.

SLIPPAH: Ha, ha. You mean, you no can fly!

CACAROACH: Bettah safe den sorry. My grandfaddah went tell me da story of Icarus Roach went fly too close to da sun . . .

SLIPPAH: And went burn up?

CACAROACH: Naw, was florescent light. Went hit his head and fall down. Only to be slippah-ed. Roach-In-Peace, Icarus.

SLIPPAH: Okay, I going do you one flavor. Stay away from da blue light.

CACAROACH: My Uncle said something about dat. Get one blue light and plenny dead termites at da bottom. Some fresh, some rotten. I like rotten. Ho, all-you-can-eat buffet he said. "But no go by da blue light," Uncle said. Dangerous. If you misstep, zap, you pau. Goners! Some even get one vacuum when you come close da buggah suck you in.

SLIPPAH: Like da ladies at da bar . . . come close and dey suck you in, "You buy me drink?"

CACAROACH: I not scared of dat. Das fo da flying insects fo get electrocuted. Da electricity inside too weak. No even tickle.

SLIPPAH: Watch out, might curl your antenna. Or fry your feet.

CACAROACH: Naw. Us guys no die. We jes dehydrate. Das da killah, when no can find water.

SLIPPAH: Das why Hoy Hoy so dangerous. If you get stuck, no water.

CACAROACH: Look, even if I wanted to eat dat bait, I wouldn't get stuck.

SLIPPAH: How come?

CACAROACH: Walk on da ceiling of da Hoy Hoy. Reach down wit da feelers, smell, smell, aroma. Sniff, sniff, sniff. Snack on da bait. Figgah out das not real food. And move on.

SLIPPAH: You tink you can resist da Hoy Hoy calling to you, "Hui, hui. Greggie, I know you like eat my stinky bait. Come, Big Boy. Come eat me . . . "

CACAROACH: You tink I was born yesterday? Das da worst kind of death. Slow, agonizing, and painful. Death by dehydration. So cruel. Violation of da Geneva Conventions, I tink.

SLIPPAH: So what kine cacaroach you?

CACAROACH: Me? Ah, one good one. One smart one. One handsome one. Strong one . . .

SLIPPAH: I mean your lineage. Like me, I one rubbah slippah from my ancestors, da Zoris. You German? Oriental? American? I know you not Australian, you no mo accent.

CACAROACH: Hapa. And one smart one . . . My bruddahs and sistahs, most of dem ma-ke, die, dead. I told dem always be careful. You not as fast as you used to be. Mo bettah be smart and alive, den stupid and dead. When you hear, "Get da slippah!" no try scurry back home. Stay put, stay upside down on da ceiling, make yourself small. No try make a break fo it. But no, dey tink dey still fast, like when dey was young.

SLIPPAH: Cacaroach, you old, you slow, and you cocky. You bettah run befo I come crashing down on you. SPAA-LATT!

CACAROACH: Gimme head start. Close your eyes. Count to ten first.

SLIPPAH: Okay, okay. Ready, set, go! Ten . . . nine . . . eight . . . seven . . . six . . . five-four-tree-two-one. Ready or not, here I come! Where he went? He cannot get far. Check undah da sink, by da garbage can, by da sticky stuff behind da frig. Shouldn't have closed my eyes.

ROACH CHORUS: *(Excited)* Slippah coming, slippah coming! To da cabinet, scurry!

(Sound of cabinet door opening, then slamming. Darkness.)

ROACH CHORUS: Alert! Alert! Stay away, new Trap-A-Roach in da neighborhood. *(Antenna emerges from Trap-A-Roach. Gasps.)* Whoa! Who is dat?

CACAROACH: Hoy, hoy guys!

ROACH CHORUS: It's Greg! Look, he's alive! He survived da Hoy Hoy! He came back from da welcome mat, da glue, and da bait. How you did dat?

CACAROACH: *(Preens, brags)* Not hard. SLIPPAH stupid enough to give me head start. Hide in plain sight: **inside** da Hoy Hoy. Upside down on the top. Jes hold on like on one bucking bronco . . . jes ride um out.

> *(As CACAROACH recounts his bravery, ROACH CHORUS looks up and point.)*

ROACH CHORUS: Slippah alert! Scurry! *(Scatters, afraid.)*

CACAROACH: *(Unconcerned)* Hey guys, relax. No pop one gasket. I went pop da slippah's gasket. Put some bacon grease on da toe strap. Da buggah so old, was ready fo pop anyways.

SLIPPAH: It's your time to die, CACAROACH! *(Straightens up, gets ready to swat. Winds up and swings. Straps come loose, loses balance and misses.)* Aiya! Broken toe strap!

CACAROACH: Sorry SLIPPAH, time fo you fo go to da slippah graveyard: where only get broken toe straps and da only ones not broken stay all left side. Hasta la vista, Baby! *(Exits.)*

(PAU)

Unko Raised His Fist

• JENNIFER HASEGAWA •

Me and unko went
fishing down South Point side, near
da hahd fo see place

dat get da long ropes
tied to pre-colonial
dimensions. Unko

said fo no be sked.
Da buggah tied tight to dis
plane of existence.

Unko perched our tent
inland an den we when walk
out to da cliffs wit

our fishing gear. We
cast our lines out like missiles
into megatons

of ocean dat get
da bes kine fish fo catch, like
ulua, weke,

menpachi at night
time, perch, halalū, but deres
a lotta unknowns

that comes with that wild
innocence. I glanced back at
camp and our tent was

doing the hula
at sunset. Not 'auana
kine, but kahiko!

"Da wind," Unko said.
Den da cast iron pan we
was going use fo fry

da fish leapt into
the salty air. Then up went
the folding chairs. Da

bag charcoal wen bus
open an look like one flock
mynah birds circling

over camp. "Aisus,"
Unko said, "Da night marchers
finally come for me."

I heard the ropes groan,
tightening in the pull of
the full moon tide. "Dey

stay coming. Lie down,
put yo face down," Unko said.
Lava rock punched me

in the hard places
and drew blood from the softest.
"No look!" Unko yelled.

The clanking faded
eventually and with
that Unko raised his

fist at the dawning
place. From the dark chaos of
the beforetimes came

light : sound : substance that
woke even the sleepiest
of us. In the still

wreckage, my Unko
opened his mouth to shout, but
instead out crawled a

tiny honu. He
launched it straight off of his tongue
into the yawing

surf below: Every
atom shimmered, shook by news
of this hard-won truce.

Waiwai as Why

• LEE A. TONOUCHI •

Before time, before da accident, da Waikīkī sunrise used to be one beautiful ting. She remembered its rays would glisten on da gentle rippling blue waves making their way to da white sandy beaches. People from all around da world would spend their savings for come here for this balcony view. Nowdays da water not so blue. And tourists no would even dare venture into da dilapidated Waikīkī projects.

"Waikīkī, Kaka'ako, Kāhala, Hawai'i Kai, these used to be all da rich places to live you know," he reminded.

"Spin it anyway you want. Who cares if this used to be one fancy hotel? Who cares if Elvis stayed here once? He left dis building one long time ago."

Ignoring her, he continued getting dress for his porter job at da Wai'anae Marriot. She continued sitting at da table, writing "Mālama Pono" on top her signs with fat markers. He wen go place her front desk uniform on da back of da chair next to her. She wen go fling da gaudy mu'u mu'u off to da side.

"You not going work?" he asked. "How we going move to da promise land? We gotta save so we can come rich."

"You always say da same ting."

"We almost get enough liters save up."

"Save for what? We no can go." She hesitated. "Not anymore."

"But we agreed."

"Tings change."

"What wen change?!"

"There wuz . . . one accident."

"I know had one accident! Everybody knows had one accident. Everybody even predicted da accident would occur!"

"I not talking about da leak."

"What den?"

She nevah answer. She nevah like answer. She wuz tired of his talk.

"So wot, you going to da ting?"

"Yeah. I should. *We* should."

"No make difference to us. We going leave dis rock."

"Dey gave up Mākaha, but now dey like take over Kaʻaʻawa Valley for their *exercises*."

"From Bellows to Kāneʻohe Bay das all theirs already. Waving signs not going change nahting. We gotta accept that that side of da island all belong to dem now. Dey paid their kālā."

"You mean their *dollah*?" She shook her head at da literal-ality.

"We lucky we get job. Since da accident, everybody in Honolulu all doing catchment. We lucky. We get paid in good clean wai. All our friends wish dey can work tourism jobs up North Shore like us."

She stared blankly at da pukas in da wall, an'den at da faded landscape picture and thought about simpler times, twenty years ago, back when dey first started dating.

"Remembah when you asked me out? You nevah have money so you always suggested we go beach."

"I wanted for see you in your bikini as why," he laughed.

"I wuz one cheap date. You used to go spear fishing and cook your catch on da hibachi. I would try get us some ʻaʻama crab. Da sea wuz our refuge. For get away from it all."

"At least we get those memories. Local kids nowdays, dey dunno. All dey know is no drink da water, no go in da water. If you in Honolulu, da ocean all kapu."

"If we had keiki, how would we teach dem?"

"Why you worrying about that? We always said we wuzn't going have childrens."

"Like I said. There wuz one accident."

At first he nevah catch on, den when he did he went on about how and when, but to her nevah mattah. She already decided she wuzn't going go to da Ninth Island. She would stay. She would teach her keiki that in Hawaiian da word for "fresh water" is "wai." And da word for "wealth" or "riches" is "waiwai." You say 'em twice; das how important Hawaiians considered fresh water for be. All da lo'i growing kalo, all that depended on freshwater. Even get freshwater when you go in da ocean. Not only wea da streams meet da sea, but also when you walk in da ocean and you find da cold spot. Das wea all groundwater stay seeping up from underneath your feet. Freshwater drew fish into da old Hawaiian fishponds. Limu grew in da ocean by wea had all da freshwater. Water used to mean life. Water nevah use to bring death. So when he ask, "Why? How waving one sign going make us come rich?" "Waiwai, as why," she going stand up and say.

Baba Lepidoptera

• RASHA ABDULHADI •

...
Not since your transit have you been so large
as the mantis on the door light
outside the home where the imam washed your body.
I wondered what ritual you would have wanted,
so took this presence for a blessing.
Later under a tent in the rain,
past your old body's new dirt home,
you came swooping through
on wings butter and black:
the largest swallowtail I'd ever seen.

...
Now you take nectar
all afternoon making honey
in your airborne gut.
You multiply forms, wear
dusky dresses for the dhikr—
your great aunt once complained:
gone are the days of the real men,
those who wore the long dress
now you wear the wings
of transparent return.

...
When a snake no longer than
an open hand, for the first time sheds its skin,
when the cicada cracks its back to be born
for a day, when the grub sleeps in leather,
when we too gestate again
this time naked in a womb of clay
is there fear, does the transforming nerve
need a guide, does longing enter the organs
as they travel, can there be contentment then,
as self separates from skin,
just to know: this is the transfer station.

Search the Waters

• DONALD CARREIRA CHING •

They said it would be years. Then, the tsunamis came and the seawalls fell. Māmala Bay swallowed Waikīkī and met the Ala Wai, and a million dollars couldn't buy you a breath on Ala Moana Boulevard.

On the other side of the island, in ʻĀhuimanu, the damage hadn't been as bad, but that didn't matter to Kaʻimi. He had been born on the beach, his mother giving birth to him during a birthday party at Kualoa, had lived his life on the water, first with the Navy then as a boat captain for the fire department, and he knew what he had to do. After the reports of what had happened came in, he hiked over Puʻu Maʻeliʻeli Digging Hill, taking with him food, water, and two tanks of gas. It took him an hour to make it down to where he had hauled his boat ashore, a parcel of state land that his friend had managed for years. From there, he navigated out through the capsized hulls and jutting masts of what was once Heʻeia Kea Pier and out onto Kāneʻohe Bay.

By the time he rounded Lēʻahi, the sun was on the horizon, casting the scene in front of him in a bloom of red. A few hotels stood stoic above the flood, but most were halved or disappeared completely. There were other boats, the military, and the coast guard. Helicopters and drones flew overhead. But it was the bodies that made him cut the motor, each one a dull thud against the hull.

When one of the fireboats came around to ask him what he was doing there, he flashed the dog tags around his neck and lied, "I'm here to help." They turned him away, told him it wasn't safe, but he didn't care. He anchored and waited, listening to radio coverage from the scene. The rescue efforts continued on into the night, but by that time, Kaʻimi had put on his old firefighter jacket and was able to slip his boat into the chaos.

It was difficult to hear anything above the noise of chopper blades, boat engines, and bullhorns. But as Kaʻimi navigated away from the luxurious rubble along Kalākaua Avenue and down the side streets, now waterways, he could make out screams and cries for help. He had brought night vision goggles, a swap meet find, and used them to sift through the shades of green.

The first person he pulled on board was James Cross. Jimmy had been living in Waikīkī for three years. He was a retired stevedore and was still collecting the checks they sent to his P.O. Box. He had a house and a wife, then he didn't. A drunk driver took his wife. The bank took his house. He couldn't live there anymore, so why pay? Now, it was just him and his Jenny Girl.

"She stay out dea," Jimmy insisted. But if there was one thing that Kaʻimi hadn't seen breathing yet, it was a dog.

Kaʻimi stuck to the areas he knew. Most tourists had heeded the warnings and had gone to their hotel rooms or to the roof tops. Locals had found themselves in traffic, only to abandon their cars and scramble on foot. Yet, some stayed. "Where was I supposed to go?" Lei asked him. She was new to the streets. Lost her job and ended up in Kakaʻako. The sweeps took most of what she owned, so she moved. She figured at least there were showers, the beach, places to keep clean. "I tried the hotels but was madness. When I got to the door, they said guests first, like they don't have the room."

He had found her lying out on a McDonald's sign, a cigarette in one hand, her arm dangling between the arches. Now, she was gulping down a bottle of water and eating chips with a pair of chopsticks she had retrieved from her hair. "I came back, you know. A bunch of us did, but you know what?"

"They had locked the doors," Kaʻimi answered before she could. He had heard the same thing already. At first, he wasn't sure if he believed it, then he found a valet who hadn't made it in on time.

He got stuck on his way to the parking garage. By the time he ran back, all he found was sandbags.

"Where were we supposed to go?" Lei asked for the third time.

Ka'imi didn't have an answer. Though, he knew they weren't all like that. Some hotels kept their doors open all the way until the first wave hit. A woman from Tacoma told him that she had been the last one in, that she had turned around and saw the water rushing down the street like rapids down a canyon. "Right then, I saw God's face in the flood."

"Did you pray?" One of the other passengers, a teenager with a New York accent and little tact, asked.

"I ran." She laughed until she had to wipe her eyes. She was on the third floor when the water rushed over her head. "Thankfully, I found a window."

Ka'imi kept at it, pulling people up and taking them to rescue services or helping them troll the water for people they knew. He barely rested, taking short naps only when his vision started to blur or his hands couldn't hold the steering wheel steady. By the third day, one of the firefighters had given him a radio and he started to coordinate pick-ups, but those occasions became rarer. Then, on the fifth day, they gave him a helmet and an axe. He anchored his boat and started to join the efforts inside the buildings. He was part of Station 7 again, where he had worked when he first started out. In the breaks between light and darkness, when the spaces were filled with nothing but smoke and ash, he felt those ghosts come back in tremors and small gasps of breath, and he thought of what brought him there.

Breaks were brief. Every second was a second too long, so he continued to break down doors and drop into flooded hallways. When he pulled bodies out, he followed procedure, he did what he could, and he moved on to the next section to be cleared. But before he tagged the X code on the outside of the room or in front of the hole in the floor, he took the time to really look at the faces just in case someone asked if he had seen a mother, a son, a friend. Just in case it was his daughter he was holding but didn't recognize.

A week after the disaster, Ka'imi took a photographer from the paper out into the fray. When she asked, he said no. "There's more to do here than take pictures." She agreed but that wasn't what she was there for.

"My father was working when the wave hit," Maka said, checking the battery on the camera before checking the lens. "The Royal."

Ka'imi nodded. He knew no one there had survived.

"I just need to work," she added. Ka'imi obliged.

They spent much of the morning and afternoon touring the aftermath. They spoke in small bursts and slips of Pidgin. Most of the time, they discussed the state of things before. A month ago, rather than invest in building up the seawalls and other precautions, the state had spent 13 million dollars to add sand back to Waikīkī. There was nothing anyone could have done to prevent what had happened, but still they laughed at the irony.

"You got to look years back, decades, generations. All the cracks they didn't fill."

"Or filled them with."

"Or put to the side or somewhere else."

Ka'imi nodded, but he felt the weight of the discussion in his shoulders and the rest of his body. The days on the water were heavy and he was beyond aching.

Maka took a picture of him and he looked up. She checked the display. "How long d'you think it'll be?" she asked him. "Until it's over." It was the first time the future had come up. He just shook his head.

"And what about for you?"

"I dunno, there's still plenty to do here."

"That's really why you came here?" she prodded.

"That's what I'm doing," he was quick to reply.

"Yeah, but to just come out here like you did, to do what

you're doing," she looked at the display again. "I'm not so sure."

He started the engine and they headed back.

When they got to the shelter where she was staying, a cruise ship that had been out on the water and survived, Kaʻimi asked to look at Maka's pictures. She let him borrow her laptop to scroll through everything that she had seen over the last several days. Although the Ala Moana and Waikīkī areas had seen the most damage, Ward, Kakaʻako, Iwilei were all underwater. Other areas of the island had fared better, but the damage stretched up the Leeward coast. People said it was worse on the other islands.

"There's a list, you know, of people they've identified. They haven't released it yet, but I could probably get a look."

He understood what she was offering. "She won't be on it," he admitted.

"You can't be sure."

He shook his head. "No tattoos, probably no ID, no way to identify her."

"They take pictures."

"Maybe then," he agreed.

"She lived out here?"

"Can say that."

"Houseless then?"

"Five years now," Kaʻimi closed the laptop. He had only gone through one folder, but he didn't know what he was looking for anyway. "She struggled with some things, after the military," he clarified. "She got help, got some pills, but she didn't like the way they made her feel. Said it was worse than when she was off them. So she got off them. On to other things, you know da kine, then other things lead to other things."

She took the laptop and put her arm around him. "They still haven't found my father," she admitted. "They probably never will."

"She's my daughter," he finally said, holding back the urge to collapse.

After they talked, Kaʻimi left to spend the night on his boat. After so long on the water, it felt uncomfortable being on stable ground. By then, he was so tired he didn't bother to spread out the wet towels to dry or prepare the motor for the next day. Instead, he lay down on the deck and let the waves carry him to sleep.

But it wasn't long before he woke. A scream he thought, or an echo of one. For a moment, he listened for a boat motor or a helicopter, but there was none. It was late and there was little light. Most of the solar spotlights that the rescue teams had set up were off. The noise of the day gone or limited to the crackle of radios or the buzz of drones. He closed his eyes, but he couldn't hear anything.

Still, he started out anyway, searching with his gut. He coasted through the maze of makeshift caution signs and way markers that had gone up in the aftermath, using his goggles or a handheld flashlight to search the waters. He had gone beyond the possible range of the sound, but he continued until the motor died.

He had almost made it to the Ala Moana checkpoint. Below him, he imagined Ala Wai Boat Harbor, and a short distance away, Kahanamoku Lagoon. It was a wading pool for tourists, but Kaʻimi used to bring his daughter there to watch the fireworks, especially when she came to visit him at the firehouse.

Kaʻimi wanted to scream. Instead, he grabbed a flaregun and climbed up onto the bow. He raised it in the air with his finger on the trigger. He just shook, his other hand holding the tags around his neck, wishing he hadn't taken them from her, wishing he could take back the words he had yelled five years before. "You're a disgrace," he whispered them to himself, salt on his lips.

He stayed there until light was on the horizon. Then, he climbed down, filled the gas tank with what was left of his reserves, and drove to the shelter. He anchored there and waited for the noise and scramble of another day, and for Maka to wake up. She still had work to do. They both did.

The Promise (III)

• MELISSA MICHELLE CHIMERA •

Midnight, Water City excerpt

• CHRIS McKINNEY •

I'm flying at top speed above the ocean. Looking down at the pleats of breaking water, I am amazed at how well-organized something as chaotic as the sea can look from afar. I break to the west side of the island and dip down to the well-lit coast. Oceanscraper cabana beach caps to the right, the giant aquatic theme park connected to the beach, shaped like a giant oyster with a pearl-like dome in the middle. Golf courses. A couple of shabby ones for the OBB, the rest exclusively for The Money. This side of the island is where a few of The Money live, the older ones who prefer land under their feet, who own prime acreage cut from lava rock fronting vast manmade white sandy beaches. I'm gliding over the estate of Idris Eshana, inventor of the iE. He died a few years back at 121. His château is being converted to a museum, soon to be another stop on The Savior's Eye pilgrimage. It's next to the shuttlefield where people transport to the continents and other faraway water cities. The whole scene probably looks like any point in the history of civilization, really, the past smeared with the present.

I remember that when Sabrina and I first started dating she was in awe of the people I knew. Of course, there was Akira, but when this island became the center of the world, I also knew top brass like NASA Director Parker and tech moguls like Idris Eshana, who came to help plan the construction of Ascalon. This is when a lot of The Money showed up to try to pitch in, or if their help was turned away, to witness. After Ascalon did her thing, a lot of The Money ended up staying. The island is conveniently located between the Mainland U.S. and Asia, the world's two financial, recycling, and tech giants. I stayed friends with some of these people. I may have even saved a couple of them back in the day, when zealots came and tried to blow up the entire mission. The crazies who believed that the apocalypse was meant to be. Sabrina heard old Idris tell the story of me pulling out my rail gun and seemingly firing at random into a crowd of protesters. My own security team thought I had gone crazy and almost gunned me down. The truth is, I fired once. And it wasn't random. I saw green. And the kid I shot was packing a dirty bomb in his backpack. But to hear Idris tell it, I performed like an action hero, and Sabrina was smitten. Idris winked at me after she walked away. Nothing like having the richest man in the world wingman for you.

It's easy to drift into nostalgia up here in a SEAL. Not many fly them, so there's never really traffic. SEAL licenses are only granted to first responder, military, and science personnel, and even then, you need to be of a certain rank. I own mine, but I put it up for collateral to buy the float burb unit, so who knows for how much longer. Kind of like me, it's becoming obsolete anyway. There aren't really serviceable roads on the island anymore, and vac tube trains, hovers, and heli-taxis get everybody where they need to go. The Money still have their SEALS and employ ex-cops and ex-military like me to chauffeur them around, dangling supplemental pension and all, but even they hardly use military-grade flying vehicles anymore. We just don't gotta go that high.

Maybe I'm feeling weepy about the past because of the death of my best friend. Maybe it's the mess I just made back home. But most likely it's because I've called in a couple of favors from The (old) Money pals, and it's always been painful for me to ask anybody for anything. Another of my personal flaws that eighty years of supposed learning never stomped out. I'm hovering over a prepubescent sweep of native trees now, a forest once wiped out and then replanted. They take three hundred years to hit full, majestic maturity, so these are just twenty-foot saplings that are about my age. Right now, I'm heading to see Jerry Caldwell, a retired attorney from Mile High who's also one of the heirs to the biggest corn syrup company in the world. Like Big Tobacco before it, the industry took a giant hit in the U.S. when there was outcry that these companies were knowingly poisoning the children of the nation with GMO junk food. And like Big Tobacco, her family's company simply concentrated production and sales abroad and continued to thrive by poisoning foreign children in countries who supposedly weren't as free as in the U.S., but let their people poison themselves all they wanted. Jerry came here with her parents when the rest of The Money did, offering to throw their fortune into the Ascalon Project. But they were among the rejected who ended up just staying in their brand-new deep-sea lofts to watch. Akira was downright mean about it to Jerry's father—the thought makes me laugh to this day. What she said to one of the richest men in the world was, "What are you proposing we do? Bribe a carbonaceous chondrite meteorite with a carbonated beverage and ask it to smile and go away?" The old man never got over the insult. But like everyone else, he stayed for the show. Jerry and I go way back. I actually met her through Akira.

They'd gone to grad school together on the East Coast. Princeton-Columbia U. After Akira finished her undergrad degree in Japan, she split and went on to do her PhD in astro-physics. Jerry was a freshman at the time, double majoring in physics and economics. There are thousands of books on Akira's life, but most concentrate on the crazy days of Sessho-seki, while others attempt to recreate her experiences as a childhood genius. Her piano story has been written hundreds of times, on the same level as Newton and his apple at this point. But none of the biographies delve into Akira's college days, when she was actually learning. People aren't into that sort of thing. They want to know what was going on when someone was doing, not learning. Besides, Akira has always been a private person. Jerry, too. So any recounting of this time in Akira's life is speculation. And despite the fact that Akira and Jerry were best friends in college, Jerry taking this tween under her wing, hardly any of these books mention Jerry at all. When the world was ending, Akira hired her old PCU friend as one of her attorneys. Insult to injury for Jerry's old man. But a couple years later, they had a falling out over what Jerry called Akira's "psychopathic ego." She added that if it weren't for the fact that Akira had to live on this planet, she'd have had zero interest in saving it. I found this hilarious. There was probably some truth to it, but Jerry was bruised over the whole thing. Akira, on the other hand, seemed completely indifferent, which was consistent with how Jerry saw her. It's weird having two close friends who hate each other, but neither ever seemed to mind that I hung out with the other, unless you counted silent judgment.

Jerry's the one I called to get me released from interrogation. But I'm not heading to her place now to discuss the case or Akira and the bad old days. I just need a couch to crash on, which through forty years and two wives, Jerry has always provided. She lives on the next island over, the one packed with skyscrapers built by all the rejected Money years back, years after the Great Sun Storm, when storms in general were the least of our concern. The entire place is lit up and reaches into the sky, cloud-breaking bouquets of tech mounted with telescopes that each resident can patch into from the comfort of their high-altitude homes. Besides Akira's Telescope, this place offered the best bird's-eye view to an extinction-level event. When Ascalon's Scar first lit up the sky, some thought it was Sessho-seki coming and jumped. Human feet, broken at the ankles from impact, washed up onshore for weeks after the world was saved. A page-three story to anyone but a cop who had the task of matching feet with names while the rest of the world celebrated. It sucked, too, because we stopped keeping toeprint records by then.

My iE goes off. A reminder to take my blood pressure and anti-plaque pills. I think about my 3D-printed fake teeth, fake hips, fake hair. Neck and jowls nipped and tucked. Already on my second heart and liver, benes used up from military service. The entire thing propped up by titanium in my spine and left leg. Unlike my pain, memory, space-travel grade anti-anxiety and anti-insomnia pills, these BP and anti-plaque pills I take. This is what getting old is, expecting our second or even third livers to hold up the messes we call bodies as we weigh them down a pill at a time. I pop my pharma and descend to the ocean-generated bioluminescence that lights up the scrapers. I head toward the biggest one, the tint of the whale-tail–shaped tower breaching two layers of clouds moving in opposite directions.

The Day the Land Spoke

• ZOE C. SIMS •

After silence so long, I had started to doubt
the stories. I had heard nothing: only dishes shattering
the day we watched the ground shiver, koai'a in wind.
Only the crush of quiet the sweltering summer the reef
turned white as pages, a field strewn with bones.
Only the choppers' patter as flame resurrected the grassland,
thick black billows, into the sky.

The day the land spoke—and I heard—
the sound started
as a valley murmur,
thrumming thunder in summer,
thunder in a body, thunder sustained.
A flash flood sweeping down streets.
The rattle the breath gives just before the end,
if sky were lung. The boiling birthplace of Lō'ihi,
piercing, becoming

memories:

The shafts of bamboo I used to slip between
to hide in the grove's heart, looking up
to watch leaves dance their jig with the wind.

The banyan roots buckling the sidewalk.
The coil of the 'auwai, slow and quiet power.

Bending down to a breadfruit, smooth green bounty,
between two parked cars, the tree I don't know where.
Later, spooning its soft, warm flesh onto my tongue.

Heavy air condenses into a mountain
of clouds. Surging water curves into
crest. Ocean births the live and rising
ground, and so her sound resolved

into words I knew, a voice close as my own.
My child. My child. You are my child
still.

Calls to Announce a Survived Existence

• LEHUA M. TAITANO •

Look! Here
is my
graying
crown.

Sigi magi!
See how my
belly has
stretched
and sags.

Tsch! Tsch!
My throat
has made a
blossom
out of scars.

I am still
here.

[1]

California Scrub Jay

---

[1] Ornithological spectrogram still of a California Scrub Jay (*Aphelocoma californica*), sourced and reproduced with permission from the McCaulay Library at the Cornell Lab of Ornithology, as recorded by Geoffrey A. Keller. This jay is a nonmigratory species endemic to Western North America, whose call is often referred to as "scratchy" or "nasally" and "shrieking."

The Return of the Ko'ko'

• CRAIG SANTOS PEREZ •

Ko'ko' Reyes used to hate her name.

In the third grade at Carbullido Elementary, her homeroom teacher, Mrs. San Nicolas, taught them about "The Native Birds of Guam" to mark the coming of Easter. The colorful Micronesian Kingfisher, *sihek*, the austere Mariana Crow, *åga*, and the flightless Guam Rail, *ko'ko'*, which also happened to be the school mascot. They colored drawings of the birds to learn feather patterns. Memorized what insects each ate. Drew timelines and charts to map their growth, from egg to maturity.

"Mrs. San Nicolas?" Ko'ko' raised her hand. "I've never seen these birds before. Do they live in our village?"

"Sadly, they're all extinct. No one's seen them here in Barrigada for a long time."

"What does 'extinct' mean?"

"'Extinct' means . . ." Mrs. San Nicolas paused, uncomfortably. "'Extinct' means they all died. Like the dinosaurs."

"How'd they die?"

"The brown tree snakes. They arrived to Guam aboard military ships in the 1940s. One hundred years ago."

Steven Sanchez, the boy who sat behind Ko'ko', blurted out: "I've seen hundreds of snakes, Mrs. San Nicholas. My dad hunts them. That's his job. He said there's more snakes on Guam than any other island in the Pacific."

"I've seen snakes, too," another student exclaimed.

"Me too!"

"My dad said the snakes cause power outs," Steven spouted. "He said they even attack babies in their cribs at night!"

"I heard that too!"

"Me too!"

"Okay, okay, quiet down," Mrs. San Nicolas commanded.

"It's almost recess. Don't forget to gather material from the playground for our nest project."

Ko'ko' stared at her drawing of the bird she was named after. Small, round. Just a foot in length, a foot in height, and about half a pound in weight. Brown head and back feathers. White stripe across the eye. Gray neck, throat, and upper breast. Black breast and abdomen with white barring. Sturdy legs, wide feet. Thick black bill. Red eyes, black pupils. Ko'ko' imagined brown tree snakes crawling under her desk, wrapping around her feet, whispering "extinct."

When the bell rang. Ko'ko' jumped from her seat, left the classroom, and focused her attention on finding leaves, grass, and twigs. She didn't notice Steven and a few other boys following her.

"Ko'ko' is named after a dead bird," they teased. "She's so dumb she can't even fly," Steven grabbed Ko'ko's long brown hair, wrapped his dry, scaly arms around her and squeezed. Her re-framed glasses fell to the ground. The other boys laughed. "I'm going to swallow you," he hissed, with his slicked-back brown hair, large head, tall and slender body.

"Leave me alone," she yelled. Ko'ko' was much shorter than Steven, but she was still able to wriggle away. She ran to hide in the girls' bathroom.

Throughout the rest of the month, the students decorated the classroom for Easter. The walls were filled with vibrant drawings of extinct native birds. On each small desk, a nest. Despite the joyfulness of the upcoming holiday, Ko'ko' was miserable because every day the bullying continued.

On Easter Sunday, Ko'ko' attended mass with her mom, Frances, at the San Vicente Catholic Church in Barrigada. She was grateful for the weekend, the reprieve from school. Plus, decorating eggs was one of her favorite activities.

As Frances put a pot of water on the stove to boil, she asked her daughter, "Is something wrong. You don't seem like yourself today."

Ko'ko' tentatively answered, "I want to change my name."

"What? Why, *nen*?"

"The boys at school tease me. They hiss when I walk by. They say I'm dumb because ko'ko' can't fly. They call me extinct. Why'd you give me this name?"

"I'm sorry kids are teasing you. But Ko'ko' birds had powerful leg muscles and could run through the jungle without making a sound. They could even swim and dive, using their wings underwater. They're very resourceful and smart, just like you."

The water reached boiling. Frances carefully placed a dozen eggs into the pot. Lined up six small bowls, vinegar, and the food coloring package on the table.

"Before you were born," Frances continued. "I worked at the Guam Bird Recovery Project. In the 1980s, zookeepers came to Guam and captured the last wild birds. They took them to zoos in San Diego, St. Louis, Chicago, Honolulu, and other places, to breed them in captivity. Years later, several birds were brought back to our islands. Some on Rota, Cocos, and Guam. In 2019, the ko'ko' became just the second species after the California condor to go from 'extinct in the wild' to 'critically endangered.' We kept some of them in an aviary, a large bird house. Others lived in the wild, but we tagged and watched over them too. We tried to keep them and their offspring safe."

"How many birds did you take care of?"

"Twelve birds. Four sihek, six åga, two ko'ko'."

"What happened to them?"

"They got sick. A new strain of bird flu."

"Birds get flus?"

"Yes. Millions of birds around the world died. Even in zoos. The off-island Guam birds all passed away. So did the re-introduced birds here in the Marianas." Frances paused. Took the eggs out of the boiling water, placed them in a bowl of ice. Poured water, vinegar, and dye into the small bowls.

"Our birds in the aviary were the last of their kind. First, the åga got the flu. Then the sihek. Then the male ko'ko'. The female ko'ko' survived, though. Somehow, she recovered. The last native bird of Guam on the entire planet."

"What was her name?"

"Her name was . . ." Frances choked up. "*Pudera, Hope.* I spent every day with her so she wouldn't be lonely. She lived a few more years until her kidneys failed. She was eight years old. That's why I named you Ko'ko'. Also, your beautiful brown skin reminded me of their feathers."

"What happened after Pudera died?"

"The government shut down the project. I lost my job. And then I found out I was pregnant with you. I moved back into this house with grandma and grandpa. You were born, and I just took care of you."

"I'm sorry, nåna. Sorry about the birds. Sorry about wanting to change my name." Frances handed Ko'ko' one of the eggs. Kissed Ko'ko''s forehead. "Don't worry, *nen.* Let's decorate our eggs so you can take them to school tomorrow for your nest."

The next day, all the kids in Mrs. San Nicolas's class were lined up outside waiting to enter the classroom. As Ko'ko' walked past Steven and the other boys, they hissed at her. "Hey, stupid ko'ko' bird! Did snakes eat your Easter eggs!"

Steven lunged towards her, but right before he could enclose her in his sweaty arms, she kicked him between the legs with all the force her small frame could summon. Steven keeled over, grabbed his balls, and fell to the ground. He screamed in pain. Cried, like a sissy.

Ko'ko' pronounced: "If anyone ever teases my name again, this will happen to you. I may not fly, but I can kick." She feigned kicking the other boys, who closed their legs and covered their crotches. She strutted to the back of the line, triumphant.

Mrs. San Nicolas ran to the scene when she heard the commotion. She was one of the oldest and shortest teachers at

Carbullido, standing at a mere five feet tall, with a bun of gray hair. In her auntie voice, she interrogated, *"Who did this*?"

No one answered. Until Mercy Manibusan, a short, chubby girl with pigtails, spoke up: "I did it. I beat up Steven."

Ko'ko' was surprised by this false confession. She once worked with Mercy on a group project, so they were friendly to each other, but they were not close friends.

"*Maila*, come with me, Mercy. You're in *big* trouble."

"No, she's lying. . . ." Steven finally mustered enough breath to say. "It was Ko'ko'."

The other boys echoed: "Yes, it was Ko'ko'."

She was sent to the principal's office. The verdict: suspended for the rest of the week. "I'm so sorry, nåna," she said when Frances picked her up.

"Don't be sorry, *nen*. The principal told me what happened. I'm glad you didn't let those boys push you around anymore. Let's go to Shirley's for breakfast. We'll share fried rice and eggs."

No one bothered her again for the rest of her time at Carbullido Elementary. At Untalan Middle, the legend of Ko'ko' grew. Instead of beating up one bully, it was five. At Tiyan High, the story grew into a mythic battle in which she defeated ten adversaries. Either version, she ultimately escaped capture from teachers, principals, and police officers, disappearing into the night.

Despite her legendary status, she did not have many close friends. She burrowed herself in school and books. Her most passionate subject: animals. By the time she was a senior in high school, she dreamed of working in a zoo. So she applied to colleges where she could pursue her goal. Her top choice: the University of California, San Diego (UCSD), which had a world-renowned Zoology department.

"Nåna! I got in!" Ko'ko' celebrated. She showed Frances the acceptance letter.

"I knew you would, *nen*! I'm so proud of you! But . . . I'm going to miss you."

"Don't worry, nåna. I'll come home every holiday and summer."

A few months later, Frances drove Ko'ko' to the airport. She parked because she wanted to come in and spend every last possible moment with her only child. As they waited at the security area, Frances pulled out a plastic Ziploc bag from her purse.

"I have a gift for you, *nen*. Remember Pudera? The day she died, I plucked this feather from her wing. I've held onto it for more than twenty years. I saved it. For you."

Ko'ko' gently held the brown feather. Ran her fingers along its vane. The barbs as soft as hair.

"As you spread your wings," Frances advised. "Don't forget where you come from. Don't forget what your name means."

"Saina ma'åse', nåna. I won't forget."

Flight 22, San Diego, is now open for pre-boarding at Gate 9.

They clutched. When Frances finally let go, she cried as her once fledgling, flightless daughter boarded the one-way flight across the ocean, far away from her island nest.

Ko'ko' declared a Zoology major as a freshman, joined the Zoology club on campus, volunteered at an animal shelter, and secured a work-study job in the aviary at the San Diego Zoo. She even became a vegan, which is an extremely rare species amongst the Chamoru people. Ko'ko' did not have much time for socializing or partying, and she was too busy to travel home during holidays. Her plan to return home after the academic year was thwarted when the zoo offered her a full-time summer job.

"Stay," Frances told her over the phone, hiding the disappointment in her voice. "This is your dream job. You can come home next summer."

Ko'ko' remained in San Diego. Her sophomore year was

even busier. She became vice president of the Zoology club and joined the UCSD campus chapter of PETA. The next summer, she continued working at the zoo. During her junior year, she overloaded on science, animal, and veterinary labs. She spent that summer working again at the zoo. As a senior, she was voted president and completed her final major requirements. Before she could catch her breath, she was on the verge of graduation. *She had not been home in four years.*

In the beginning, she tried calling her mom at least every other day. But soon this decreased to twice a week. Then every weekend. Twice a month. Monthly.

"Nåna," Ko'ko' said over the phone. "I have good news. I got accepted to the master's program in Zoology here. Full scholarship. I'll be studying bird genetics."

"That's wonderful, *nen*! You deserve it. You've worked so hard."

"Thanks, nåna. I know you don't like to fly, but did you get your ticket yet for my graduation?"

A heavy silence hovered over the static of the long-distance phone call.

"Oh, *nen*. I've been trying to find a good time to tell you, but you've been so busy. I can't come to your graduation. I'm so sorry," Frances wavered. "The cancer came back. It's spread. Stage four."

Ko'ko' submitted her final projects early, quit her job at the zoo, and flew back to Guam to care for her mom. She missed her graduation ceremony, but it did not matter to her. What mattered was that she spend every day that summer with her mom. Frances was a strong Chamoru woman: stocky, with thick legs, short arms, and a curved frame. She had beautiful brown hair with a graying stripe along the right side of her plumage. Her skin was a darker shade of brown than Ko'ko', but given their similarly-shaped bodies, lips, nose, and eyes, you could easily recognize they were mother and daughter. As Frances weakened and lost weight, Ko'ko' cooked for her, helped her shower, and cleaned the house. When Frances was confined to bed, Ko'ko' fed her, changed her diapers, sponge-bathed her. Towards the end of that summer, Ko'ko' was brushing what remained of Frances's brown and gray hair, when she said: "When I die, I want you to go back to San Diego. . . ."

"No, nåna, I'm not leaving again."

"*Nen*, listen. I want you to finish school. Get your Master's. PhD. *Then* come home. I made my will. You'll inherit this house. I want you to live here. Start a family. Promise me, you'll go. Promise me, you'll return."

"Okay, nåna. I promise."

That night, Frances died in her sleep. She was 48 years old.

Ko'ko' completed her master's thesis in two years. Her research focused on bird genetics and the history of the avian gene vault at the San Diego Zoo, which was established during the bird flu pandemic. Then Ko'ko' enrolled into the PhD program, where she worked in a well-funded, experimental lab run by the preeminent Dr. Orn, who specialized on the genetic sequencing and modification of the critically endangered American eagle.

Even though she dedicated five years working on her dissertation in Dr. Orn's lab, her real passion was something that she labored on in secret, without authorization or funding. She would have been expelled if anyone ever found out that she had been sneaking into the lab late at night, covertly using the equipment and stealing supplies and resources. Her true project: to bring the ko'ko' bird back from extinction. To re-wild her namesake.

De-extinction was still a fringe subject within the Zoology community. Even though the technology made it possible, the ethical and ecological questions prevented scientists from pursuing its full potential. Even Dr. Orn, whose research laid the groundwork to bring back the iconic American eagle when it inevitably went extinct, was apprehensive. He always emphasized the "precautionary principle." What right did we have to bring back species? Which species should be resurrected? How would their reintroduction impact existing ecosystems?

At first, Ko'ko' read every study on de-extinction just out of sheer intellectual curiosity. Then she started to daydream: *what if I could access its genetic code?* But she knew, from her thesis research, that the avian gene vault did not contain any material from the ko'ko' birds that were once housed at the San Diego Zoo. Dead end.

Then, on the seventh anniversary of her mom's death, she took out Pudera's feather. She privately tested the feather and, to her amazement, it contained enough genetic material for a complete sequencing. She wondered: *what if I modified the code and inserted two sequences from an eagle? One for flight, one for predation? What if I could modify the sequence further, so that the female bird could self-reproduce? What if I artificially inseminated a dozen eagle eggs? Stored them in a transportable incubator? Shipped them to our family house in Barrigada? What if I bought a one-way ticket home?*

Ko'ko' transformed her mom's old bedroom into the incubation room, where she cared for the eggs. They hatched about three weeks after arrival on Guam.

"Håfa adai," she whispered to the newborns as they emerged from their shells. "Welcome home."

Ko'ko' hand-fed the downy black chicks slices of brown tree snake. The birds were notably aggressive in appetite and behavior. Perhaps extinction made them even hungrier for life. Juvenile wings developed on their bodies in four weeks, and they reached adult weight in seven weeks. At that point, Ko'ko' brought them a whole, live brown tree snake. The birds made loud, piercing screeches— *kee-yu, kee-yu*—and short whistles—*kip-kip-kip*—as they ferociously ripped apart its flesh with claws and beaks. All that was left was a clean carcass of skin and bones. The next day, Ko'ko' released the twelve birds into the jungle behind the house. In two months, they returned to lay their own clutch of eggs inside the house, where Ko'ko' would care for and raise them until they, too, were ready to leave the nest.

"Håfa adai Guam! Today, more than fifty dead brown tree snakes have been spotted here in Barrigada. In the middle of the road, strewn across playgrounds, and even hanging on power lines. Some residents think this might be a prank by teenagers, others suspect it's related to gang initiations. If you witness wrongdoing, please contact the Guam Police Department, which currently has no leads. Reporting live for KUAM news, this is Mercy Manibusan."

Mercy attended the same schools that Ko'ko' did until their flight ways diverged as Mercy attended the University of Guam, majoring in Journalism. She had been working at Guam's major news network since graduation. A well-trained reporter, Mercy interviewed countless people from her old neighborhood, but no one saw what happened to the snakes.

More dead snakes appeared in the following days and weeks. Soon, dead snakes were found in the northern village of Yigo and all the way to the southern village of Merizo. After four months, a thousand dead snakes. After eight months, 10,000. After a year, 100,000. The cause remained a mystery.

"Håfa adai Guam! We're here with Steven Sanchez, my former classmate and now the director of the Brown Tree Snake Control and Eradication Project. There are rumors that you have developed a covert and effective operation to eradicate the snakes? Is this true?"

"It's good to see you Mercy. I almost didn't recognize you since you lost so much weight," he chuckled. "I wish I could take credit for what's happening. Whoever's doing this has accomplished something we've been trying to do for decades. But I hope they stop soon. Because if they don't, I'm going to be out of a job."

A million dead snakes on rooftops, gutters, beaches, trees, churches, swimming pools, malls, and parks. Some thought it was caused by climate change, others believed it was a sign from God of an impending judgment day. Scientists tested the dead snakes and found no toxins or pesticides in their system.

Then, one day, it stopped. For the first time in eighteen months, there was not a single dead brown tree snake sighted anywhere on the island. The phones at KUAM, animal control, and the Guam Police Department were silent. For the first time in over a century, there were no more snakes on Guam.

"Håfa adai Guam, I'm at Carbullido Elementary, where the once-thought-to-be-extinct ko'ko' bird has miraculously re-appeared today! A flock of a dozen have been spotted running and yes, *flying*, around campus. I'm here with Dr. Orn, a bird expert from the University of California, San Diego, who's on island to study this unique case. Dr. Orn, how is this possible?"

He cleared his throat. "I believe these very special birds might have survived in caves and evolved to fly as a survival mechanism against the once prevalent brown tree snakes." "Thank you, Dr. Orn. Hopefully, these ko'ko' birds will continue to thrive. This is Mercy Manibusan, reporting live for KUAM news."

Residents were astonished. They had only seen the ko'ko' in pictures and books before. But soon, more flocks of ko'ko' birds were spied in other central villages, then in northern and southern Guam. Hundreds, then thousands, then tens of thousands of ko'ko' bids roosted on houses and cars, walked across streets and blocked traffic, entered grocery stores and restaurants, even invaded Wednesday night market at the Chamorro Village. They whistled, screeched, and kipped. The sense of amazement quickly turned to annoyance.

Similarly, the tourists loved taking selfies with the ko'ko' at first. The Guam Visitors Bureau even promoted the island as a "Birders' Paradise." However, the love affair with the ko'ko' ended when hundreds of thousands of them chose Tumon, the main tourist village, as their preferred pooping grounds. Visitors could no longer shop duty-free, sunbathe, get married on the beach, or watch the sunset from their hotel balconies without getting shat on. Tourists stopped arriving, disappearing like the brown tree snakes, vacationing on other tropical islands not infested by native birds.

The ko'ko', exceeding a million in population, also occupied the military bases, easily flying over the barbed wire fences like *I Nasion Chamoru*. They disrupted the firing ranges, tripped the marching soldiers, slept in fighter jet engines and missile defense antenna satellites, and boarded the aircraft carriers and other warships docked in Apra Harbor. The Department of Defense was forced to transfer their troops and fleet to other bases in Asia and the Pacific. The ko'ko' was declared a national security threat—*enemy of the state*.

The government of Guam was in turmoil. Losing its dual economic base of tourist and military spending, it laid off most of its employees. Private sector businesses went bankrupt. The recession sunk to a depression. More than half of the island's population, desperate and hopeless, migrated to Hawai'i, California, Washington, Nevada, and Texas.

To address this existential crisis, the Native Bird Control and Eradication Project was founded, helmed by Steven Sanchez. It organized daily bird hunts, sprayed pesticides in the jungle, and set up net traps. When these tactics failed, they tried something creative: "Operation Snake Drop." They laced imported brown tree snakes with poison and dropped them into the jungle from helicopters, hoping to entice the birds with a tasty meal. The ko'ko', too smart for this Trojan-horse ploy, killed then carried the uneaten snakes to the front porch of Steven's house.

"Håfa adai, Guam! I'm here at the Chief Quipuha Park in Hagåtña, where a group of activists are protesting the bird eradication efforts. As you can see, hundreds of people are standing alongside thousands of ko'ko' birds. This is Veronica Cruz, one of the organizers of today's march. Why are you here, Veronica?"

"I'm here to *prutehi yan difendi* the ko'ko' birds," she said, pointing to her screen-printed T-shirt with the image of a ko'ko' bird and a raised fist. "Ko'ko' aren't an invasive species. They lived here long before people. They're endemic to this island. *Respetu* indigenous animal rights!"

"Veronica, what do you say to those who are concerned about the negative economic impacts of the bird presence?"

"I say the positive *outweighs* the negative. The ko'ko' eradicated the snakes. They're spreading the seeds of endangered native trees. They're eating invasive spiders, rhinoceros beetles, and fire ants. They got rid of the tourists and the soldiers. They're a symbol of justice, sovereignty, and independence!"

"Biba!" other activists chanted in unison.

"Si yu'us ma'åse', Veronica. This is Mercy Manibusan, reporting live for KUAM." The return of the ko'ko' bird divided the Guam community. There was a vocal minority of Americans who feared that the presence of the ko'ko' would strengthen the decolonization movement, so they advocated for the re-introduction of brown tree snakes. There were foreign corporations who proposed ways to monetize the ko'ko' birds, such as creating guano, exotic meat, and feather work industries. The tense situation became the main wedge issue for the upcoming gubernatorial and legislative elections. No matter where you landed on the issue, one thing was certain: the ko'ko' birds were here to stay, and those who remained on Guam had to learn to live in this new reality.

Mercy was sitting at her desk, preparing questions for the political candidates when her phone rang.

"Håfa adai. This is Mercy Manibusan. KUAM news."

"Greetings, Ms. Manibusan. This is Dr. Orn from the University of California, San Diego. I spoke with you last year when I visited Guam to study the ko'ko'."

"Dr. Orn, it's good to hear from you."

"I'm calling because we completed our study. We discovered some troubling facts that you might want to report on."

"Troubling?"

"Yes. Of the two thousand birds we examined, *all* were female. Not a single male. Yet they're reproducing at a staggering rate."

"That's strange. Could the males be hiding? Exhausted from breeding?"

"That's possible, but highly unlikely. Our second finding is even more troubling, though. Every bird has identical DNA, as if they're all cloned from a single bird."

"Identical?"

"Yes. We also mapped two anomalous genetic sequences. We're still analyzing them, but it's clear these birds have been . . . *engineered*."

"So, in your expert opinion, they didn't survive in caves or evolved to fly, as you previously thought."

"I was wrong. These ko'ko' were *definitely* created in a lab. They either escaped accidentally, or someone released them into the wild without approval."

"Is that legal?"

"It's not only illegal. It's unethical. Once we finish our analysis, I'm required to report this to the FBI. This could be prosecuted as an act of environmental terrorism."

"Thanks for calling, Dr. Orn. I'll do some research on my end. Please let me know when you finish your analysis."

After Dr. Orn hung up, Mercy ruffled through her files to find her notes. The dead snakes and living ko'ko' sightings both started in Barrigada, then circled outwards to other villages. She took out a close-up map of Barrigada to highlight every residence that filed a report. In the center: a single, unhighlighted home. Mercy typed the address into an online real estate database to identify the owner.

Rusted chain linked fence. Crooked "No Trespassing" signs. Padlocked gate. Mercy climbed over the fence, nearly tearing her skirt. Dense, waist-high grass in the front yard. Soggy, old copies of the *Pacific Daily News*. Something crunching under her feet. *Broken eggshells.*

The single-story, flat-roofed concrete house seemed abandoned. The paint of the white walls and brown trim was peeling. The windows still had typhoon shutters up, even though it was the dry season. The front porch was strewn with dead aloe vera plants. The only sign of life: the air-conditioner units hummed.

"Is anyone home? This is Mercy Manibusan, from KUAM news."

She knocked on the front door. No answer. She knocked again.

"Ko'ko' Reyes? I know you're home. It's Mercy. From Carbullido. Mrs. San Nicolas's class. Please open the door."

Footsteps. The door slowly opened—a rush of cool air. Ko'ko' peaked her head out.

"I can't believe it's really you, Ko'ko'. How many years has it been? I heard you moved to San Diego after high school. When did you get back?"

"Hi, Mercy. I see you on the news all the time. Yes, I went there for college. Was away for eleven years. I came back about two years ago."

"Are you working? Is your mom home?"

"No, she died a while ago. Ovarian cancer. I'm just tending this old house now. What are you doing here?"

"I'm sorry to hear about your mom, Ko'ko'," she paused. "I'm doing a new report on the birds. . . . How'd you do it, Ko'ko'? Why did you bring them back?"

Ko'ko' opened the door wide enough so she could step outside. Before she was able to close the door, Mercy glimpsed countless, unhatched eggs in the background. *The nest.*

"Mercy, I . . ." Ko'ko was on the verge of a confession, but then a flock of ko'ko' flew above them, swooping into the yard, then to the back of the house. *Kee-yu, kee-yu. kip-kip-kip.* "Mercy, I never asked you this, but why'd you try to take the blame for me? When I kicked Steven Sanchez?"

Mercy was not prepared for this question. As the reporter, she was more comfortable asking questions than answering them.

"He bullied me too," she admitted. "You remember, I was overweight then. He always called me a pig. Made oinking sounds around me in the cafeteria. I was too scared to fight back. When you kicked him . . . I don't know . . . I wanted to protect you."

"It was brave of you, Mercy. I didn't say it back then, but thank you."

"Ko'ko', I came here because Dr. Orn called me. He told me the birds had been created and genetically modified in a lab. He's going to alert the FBI soon. If they catch you, you'll go to federal prison. Life sentence."

Mercy let her words sink in.

"You need to destroy any lab equipment you have here. You need to run. Leave Guam. Never come back."

Ko'ko' woke before dawn to visit Guam Memorial Park.

"Nåna," she whispered. "Dispensa yu, but I have to leave Guam again. My flight's this afternoon."

She took the feather out of her pocket. It reminded her of her mom's hair.

"I brought them home *for you*, nåna. They'll be here with you, *forever*."

She placed the feather upon the grave. The sun dyed the sky the color of purple, orange, and red Easter eggs. Thousands of ko'ko' birds rose from sleep, stirring the plumeria trees. They stretched their wings, ready to forage. Some ran. Others flew.

Daughter Moon

• NORMIE SALVADOR •

0.
Through the Never there is no annunciation.
Crossing elliptical orbits, Theia tries to touch sun,
instead it collides and penetrates a nascent Gaea coalescing
to inure her to the absolute.

Gaea, a birthing stone, gives birth to a daughter moon
trailing a molten umbilical. This child so takes after her father:
an only child, a lonely child, stillborn.

1.
In her home every door is ajar and beckoning. In one room
stands the Maiden, in another the Crone. She stands in-between
rooms, holds aloft a bowl; suspended within is a constellation
              of milk and menstrual
blood diffusing into a nebula. In this translucence, she will scry.

2.
First are the kindred of Sirius, conceived in cirrus cloud
dispersal and shards of eons-agéd stellar flame,
cavorting on colloidal ice-powder halos of the fourth stone
              from the sun.

Inch by inch, the distance between Mother and daughter moon
increase with her spiraling gyre. Second and shadow lengthen
on Tycho's crenellations, hidden below curvéd lunar horizon,
its radiants distinct in any month's closing quarter.

She calls down the breathless moon.
Upon Maria Tranquillitatis, even regolith, smallest of the storytelling
stones, still responds after human generations of neglect.

Within apogee, this Princess of Tides descends,
bridging a frost span of evanescent luminescence,
and once again breathes her Mother's breath that she lost so long ago.

And she strides upon the true moon glimpsed by Herschel,
who believed in hills pinnacled with tall obelisks of fire-struck
quartz, and where rise slender pyramids of monstrous amethyst—
a dilute claret—spanning permafrost deserts of chalk and flint.

The scent of salt permeates this promenade, a colonnade
of crystalline caryatids offering up canopic urns.
In each, a soul curled up in lachrymatory ice.
Rims overflow with tears from their mothers.

Forged through a nine-month lifetime, she and her daughter are
linked by an umbral umbilical, a silver-burning-skin insistence.
At this silver cord's end will she find her daughter.

Cold stone hands warm at her touch; she relives
her months of grief as her tears are lost in the cascade.
The ice is scalding; the pain familial and fleeting.
In her intertwined hands rests her daughter's soul.

3.
Unregarded, the bowl drops from her hands. She blinks.
She places her hands upon her belly. And there, a fluttering
again so like the first quickening. She cries
as Maiden and Crone embrace the Mother once more.

Hala Yah

• KAHEALANI MAHONE-BROOKS •

The Daughter of Chief Taga

• YASMINE ROMERO •

"Something's changed in Tata," Attau thought out loud, "or perhaps," she pushed the pandanus leaf up and over, "something's been changing all along." She pulled down, hard, watching the leaves bind one another.

"Something's caught."

Attau scrutinized the web of leaves across her hands: they were supposed to form a durable basket. Instead, the basket resembled birds' nests destroyed by the village boys. She ground her teeth. She had forced the concave center too far with her right fist, splitting the edges.

—Try again, said the tinny voice of Tiha.

Tiha Taitasi died on the night of an inconceivable typhoon. She ran out onto the beach, letting the wind and water overcome her. Her long hair lapped against her like the waves as she sang. They, the villagers, spoke of the smile she wore that night. Your tiha offered herself, they said, to the Siblings.

Now, Tiha Taitasi was a skull amongst three that lined the cleanest part of their house. Mats ran along, left and right, for the numerous children, twelve; the wife who obeyed her father; and her father himself. Attau had had two mothers, but one had canoed back to Saipan. She had had a freer spirit than anyone, and a resilience that no chief—man or woman—could match.

Tata refused to talk about her, but Nana did. Sometimes in cooing tones. Other times in tears when she believed no one else was watching.

The sun was dragging itself over their hollow eyes; it pressed up into the backs of the skulls, making it seem as though they were breathing light: Nang, Tiha, and Bisaguella. They spoke to her, often, in afternoons like these. Their words became whispers, however, when the sun set fire to seafoam.

Sometimes, Attau would become frightened that they had left her. She would sit up and scan the area around her. If everyone was sleeping, then she would crawl over, touching the skulls: eye sockets still gaping. Jaws still settling in their final swoon. Bones still smooth and uncracked, save Bisaguella's left temple.

Once she outlined each skull in the dark, Attau would lean forward to sniff, "ñora." Her heart would, finally, relax.

—Listen to Fu'una. She sings.

—She calls.

A rare gust of wind tosses the thick black of Attau's hair.

—For you, neni.

Tata always frightened those around Attau and her family. "Even the foreigners," he'd snicker, "are frightened of your tata." Those light-skinned bringers of an entity named "God," which Attau did not understand.

"Fu'una yan Puntan," she said to the figure in front of her, "I can see." She pointed to the sun and then the rock outcropping nearby. The white and black cassocked individual was looking elsewhere. His eyes were not on her. They were on the men and boys crossing paths from daily casts of fish nets, stonework, and carving.

"Father," she asserted. The missionary turned, startled. His beard was long, rugged. She reached towards it, thinking that he must need to touch to hear like her older sister, Maiana. The whites of his eyes reminded her of bone, *and that bone does not move. It turns and fractures.*

Tata brings me colorful feathers that smell of death. Bright emerald and darkly red plumage cross-cuts with browns and blacks that are familiar, comfortable. Her fingers dig into the soft of these gifts, and then up to his knowing, strangely warm stare.

"Kirida," and he smiles, revealing a line of sharp teeth that intrigues.

That pulls.

Chief Taga was tall and broad. He lumbered rather than walked. Every sunrise, he made his way to their makeshift quarry by walking through the surrounding latte houses. Attau, not soon after she could walk, accompanied him in a stumbling sort of way.

Tata never offered to carry her, and so she quickly adapted to the ever-shifting terrain. Earth and plants alike favored her: curling into her toes to prevent her from falling or catching her hair to stop her from encountering dangerous creatures (feral pigs, flying foxes, and rats). Even when the rain softened the dirt, creating sucking noises as she lifted each foot, Attau was nimble enough to stay, at the very least, three steps behind her father.

Sometimes the adults would greet her.

Sometimes the children would make faces.

Attau made them right back because

—She is Taga's daughter.

Nang's voice was melodic, almost always sounding amused. Attau had known Nang. Her strong set of hands. Her chants that moved others to tears, even her own tata. Her body moved to the sound of wind coaxing coconut tree leaves to shake, to shiver. Her eyes were a deep, unnatural green-blue that saw lies before they even bubbled up. Some of the elders said that it was rumored Nang was more fish than woman.

Attau saw that in Nang's restlessness. Bisaguella spoke of her restlessness often, and how she outright refused her. "No daughter refuses her mother," other than Nang. She was impenetrable like a reef and that could have been why Tang died so young. He always followed Nang's lead: what to do, where to go, and how to do it. And so, on the night that Nang took sick, and Tang had to find his own way in scattered thunderstorms from the standing house to the canoe and then back, he was struck by a tree.

Nana always began to cry when talking about Tang, even though Tiha Taitasi comforted her with, —no, no, he's still here. Somewhere.

Nang did not remarry, but created wealth in Tang's stead. She fastened fishing nets that villagers mouthed never broke. She sang ayotte' with such feeling that the jungle shook in honor of her. She transformed her daughters into powerful women: one married to a chieftain (Nana) and the other mistress to Fu'una and Puntan (Tiha Taitasi).

"You have to keep moving." Nang grinned past blackened teeth. Her leathery hands wrapped about Attau's face. Her eyes were the scales of parrotfish. "So that you don't end up like the banana trees. Rotten, after a short life."

Taga tended the quarry so that he could continue to build for his family and village. He also enjoyed working with stone more than challenging people to tests of strength (which he would never admit). His hands forced limestone to bend, submit, yield. His fingers felt the beat of Fu'una's heart and encouraged her to beat faster, slower, stop.

Attau often watched him, under a blooming tiger claw, seeing how the lines of his body bent and straightened in their craft. She wondered if she could be like him, someday. Attau eyed limestone nearby, unshaped.

—Moving, neni.

When not working stone, Taga's upright posture was imposing. His brown skin glistened with sweat. His brows furrowed in a constant state of seriousness, as though a typhoon would come unannounced upon them. Spread its wings. Wrap them in the whirls of water and wind. Bring them to Tiha Taitasi's side.

While Attau's tata did not complain about the work, he treated his hands meticulously. Tata would rub at the base of his palms where wrist met hand. Pain softened the corners of his eyes, though fleeting, and she knew that he was still grounded in their island. He was still her father.

"See," Tihu said, "Your tata thinks he's the strongest." Tihu laughed heartily. His dark shoulders shook into the memory.

"He's always been this way."

Tihu folded his legs, so that he could animate the story of the canoe-turned-swimming race from Tinian to Luta, its tensions, and its conclusion: a draw. Tata never boasts again. Tihu feels redeemed to be recognized as just as strong. Just as worthy of chieftain. Attau had heard the story, since it occurred, at least a dozen times. But she could not deny Tihu his narrative; his source of strength:

"Your tata said, we each have four Puntan sleeps to prepare. Your brothers were put to work, and your mother and eldest sister tasked with providing food, ya? I, on the other, put to work some of the men that owe me in the village."

Attau nodded.

"When the sun rises, that beautiful Puntan left eye, I assembled the men. We worked just as hard, and prepared the dokdok properly in the span of a day. My muscles hurt, as did your tata's I am sure, although I don't think he'd admit."

"Confess," Attau blurted.

"Don't," Tihu said, "don't talk like them." Something changed, then, in Tihu's mouth and eyes. A tightening of his upper lip. "We don't confess; we share; we say; we . . ."

—Inafa'maolek, inafa'maolek.

When Tata allows me to follow along, I am ecstatic. I dash from our house into the center of the village, and then to its outskirts; I am nearest the guma' uritao that my older brothers, Yonanai and Guifi, have been sent to. I can hear the voices of men and women; their bodies move differently across the floor and into the walls nearby. These heavy sounds weigh into the building's thatched roof, which becomes smaller as Tata and I approach a ring of men.

Some I recognize immediately, and others I do not. It seems the clan is not as important as the creatures they have blindfolded. These creatures are held before them. Four more steps, and we are surrounded by these shapes.

Some watch me reproachfully. Others wonder if Tata will give them my blood. I try to grab at my father's wrist, but he shrugs me away so that he can start talking.

Gesturing.

Bargaining in ways that position one another: whoever is largest can claim the best view. This rule results in the collected men scrunching up on either side of Tata's body. My own is behind his. A shadow in a shadow. A glimpse.

In front of us is a patch of dirt, with the circular edges firmly carved into the ground. The blindfolded creatures are lowered, and the pandanus leaves are untied. I notice two pointed beaks, as orange-yellow as ripened mango, first. I then see each bird in brilliant colors of apprehension. They look at one another. Craning their long necks to the side, each rooster's eyes are obsidian: shiny and unreadable.

Without warning, they come together in loud, shrill screeches of madness.

Tihu's hands flew up in front of Attau. "Your tata thought he had the best dokdok, but he was wrong. I carved, alongside the chamorri who wish to make something of me, a canoe fit for the high chief."

He smiled, wide.

"Like me."

Blood pools at its spasming feet.

I look up into their faces, and I see resignation in some. I see defiance in others. In my father's, I see curiosity and fear.

"Tata," I whisper.

He glares down at me, pressing his palms to my cheeks. I am crying. Tata pinches my cheeks hard, as the realization settles in, and I bite down on my lower lip; I cannot cry now.

Never again.

"The tide is coming, Tihu."

Her uncle raised a brow. His mouth was open in surprise and pain. The colors of his irises were a thick brown. "But," he stammered, "I have not finished my story." Attau was already parting from him. Her steps were taking her to the main house, which he rarely haunted. Tihu was always looking in.

Attau made her way to the youngest of their family: her brother, Mahoyu. Nana thought he would be their tata's strongest. She was wrong, especially on a day like this when Mahoyu whined about his pet ayuyu. Attau immediately regretted leaving Tihu mid-story.

"Attau," he said, "he's run away again. Please help me look."

"Attau," he cried, "he's hurt, I think, please fix him."

"Attau," he thrashed, "Tata won't help me! My ayuyu went under that coconut tree!"

Attau followed him to the large tree behind their standing house. She held its ribbed trunk. Her fingers fanned against its texture at first, before bending at the joints. The coconut tree groaned. It sounded fatigued and weary like Nang when her back hurt.

—Asaina!

Attau pulled the tree free, roots and all. At first, there was a noise like stone being disturbed. That noise transformed into a sharp sigh, which gave way to dirt and water underneath the tree's tangle of roots. Somehow, Mahoyu's ayuyu, a bright blot of purple, floated there. Its large claws moved lethargically, as though awakened from sleep. Coconut crabs burrow there? Attau thought.

Mahoyu jumped in, grabbing his pet with a "you're not getting away again!" Attau laughed. Her legs were wet from the splash. The water was cool, and so she slid down to sit with her feet dangling in the pool. The sensations made her forget the look on Tihu's face. Mahoyu's dark skin shone in the sun. His neck was long. His waist was small. His shoulders and back weren't as big as the other boys in the village, and she knew he envied them.

Attau envied them.

When the sun began to lose its ferocity, a bulky shadow came from behind them; it overwhelmed their laughter. It stretched across the pool and the raised ground. Mahoyu froze. Attau glanced over her shoulder. Tata, she thought.

He eyed the boy, accusatory: "Did you—"

"No," her brother exclaimed; "it was Attau!"

"Don't blame your sister," he snapped. "I told you to leave the tree."

"But." Her brother's crab ran away diagonally. Its taro color dissolved into the brown brittle of their surroundings. Attau saw the bushes shake once, twice, and then no more.

Mahoyu began to cry.

"It was me, Tata."

Attau's voice was a rasp, as though she had not spoken to her father for a very, very long time. She hadn't. Tata turned to her. He removed his hand from Mahoyu's shoulder. His glare, in her direction, shook away Puntan's white-yellow rays that drifted down his arms and stomach. His muscles tightened, knotted in the center.

Attau did not repeat herself.

I am alone, and I am worried. Tata has been, more than ever, avoiding me. Lately, he follows the man from the ship. He even speaks their language, pressing their words into our ears and mouths. He makes us say things that we would not otherwise like, "God is always watching."

I cannot shape this language like I can rock.

I cannot hear this language, but I can see what they think of us.

I cannot speak this language, yet Tata forgets who we are. They are right, he says. Puntan is God.

But what of Fu'una?

I am shouting in my mind: what of the Mother-Sister who brings song, stone, and life?

Silence follows because I will not say it. I dare not say it across fourteen pairs of eyes. But Nang, Tiha Taitasi, and Bisaguella have not left me. They say what I want to say in unison for once, in increasing volume, in an attempt to make my tata listen:

—Stop!

The villagers of all castes were following Taga (even Tihu) to seagreen surrounded by aging limestone. Attau descended the incline where sand lined the ocean, drinking the salt of the earth whenever the waves rolled in. "Never the same," Attau said out loud.

Maiana glanced at her youngest sister with Mahoyu clutching her side. She mouthed questions: What is happening? Did you know? Attau did not see the attempt. Her eyes were far too lost in the words of their tata.

"Come, and let God save you!"

Taga stood resolute against the sun. His shoulders hiked up in a demand to listen to the man beside him: the same man that ignored Attau no matter how many times she asked him questions about his god. The foreigner stared out at those gathered like shells in a basket, and then, beckoned Tihu forward.

Attau saw Tata smile in that moment, as though he had found some sort of redemption.

Tihu walked forward straight-backed, tall. He stood at the mouth of the water. His feet were on top of the sand. All present watched with their breaths held as the man dressed in white and black took Tihu by the shoulders. He led him into their waters, and then spoke incomprehensible words. Tihu was then, ceremoniously, dunked underwater.

Attau could not tell if the movements were harsh or soft. Her sister leaned into her side, "What is happening?" But, again, Attau did not reply. Instead, she turned towards the jungle. She left her family, extended family, and the villagers she had known all of her life clustered in the sand. Her body shook. Her eyes burned. Her mouth was full of blood. She had bit down on her lower lip when Tihu surfaced in three consecutive gasps exactly two seconds apart.

Taga watched his daughter disappear into the trees as each of his family members (those that remained) and his villagers (those that were too afraid to speak out) succumbed to baptism. The chieftain's expression was lighted out by the sun.

I find a tataga split open in rot. The sun has eaten its eyes to a deep, navy almost black color. It stares, soulless.

Little bugs glitter across its now leathery, sunken skin. I press my bamboo stick into its gut. The insides ooze like decaying sticky mangoes.

I can see the bones, thin and scraping. "Stop," he says, "it's no longer ours; it's hers. Si Fu'una."

Tata points to a scuttling crab wrapped in shades of bluish gray.

"They must go, che'lu," Tihu said even though he'd gone underwater for them.

"Everyone grows sick."

Tihu was standing near the entrance to their house. His shoulders drooped, and tiredness lined his eyes. He wasn't wearing his usual hat with scrawls of Fu'una's blessings underneath. *When,* Attau thought, *had he started looking older than Tata?*

"Everyone must bear their sins, che'lu. It will pass."

Tihu raised his voice, "No, no, no stop saying that."

Attau watched their similar faces turn red.

"Stop talking like them!" Tihu roared.

Attau's latest attempts at weaving were in her lap.

"I saved them." Her tata's voice sounded higher than usual. His pitch had thrown itself into the thatch roof, unsettling the coconut leaves. Attau wondered if it might cave in.

"Tihu." Attau pushed up from her seat, so as to reach her uncle in time. But he was already turning. He was already leaving.

Tihu was saying goodbye with his back to her.

I sneak into the quarry when Puntan cries in the dark. I see streaks of his tears across the punched-out sky. It is as though I am watching through trees, and all that is left is to feel the earth at my feet. To feel the stone my father has left to fend on its own.

It is slack in my hands, and I push and prod into its texture. At first, I create the canoes of Tihu's story. I make Tihu's larger, but Tata's narrower. I then refasten it with a knead or two into a flat surface from where I tug up five corners to imitate a seastar.

The seastar crawls from my knees towards the other stones that lay, forgotten in a desire to be, to become, to face the world.

I watch as it disappears amongst its folding aunties and uncles, its mothers and fathers, its sisters and brothers, its cousins and warring friends. It becomes as gray and unrecognizable as the rest: a mass of not yet.

Mahoyu retched, and Tata, at first, denied the severity. He'd tell Nana, "He'll be fine. Give it two sun rises."

But Attau's little brother did not recover. He was covered in sores. His skin resembled flesh-colored limestone, and scratching left drips of red and yellow fluid.

Nana instructed her children to stay away, and yet one by one they each fell. The pandanus mats were not enough to soothe their pain. Wind grew fainter, until it was a whistle across ferns of green. The sea, Tiha Taitasi's singing place, smelled close and dead.

Tata walked back and forth as though Nang's "keep moving" would stave off the loss.

"We need to do something else," Nana called out. "They say Tihu is gone, Taga." Nana's eyes were watery. Her cheeks flushed. Attau moved towards her, and she raised her hands in front of her. "No, kirida, no."

"But you are sick, Nana." Attau heard her voice echo like a rasp. Nana smiled at her, which was always how she remembered her: dark hair loose and wild past her breasts. It was the same kind of hair that Attau had: thick and ropey.

She wanted to touch the light that colored the fringe, but her wrist was violently tugged back.

"Your nana needs sleep," Tata said in a panic.

Attau looked up at him. He was aggravated. He was hurting her. Nana followed up, perhaps to soften things as always, and that very thought brought the sea across her daughter's face.

"Your Tata is right, Attau, I'll be fine. Soon."

Only then did Tata let go of her.

They say the foreigners are gone. They say I will be gone, too. It's only a matter of time. Tata says we should have changed our ways. We should have found God.

But here I am, sleepless as fires burn into the night. Shaking.

Attau was left alone, with her tata and the skulls of her ancestors.

Wrapped in their sleeping mats, and whatever else Attau and her tata could find, was their family. Nana had been the last to die of fever and sores. The stink of death crept past their bones, swelling where the flesh had gone rotten. Their skin boiled and braised from the heat and humidity of Tinian. Blood and pus seeped through some of the mats. Attau regretted not refining her weaving skills.

"How many more?" Hunched over Chatongo's lifeless form, Tata's shoulders were shaking. "How many more must you take?"

Attau did not know who Tata was addressing, but she did not think it was Puntan.

"Tata," she said angrily. "We must bury them in the stone."

He turned to see her, really see her. His face was full of fear and shame. He was no longer her tata, but an echo or memory of one. The one that emerged after settling for a draw between himself and his brother at the end of that infamous race.

Tihu was dead.

Tata knew he was dying, too.

"But the stone will not listen any longer." He swallowed.

"I will take them," Attau resolved, "and I will make sure each of us are seen to. I will not ignore them. I will listen to their spirits. I will find a way to keep them strong, Tata, keep them remembered.

"But know this, Tata, I am not afraid. You taught me well. I can shape stone. Did you know? I can move mountains. I can do all the things you should have done for them, for me before this happened.

"And you, look, are falling to it as well. Your skin is breaking apart, and you try and hide it. But I know, Tata. I know.

"Fu'una told you she would watch over you like she watched over Puntan. But you refused, you ignored, you began to believe she no longer exists."

Attau slammed a fist to her chest. "I love you, but you have destroyed our family, and so I must rebuild. I must find a way forward. It is what we, as chieftains, do."

She raised the spear in her hand. Her brothers had found the materials, and Tata had carved it for her. Nana and her sisters had decorated it blue, green, and red. Tata lowered his head, unable to meet her eyes. Fatigue shadowed his angles, most especially in his face.

He had lost hope, and, in this moment, Attau knew her tata was no more. She plunged the spear deep into his heart. Attau held it, watching the blood swell around the head of the spear; it leaked from two spots, forming rivulets of heat down his torso to curve about his hips, and then pool in his lap.

On her knees, she held her tata in his last gasps of life. Attau's eyes were closed, but she did not cry.

—Listen, neni, listen.

Bisaguella's voice surfaced papery and thin, as though dried out in the sun for far too long. But the splinters of pitch were as beautiful as triggerfish.

—Take care of our family. You must follow through and bury each of them in stone, including your tata. You will be able to watch over their spirits. You will need this strength because you are now tasked with watching over the villagers, all of them.

—You will die old and loved, my great granddaughter. You will turn sorrow into strength. You will make vulnerability valuable, and carve out a new place, a new life for those dead, those now, and those before you.

—You are not alone.

—But know that your spirit will forever live, for this is why Fu'una is a constant, because others like the priests on those ships will tear our people apart; they will burn our huts down; they will destroy our fields; they will break stone.

—You, neni, will have to watch, to listen, to keep your spirit in our people.

Attau laid her father's body against the base, the haligi, of the twelfth stone; her hands pressed him into the material just as she had for the rest of her family. Tata's flesh turned from red to black to gray.

The stone invited her to push and prod, to form, as though it was as malleable as sand and mud, the likeness of a Chamorro into the masonry. Her hands came away covered in bits of limestone. These miniature breaks moved, practically danced, across her palms and finger pads.

The stone was, and always would be, alive.

Her brows furrowed at the realization. She glanced at the sky for signs of typhoons. Attau proceeded to rub at the middle of her palms. Her eyes creased when pain blossomed like plumeria: fragrant and sweet throughout her skin, bones, and muscle. But like her tata, the pain lasted seconds, and she knew that she was part of their island. She was still Chief Taga's youngest daughter.

Philodoria

• JOSEPH STANTON •

So much depends upon a rare bug
as tiny as a single eyelash,
a micromoth on Moloka'i

radiated from its ancestor
millions and millions
of years before *homo sapiens*

even dreamed of arriving,
a micromoth
that lives for and in

a plant, also rare,
that needs the moth, too.
For lack of one or the other

a forest might be lost
or might
never have been.

Before the Naming

• KALEHUA KIM •

Before the naming there is the dream.
It comes without warning or prayer.
It comes before anyone has uttered
the words, *longing* or *want* or *please*.
It comes very close to the hour of waking,
yet in the dream, one feels awake.

That is how Tūtū explained it to my mother.
It is how my mother explained it to me:

Da first time is preparation,
You goin' build yo' armor, choose yo' weapon.
Sometimes you have to fight fo' one name,
but you goin' know what you need.
Da first dream will come with your first ma'i.

And it did.

My ma'i came when I was ten,
So young, Tūtū tsked,
Too young? my mother asked,
as I dealt with the rust between my legs
Everything will be different now,
I murmured to myself.

Sail Bone

• KALANI PADILLA •

In my dream last night my grandmother's voyages
were visiting my other etymologies. She said
Your children's names will mean

they have
Ancestors.
they have ancestors
to answer for.

In my dream she called me
to chart our bones and where they
continue to go—
As they smooth out like mountains between
shoulders of wind—
Giving battles for immortality
A way away to the ocean, to time.
tarsals planting themselves
like oars in the sea,
mustard seeds over and over,

And I hovered with my sisters
on the old reef, belly down,

and with my brothers knocked
On the bamboo
as bamboo knocks on each other
culm to culm; year to year.

In my dream I learned pain's map
of healing.
Of the jigsaw borders of forgiveness
Where love of that traveler
that transgressor still exists.

Stay

• MELISSA MICHELLE CHIMERA •

Stars May Hunger, Suns May Still

• SLOANE LEONG •

A flaying wind off the mountain glacier batters Sangee's back with icicled fists. Each strike hits wild and sudden, with the same unconcerned familiarity her mother might have after a long hunt and longer indulgence of moss wine. It is only right. The land had bled, feverish and thrashing, through her tribe's birth and anything brought forth in pain deserved pain in turn. Pain was the seed of strength and anything you wanted strong, unbreakable, you loved.

When her mother struck the sound from her ears, that was love.

When the ice blushed the skin of her nose black, that was love.

The spear in her hand, the honed tip: love.

Sangee treks through the tundra with the touch of many mothers at her back and her front, in bruises and cuts and ice-burned skin. Her quarry, an older delver, churns through the snow at a steady speed, losing its footing every so often when its wide hooves hit packed ice. The beast is shaggy and fat, its segmented shovel of a face hidden beneath the knotty wool of its coat. The delver is not made to run but Sangee has already struck it once, the spear slanting through its nasal hood.

Shouts from Sangee's hunting mates barely break through the windy roar, faint pleas for her to stop, turn back. Even the delver is flinching as hailstones nick his muzzle and strike his calloused nasal hood. Sangee ignores them, taking the storm's whipping as a challenge and grinning whenever pain blooms in her shoulder or knee. Her thighs burn as she withers the distance between them.

Spear back, twisting at her waist to gather power. As she flings the spear, a large hail stone hits her mouth, jerking her head down. Her vision flashes white, bittersweetness coating her tongue, but she lets the spear loose. She ignores the blood, blinks away the false white.

Her weapon always flies true. She can't afford for it not to.

It lands with a wet thunk, piercing through the back of the delver's thick neck and out the front of its fleshy throat. Lowing, air gurgling through the wound, the delver crashes to a stop in a cloud of ice dust. Sangee drops to her knees and watches the beast spasm and choke, taking deep breaths to ease her overworked lungs. She wishes she had gotten it the first time, in the eye; she can always be sharper, more precise. The delver stills. Sangee spits red into the white, brushes the bloodied rime from her chin.

"Sangee!"

A scowling mouth is the first thing she sees through the snow. Her mother jogs towards her, forearm held overhead to protect from hail. Sangee is taller than her mother, than most of her tribe even at her meager sixteen seasons, and yet she still feels her heart flinch away at the woman's voice.

"We're too far out of our territory for a catch this big," Meleq growls. "You killed it for nothing, child."

Child.

The word stings as it's meant to. At sixteen, Sangee is several seasons past the age she should've had her first blood, gone through her rites to be an adult wahinaq. She is a bloodless babe, stretched to disgraceful heights. Sangee hates being an overgrown child in her tribe's eyes. She shifts her weight in the snow, looking down at the space between her mother's feet and her own, wishing it would grow.

"Next time, stop when I tell you, lo. Now we have to spend all night in the storm cutting it up and dragging it back."

"Sorry, ama." She could never win with her mother. There was always too much blood between them or too little. Squinting past her mother, Sangee spots a dark hazy line stretched across the horizon, a wall of volcanic stones, a curtain of smoke—No. The ocean.

In the black of it, she makes out white crests, seafoam, and glacial fragments. A ripple that is towering waves. And then among the darkness, another dark shape rising up from the narrow strip of sea, its figure unfurling into every direction like a blot of swelling ink, a black sun glowing. It sinks back down, quick as it's risen, the stark line of the black sea once again unmarred by its presence.

Behind her, the other hunters are already quartering the delver into cartable pieces. With Sangee's help, they finish and tie the delver's cuts onto the wooden packs. The long trek back to the village is silent, save for their panting. They walk with their faces away from chilled oceanward winds, away from the watching sea.

Sangee doesn't look back.

The smoky scent of charred meat and boiled river grass drifts out from her grandmother's burrow hut. Sangee kicks the snow off her boots before ducking down inside the narrow entrance, emerging into the spacious excavated dwelling. Radzi turns the meager stew over with a bone spoon, flames blackening the bottom of the small stone pot. Beside her sits Sangee's younger sister Nnasa, twelve seasons old and inevitably petulant. Sangee bends and kisses Nnasa's forehead, pleased to receive a predictably grumpy hum in turn.

"Good hunt?" Radzi asks. The sleeves of her wool robe are shucked up above her elbows, white hair hanging around her shoulders like a cape.

Sangee kisses each of her grandmother's cheeks with a tired smile. "I thought so but ama disagreed."

"That's the nature of mothers and daughters."

"You were like that, too?"

"Always."

"Atu, I'm hungry," Nnasa whines, leaning onto Radzi's shoulder.

Radzi smiles, pats the girl's cheek hard. "You mustn't whine, Nnasa. If the qalipuk hear you, they will take you down under the glaciers with them."

"At least they'd kill me quick instead of letting me starve," Nnasa mumbles. The older wahinaq liked to warn the younger about the ocean people and how they liked to snatch up naughty children and hide them in the center of the deep-sea nests. It was a solemn jest because it had once been true long ago, but now peace had been brokered between the two people; stolen children could once again be a joke.

"Oh, they'd feed you good," Radzi says, stirring the coals. "My qalipuk once brought us a shoal of fish so huge, we had to leave most of it on the beach! It stank for weeks until the birds came and ate it away."

Nnasa says nothing; she is distrustful of the qalipuk, as are many of the wahinaq. There were rules between the wahinaq and the qalipuk, their pact of peace like an impossibly long fishing net filled with twisting, savage eels. It felt on the precipice of tearing, all of Sangee's tribe's hopes just a thread away from unraveling, dropping back into the dark depths. Because with peace came sacrifice. Certain hunting grounds were made off limits, types of prey forbidden for them to hunt or fish. And wahinaq or qalipuk were forbidden from fighting or even interacting outside ceremonial meetings.

Some people don't take well to rules; Nnasa was one of them but Sangee knows there are more grumblers in the tribe, unsatisfied with the treaty. But there was no fighting it.

No fighting them.

The qalipuk were massive beings, bigger than a hundred wahinaq pressed together into one body, one weight. Impossible to defend against, almost impossible to kill. And if Sangee's people held grudges over this pact, then it stood to reason the qalipuk must as well.

Between the two, there were debts and memories, bitter as smoke, sweet as river grass.

It was as a child still strapped to her mother's back when Sangee first saw one of them. A towering, foamy black-and-white blur rising from the ocean, making the glacier they stood on keen and crackle with its weight. Sangee remembers a giant tendril like a finger coming to brush down her cheek, sliming down the edge of her jaw. Sangee didn't remember what else the qalipuk looked like but she would never forget its texture, slimy-slick and granular with caught sand. The tang of salt and an unknown flavor was on her tongue for days afterwards, souring her teas and moss puddings.

"I'm sick of this," Nnasa says, jerking her chin to indicate the stew. "If we could hunt the shore voles, we wouldn't be so weak."

Radzi reaches to slap her but Nnasa dodges; unacceptable.

"Rancid little egg! Your ama hears you talk like that, she'll turn your face purple."

"Tch, I'll just make sure she drinks too much bitter moss. She'll be too dizzy to beat me."

Sangee sucks her teeth. "She's still our ama, Nnasa."

"I wish she wasn't, kaiqua." She spits the last word out—the formal word for older sister—with a measure of acid. "I would rather be taken by the ugly qalipuk." The words snap like the embers beneath the soup pot.

Radzi sighs as if a great stormy cold has slipped in from the ice fields outside and draped around her like a coat. "You are getting older, little egg. You will be free of many things soon. More than you wish to be."

To the qalipuk belonged the ocean, its churning blackness, its endless ravines and the unknown life that it continued birthing forth from its depths like a vast abyssal womb.

To the wahinaq belonged the ice fields and the rivers, its swiftness and freshwater meadows, the streams like unwavering blue veins traversing the white body of the land.

Through that blueness, the women's paddles cut. Three narrow canoes slice through the crisp waters in silent procession. Sangee and Nnasa paddle beside each other with six more wahinaq in pairs paddling behind them. They are heading towards the mouth of the river where it empties into the sea: a sacred place of cyclic sacrifice that would honor the impending ceremony. They steer the boat to a makeshift dock to the south side of the river and tie off the canoes.

Iyamei disembarks first. She is small for her thirteen seasons, black braids wrapped around her head and woven with yellow reeds, green shells. A wrap of tanned delver hide fits around her hips and a wash of red clay from top lip to clavicle, from fingertip to elbow. Her belly is carefully etched with a blade, three stippled arcs curving neatly around her belly button, matching the contours of her stomach muscles. She walks out onto a jetty of black and red stone, the brackish sea slapping at her legs. Her gait is unbalanced; a side effect from her unbroken fast and the smoke of a particularly potent reed pipe meant to cloud the mind as well as the body's sense of pain. At the end of the jetty, she stands and waits.

Sangee had been invited to two ceremonial pilgrimages before. This was Nnasa's first and she feared her reaction, worried her scorn for the creatures would only grow at the sight of them.

Sangee whispers, "Okay, kaiqu?"

"Fine." Nnasa sits stiffly, hands gripping her paddle tight as if anticipating an attack. "I'm not scared, kaiqua."

"I didn't say you were."

"You might have—"

Beyond Iyamei and the jetty, a single tentacle rises up.

Nnasa inhales sharply. The first wahinaq had said the qalipuk resembled terran creatures like the salamander, the whale, the octopus, and the anemone yet none fully encompassed the fearsome air the qalipuk had. Slow as drifting ice, it ascends out of the sea. Dark waters cascade from its black spine and a musk fills the air, heavy with brine and an unfamiliar floral sweetness. It pulls itself into the shallows by the jetty, a myriad of thin tentacles rippling down along the length of its body like a bird forever ruffling its feathers. Its six wide fins, tipped in stubby claws, clutch the rocks to maneuver itself. The care it takes settling its massive head down on the jetty is more frightening to Sangee than its rows of crushing teeth.

The qalipuk's belly glints shell-white in the daylight, catching the light and refracting it into Sangee's eyes. Along its tentacled flank, three stripes color into existence: this was the qalipuk's resting markings, the same pattern that had been cut into Iyamei and every other woman that had gone through their first blood. It was the first step to their binding and the ache of the tattoo would serve as preparation as to what was to come.

The qalipuk sucks in great bellowing breaths. A low groan vibrates the pebbles under Iyamei's soles. Sangee, Nnasa, and the other wahinaq disembark and take their seat on the stony beach, ready to witness the exchange. Each wahinaq has come with a hollow gourd and together, they begin beating out a rhythm, steady as the tide lapping at the craggy coast.

Iyamei nears the qalipuk; she barely reaches the top of its shoulder. Swaying, she reaches out, placing both shaking hands against the side of its slimy stomach, just behind its foremost shoulder. The pelt of tentacles flinch then flatten into a glossy smooth surface. The echo of the beaten gourds hammer in the air.

An oily cascade of colors radiates out from where her palms rest on the qalipuk's skin. Translucent goo thickens between her painted fingers and seeps over her knuckles. The iridescence marks leap across its ribs, the deep rainbow blemish suddenly darting one end of its belly to the other. The shape blushes into symmetry, then fades a deeper color, the hue of rich soil.

Iyamei blinks.

The pattern on the qalipuk's skin blinks back, two white dots flashing red and then white again.

Iyamei stumbles back. The colors on the qalipuk move in tandem. It has painted her reflection in its skin, a living breathing mirror: a signal of kinship between their two peoples, a mating gift, a mark of acceptance. Iyamei raises her hands back to the qalipuk's ribs, her skin-painted reflection mimicking her in liquid shimmers and salted glitter. With slow precision, she signs into the wetness of its body.

I welcome you.

This would be one of the last times Iyamei would speak to the qalipuk, unless she became tribe head or counsel. For people like Sangee's mother Meleq, tribe head, they communicated frequently. The ancestral wahinaq had found speaking through tactile sign the best way to communicate with the qalipuk. Their hearing, the build of their mouths, was not made for spoken conversation, but the sensitive tendrils of their body lent themselves perfectly to tactile speech. What is it like to touch them? Sangee wonders. To feel their color change under your palms?

The qalipuk exhales a content hiss, vibrating as its dark body shifts to a searing blue decorated with intricate whorls of white. The white pigment spins and collects along its body like building storm clouds. Iyamei moves towards the qalipuk's head and strokes down the sloped muzzle, fingers dancing on the tips of its long serrated teeth hanging perilously over its lip. Tendrils unbraid across its flank and lift, revealing hundreds of opalescent disc-like barnacles anchored across its side and belly. With a tender touch, it pries one away from its flesh, loosing a cloudy green liquid Sangee knows to be its blood.

The sea shimmers emerald. Gingerly, the qalipuk offers the hard carapace to Iyamei who receives it with quivering hands. The barnacle was just barely convex, no bigger than Iaymei's hand. Fleshy coils of blue-gray meat twitched on its underside. The beat of the gourds slows and Sangee feels her heart follow suit nervously. Iyamei hesitates, then presses the underside of the shell to her belly. She is still for several heartbeats before a cry rips from her throat. This is the part Sangee has heard much of, the invertebrate sinking its penetrating tendril into the stomach to the womb, tiny filaments latching onto fragile organs. Iyamei sinks to her knees in pain, cupping the shell that has joined itself to her, given her the gift that all the wahinaq are lacking. The ability to bear children.

The gourd song rises in urgent tempo as Iyamei screams. The sea crashes a chorus and the qalipuk, hums a sweet low tone, louder than all of the wahinaq together. Iyamei's voice cuts off in a choked whine before she collapses to the jetty. The song of her adulthood rite plays on, into the light of the white sun, the shade of the black ocean. Into the jealous heat of Sangee's heart.

Meleq takes her daughters to the seeding field when they are eleven seasons and seven. It is the only place Sangee knows with colors that are neither the white of snow, the black of sea or the grey of soil. The seeding field is a charge crater, a dent in the land so deep and wide that she could not see outside of it once within. And in its center: the Sun Seed.

Sangee's ancestor Kiele had brought the Seed over five hundred seasons ago on a canoe—"it's called a starshep," Meleq had said, "because it shepherded us through the stars themselves"—so large its hull was said to stretch from one horizon to the next. The Seed boasted the same magnificent size, larger than one hundred qalipuks squished together into a pod. When Meleq let Sangee touch it, she had been surprised to feel that it was burning hot, harder than stone and smooth as ice. Metal, her mother called it. Unbreakable. Together, they would race through the orange foliage bursting from the ash-and-snow fields that surrounded the Sun Seed. When they reached the Seed's edge, they would compete to find the largest orange fronds and yank them mercilessly out of the ground, revealing their juicy yellow roots. When they had a good pile of the tubers, they would sit beside their mother chewing them into a paste, the Sun Seed glittering before them.

"My ama used to draw pictures of our mother world," Meleq says during one visit. She brings her knees to her chest, a distant look in her pale eyes. Draws a finger into the ash, making a meaningless symbol; she had no eye for drawings, not like Nnasa. "Did you know they used to drop supplies here for us once a season?"

"Who is 'they,' ama?" Sangee asks.

"You know she'd been on one once, my grandma? A starshep. She said it took her to another sky full of stars, a place with a sun." Meleq jerks her chin at the Sun Seed. "Like that but as big as a world and impossible to look at. It made all the nearby worlds green." A bitter laugh. "This world was supposed to be like that, too."

Nnasa grips her mother's sleeve. "Why isn't this world green, ama?"

Meleq takes a drink from her waterskin, though Sangee smells, not water, but fermented algae. A bad sign for both of them.

"It was supposed to be. All this." She rips up the ember

blooms by their juicy roots and shakes them in Nnasa's face. "It was supposed to grow this everywhere. All kinds of flowers and plants and fungus. Animals too. A whole ee-colo-gee."

"It did a little," Sangee says, as if the Sun Seed can hear them and needs defending.

"But it broke," Meleq snaps then gestures at the base of the Seed. "Under it, just there, is an awl. It pierced the land here, through the ice and into the frozen oceans. Made them boil and bled little creatures into the sea. It woke the grass and the algae and the ember flowers. Melted the ice and let the qalipuk see the sky."

Another reason Nnasa disliked the qalipuk: they would have never seen the stars without them.

"It did a lot," Sangee says cautiously.

Meleq smiles but it's an ugly expression, one that says she knows better and finds her daughter's stupidity amusing. "But not enough." She rasps a laugh. "A little warmer and we'd have proper greenery to live off of. And no qalipuk."

"No qalipuk?"

"None. But unlucky for us, the heat only killed their wahinaq. That's why only their kanaqs are left."

Kanaqs. Men. Sangee nods as if the words were familiar but it's anything but. Nnasa holds her half-eaten root in her lap and stares at her mother, chapped lips pressed into a small frown.

"If you want them all gone," Sangee says quietly, "Why do the wahniaq let the qalipuk put their shell on us?"

"Not shells, child," Meleq says. "It's their seed. The warm waters burned up the qalipuk mothers so that they couldn't have any children. Kiele wrote in her journals that for months after the Sun Seed landed the beaches were covered in infertile eggs and dead qalipuk. As for us, the wahinaq had no way to make children. We only had eggs, a womb, but no seed."

Nnasa crosses out her arms gruffly. "Why? Why couldn't we make eggs and seed by ourselves without the qalipuk?"

"Wahinaq are only one part, child. On our home planet, we had another part; we called them kanaq. It takes two types of bodies to make a child. If we wear the qalipuk seed on our bellies, we can make children by ourself." She thumbs Nnasa's cheek, pinches it until the girl cries. "Little copies. No kanaq."

Nnasa is quiet. "I don't like the qalipuk." She digs a hole in the soil between her legs. "They hurt the wahinaq. And the qalipuk don't do anything except fill the ocean with slime and stomp on wahinaq during the spring hunt." Nnasa munches on her fire root and crosses her legs. "I bet I could kill them all with my spear. I'll make a big one and skewer them all!"

Meleq, dazed by her fermented drink, drowses off. Sangee smirks at her sister then shoves Nnasa down before running off into the brush. She hurls fire roots from a distance, pelting her sister in the head and stomach.

"Big words from a big mouth!"

Nnasa screeches and chases after her, tears welling in the corner of her eyes.

"I hate you! I hate the seeds! I hate the qalipuk!"

"Big mouth, big mouth!"

"I'll show you! I'll hunt the qalipuk and eat their blubber and use their bones for my starshep!"

Thwack!

Nnasa yelps, her face jerked to the side, a handful of ember blooms still clasped between her fingers. Meleq stands woozily besides her, arm still flung across her chest from the powerful slap. Their mother's eyes were red and narrowed: fury stank like old, tart algae.

"Little brat. If you hate the qalipuk then fine. Stay a useless little child. A child with no children, no blood in the tribe." Nnasa's face contorts in frustration, holding back tears as she presses her palm to her burning cheek. Meleq turns to Sangee and yanks her up by her braid. "And you. I brought you here to remind you of Kiele. You come from a line of chiefs, settlers from the stars. You have the sun in your blood, girl! And you make a mockery of it with your foolishness."

Meleq throws her to the ground and turns on a wavering heel

toward the village. The sisters stay kneeling on the ground, rolling over the light taste of ember root in their mouths that had somehow become heavy and sour. The circle of bare soil where Nnasa had ripped out the ember blooms was littered with withering leaves, the orange fronds dulling to a sullen brown. Behind them, the Sun Seed scorches the air with its brilliance, but all Sangee feels is a colorless sting.

Not even a sun could burn as badly as her mother's scorn.

Almost a season after Iyamei's ceremony, Sangee finds she can't sleep.

Her skin tingles, her stomach quivers with unfamiliar nausea. Silently she hopes this is the sign of her blood coming, that her tortuous wait for adulthood is about to finally end. A handful of days pass and still nothing changes except the intensity of her discomfort. Sleep withers into an impossibility.

Sick, Sangee thinks. She's sick. Another new failure to confess to her mother. No, she'd die before she told her. She keeps her exhaustion to herself, pretends to sleep so Nnasa doesn't start asking after her.

Except one night, she can barely lay still, an itch puncturing every pore on her skin.

"Can I see?" Sangee whispers when she peeks from her blanket to see Nnasa awake and sketching.

"I thought you were asleep!" Nnasa yelps, splaying a hand over the drawing. Sangee smiles weakly. Nnasa sighs, slides the book towards her.

Sangee pulls it closer and leafs through the sketchbook attentively, knowing her younger sister's pride would be wounded if she looked too concerned. Nnasa had talent; she'd deftly sketched a variety of animals, layouts of their huts and how to expand them, strange weapons, and . . . starships.

"I . . . I really want to go to terra," she whispers once she sees where Sangee's eyes have landed. "I want to fly among the stars."

Radzi told me there might be a ship in the southern archipelago. A supply ship that crashed many seasons ago." She chews her lip. "I want to go to it. See if I can call the terrans. Or repair it."

Sangee stifles a laugh. "You're smart for an egg but you know you can't trust atu's old tales. There are no more starships or terrans." Sighing, she hands back the sketchbook to Nnasa who snatches it with simmering offense. "It's nice to dream. But you need to work on helping here. How will you catch a delver with this?" She gestures to the sketches. "Ask it to sit for a portrait? Distract it with a drawing of a female?"

Nnasa flushes. "What do I care what a child thinks."

Rage cores out all the softness of the prior moment. Nnasa had never moved Sangee's body like that before. "You . . . you little welp! The hunt matters! The tribe matters! You can't survive off dreams of stars. The sky is just as cold as it is here. It's nothing. There's nothing else but this."

"That's what a child would think." Nnasa shoves her sketchbook beneath her blankets and wriggles her head beneath the furs. "You can play in the mud with those ugly fish all you want. I'm going to the stars, kaiqua. You'll see."

Another night, another stronger, repetitive agony throbbing in Sangee's marrow. Her skin burns with a violent itch and she wants nothing more than to skin herself and leave her hide on a rack. Sangee moans and tosses on her bedroll, blinking away the subtle blur of tears from her vision. Dry. Everything is too dry. She licks her chapped lips and gags when the taste of sour seaweed meets on her tongue. The flavor turns putrid in the back of her mouth but somehow it is recognizable. A low keening echoes in her head. Sweat tickles at her cheek.

"Your bones need to stretch, egg," Radzi murmurs at her side. But where is she? Sangee can hear her but not see her. "It will hurt but you will be stronger for it."

Sangee doesn't feel strong. She feels like every bone in her body is trying to escape her skin. Shivering uncontrollably, she lifts a hand to scratch at her face. But something catches her eyes, a brief glittering. A viscous clear slime coats the skin of her hand, webs beneath her fingers. She lifts her arms up with effort: more slime, drying into a segmented pattern encrusts the entirety of it. Sangee emits a strangled yelp, scraping at the mucousy glaze, but the fluid is thick and impenetrable despite its transparence.

What was happening to her? What sick disease had she caught and from where?

She hears the scream before she can locate the sound from her own throat, her own overused lungs. Her vision crackles with white fire until her breath gives out and darkness steals her to sleep once more.

A chorus of throat-singing slowly burrows into Sangee's sleep-clotted ears. Her eyes crack open. She is lying in the community hut, her tribe watchful around her. Radzi touches her first, a cool hand pressing against her forehead. At her feet, she sees Meleq, arms crossed and a tension in her face that betrays anger and, strangely, fear. Bile scorches Sangee's throat; what had she done wrong now?

Sangee shifts, trying to push herself up but quickly realizes she can't move. Have they bound her? She tries to lift her head; nothing. She shifts her eyes, peering down at her hips and legs to see how much rope they'd wasted tying her. But there is no rope. There is nothing. She can't move because her body is not listening to her. Sangee's eyes widen and she cries out, her vocal chords searing in pain at the force of her terror.

Sangee's legs are tucked up to her chest, her arms looped around them, petrified. A foggy translucent shell encases her body up to her collarbones and the fluid inside the shell was seeping up towards her head.

It meant to entomb her whatever this disgusting fluid was. A new parasite?

"Ama . . . ama . . . please . . ."

Meleq watches her silent. Besides her sits Nnasa, her eyes

swollen from crying. Radzi strokes Sangee's head again but she spasms and gnashes her teeth, trying to escape the gelatinous casket.

"Be still, Sangee," Meleq says, her voice hushing the congregation of singing wahinaq instantly.

Only Sangee could be heard, breathing harshly. "What is this, ama? Am I sick? I can't . . . feel anything. I'm dying. I'm dying, aren't I?" Numbness creeps up Sangee's throat, a void of sensation tingling through the length of her spine.

"Sangee, listen to me."

Sangee whimpers but keeps her eyes on her mother. The tribe was as still as a wall painting.

"We've been waiting for this. What's happening to you now."

"We?"

"Us. The wahinaq. The qalipuk."

"What's . . . happening . . .?"

"You're becoming like them."

"Like yourself. There is no one like you yet, Sangee." Meleq touches the hard shell at encasing Sangee's feet, her expression a mingling of fear and awe.

"You've been doing this." Sangee can't see her but she knows Nnasa's voice. Its flatness the timbre of cold fury. "Letting them poison you. To make us into . . . that."

"You don't understand. We can't survive as we are."

Sangee hears a crash, several voices rising up in shouts and scream. A scuffle, a snarl.

"All their dead," Nnasa's hisses. "They remember. Every single one. I told you. They remember all of them. They haven't forgotten. And you want to give us over to them?"

Meleq stumbles after her. "Daughter, please—"

A slap resounds in the crowded hut. The wahinaq suck in their breaths. Sangee can feel the shock on her skin, the smack of cold air as someone leaves the room. Sangee would have cried out for her sister had she the strength but instead her throat constricts, each breath a series of blades down her gullet. Radzi hovers over her and when Sangee chokes, she can see blood spatter her atu's face. She tastes sulfur and something sweet, weightless. The slime that was solidifying just beneath her chin is now over her mouth, sealing it shut.

"Mm . . . mm!" Sangee wants to cry but her eyes are swollen so tightly shut, cutting off vision, imprisoning her tears.

"I'm sorry, Sangee-ke," Meleq sobs, the weight of her pressing over the tucked bend of her legs. "I'm sorry, so sorry . . ."

The wahinaq take up their mournful singing once more, a song she doesn't recognize: not a dirge but not a celebration. A hymn of loss. As the liquid shell closes over her head, hardening out the world, Sangee hears something lower. A single, deep bellow, rippling through the voices of her family like a tidal wave over land, forging further, deeper, until it takes the place of her pulse.

"I'm sorry," says the abyssal tone but who is offering such contrition, Sangee doesn't know.

Nothing.

Nothing and then a seashell roar.

The slow and clear thump of blood in Sangee's skull. Beside it leapt another docile tone, more faceted, dancing low. Somehow the deep rumbling vibrato calms her, as if her head is resting against someone else's warm beating heart. The first flecks of light flare blearily in the corner of her vision. Listening intently to the rolling murmur, Sangee peels her heavy eyes open. Indistinct white blurs, the murky wisps of blackblue shapes shift before her.

The wavering drone dips behind an invisible veil, quieting as the object moves around her and away. A tingle crawls down her back: a touch, contact. Sangee yelps but a gurgling replaces her scream. A sharp inhale admits a rush of water into her lungs, the thickness of it expanding in her chest like stones, fire, drowning, she was drowning—

Exhale. The water drifts out, easy as air. Sangee inhales again, the heavy water harder to draw in than oxygen but just as relieving. How? Where was her ama, her atu, Nnasa?

Again, the sensation of touch down her back. Sangee tries to turn, to see what it is but finds herself tangled up in a viscous thicket. Shaking herself free of the gooey nest, Sangee kicks through the water, trying to let her body tell her which way is up; all the light is the same here, an indigo haze. How deep is she for it to be this dark, she wonders. She can't even see her own hands in front of her face. She's only sure she's swimming because she can feel the cold wet current pulling at her skin. Finally, she reaches a lightening. A horizon clarifies in the submerged distance, the crest of an unknown mountain range inking the band of abyssal shadow. Sangee follows its peak up.

Something was wrong with the sky. The entirety of it seemed to be shimmering, the moonlight casting twirling rays of light down into the shadow world. Sangee looks down. Below her, miles and miles of impenetrable blackness. And her, easily suspended above it all, floating and wingless.

Had her family dropped her into the ocean, thinking her dead? Why?

Sangee screams in confusion, expelling her liquid breath with as much force as possible.

Tentacles wrap around her body, one brushing feather-light between her shoulder blades.

Calm.

The sign is different from how she's learned it; her atu's bony finger on her skin. The way the qalipuk sign is liquid, vaporous.

Calm.

Sangee turns, using her hands to paddle herself in the direction of the speaker. The qalipuk doesn't look as large as she expects; in fact, it's her size. It holds her almost tenderly, tentacles cupped to brace her against the currents.

Up! Air! she signs frantically onto its smooth muzzle.

The beading of its eyes blinks thoughtfully. A tendril catches her by the hands and simply signs, *No. Calm.* It touches her behind her ears, draws another word: *Breathe.*

Sangee touches where the qalipuk has and her eyes widen. On

exhale, water passes through her sinus and out the sides of her neck. Her fingers feel up to just below her ears, down her neck: five frilled open slits flutter under her fingers.

She claps her hand over the openings, accidentally smothering herself. She looks down at herself, hyperventilating: all across her body, from chest to toe, tentacles and tendrils ebbed and curled in a long undulating coat. Shakily, Sangee touches up her face to her hairline. Frictionless skin, hairless. At her scalp, a fleshy mass of filaments. She touches each one and they touch back, under her will. Her throat begins to collapse in on itself with fear.

Did you do this? she signs to the qalipuk with quivering fingertips.

It pauses in consideration, its tendriled mane flaring out in thought.

Yes, it signs back onto her arm. *Daughter.*

Sangee wants to scream again but the pathetic muffled exhalation of water does nothing to ease her. *What's happening to me?* she signs roughly onto its muzzle, her eyes catching on the clean white of its teeth.

You are our first child since the bright star fell. It pauses, tendrils dancing along her cheeks. *Our first child since the killing heat.*

Our child. The qalipuks and the wahinaqs. Sangee pulls her arms into her chest at the revelation, her own head tentacles unconsciously twisting.

Calm.

Stop! Stop . . . calm! she burbles in fury, sick of being chided. Signing furiously, she adds, *I want my ama! Up, now!*

Now, it answers. The qalipuk gathers her into its white underbelly, expanding all its tentacles and propelling them through the water with a blurring speed. Sangee gurgles a screech and latches onto them, hoping her ama is there when she reaches the shore, that her tribe hadn't just left her in the water to die.

Please, she thinks. *I'm still Sangee. Don't leave me. Don't leave me.*

The invisible ocean floor rises up to meet them as the qalipuk swims them inland. Sangee has no sense of time but she sees the light and shadow of day and night change the underwater surface.

How many days had they been traveling? She stops trying to count, drifts in and out of sleep, waking herself when she accidentally bites her lip with newly formed fangs or pinches a tentacle between her body and the qalipuk's.

When they breach the surface, Sangee stifles a sob. Above the crest of the waves, she breathes in the familiar air, light and effortless, warmed by the piercing heat from the sun. But the sky is not the white of winter she expects; it's yellow. Sea birds flitted about above her, their gawky young ones falling into the water before awkwardly taking off again. Spring. She has been gone a whole season.

The qalipuk swims her through a maze of coral and makes her wait in a lagoon offshore. It roars a request for the wahinaqs' presence, a sound Sangee knows her family would hear all the way to their territory.

A day passes before she sees them. Her tribe comes off the high plateau and down onto the rocky shore, marching out along the jetty. Sangee makes an unintentional roar, flailed her arms—fins, she had clawed fins now—excitedly. The qalipuk makes another welcoming call, waiting for the wahinaqs' voices to answer back.

Arrows fall around them like a spring shower. They whir past Sangee's ears and bounce off the qalipuk's tough hide like raindrops. Sangee screeches and waves her arms frantically for them to stop; when she tries to call out her ama or Nnasa's name, only wounded bellows emerge from her mouth. The qalipuk's tentacles bloom outwards and shake, making a loud vibrato sound that trembles the water's surface.

The arrows stop.

On the jetty, Nnasa pushes forward. Long spear in hand, ten wahinaq on either side of her with bows at the ready. Her face is hard, jaw tightened. Sangee thinks from her vantage, that her sister looks older. Much older. How long had she been asleep in the sea?

"I know it's you, Sangee. We've been waiting. We won't be a part of this—" Nnasa gestures between herself and the qalipuk, a disgusted expression wrinkling her face, "—anymore. We won't make room in ourselves for these creatures and made to suffer for their misfortunes. We're going to the south, to the archipelago where Kiele's ship lays in the ice."

Sangee's jaw drops open, revealing rows of sharp serrated teeth that even she hadn't discovered she had yet.

"Ah-ma," Sangee groans out, her new face, her new throat unable to form coherent words. She swims forward into the shallows, rocks and shells scratching at her underbelly. Nnasa was only a few arm's lengths away from her now. Besides her, the wahinaq—other young ones she recognizes as Nnasa's rebellious friends—draw back their bows and hold.

"Ama. Ama is gone. She's been gone for four seasons. She carried you into the sea that night. She wouldn't leave you. I tried to get her out of the water but she wouldn't . . . I watched her lips turn blue. Watched her eyes ice over." Nnasa swallows down her tears, clears her voice. "It doesn't matter. We had to be rid of the old wahinaq. They all knew what they were doing. Trying to make one of you. Trying to make us one of you, too. We couldn't trust them."

Every part of Sangee felt wet and impermanent, each of her sister's words chipping away at the last of her hope.

"I am chief now," Nnasa shouts over the sea's wailing. "And I am taking everyone home! Our true home. Our distant mothers were banished to this world, but we don't deserve to be. We will not sit here and die in the ice. Die like one of you, an abomination." Her eyes are wild now, hunted, haunted. "I will live in the sun and in the green worlds like we were meant to. Like we were all meant to!"

Sangee sobs and moves towards her sister, reaching out with each of her hundreds of new appendages, wanting to hold her, comfort her, anchor those lost eyes. *I'm so sorry, Nnasa,* she thinks. *I didn't know. I'm so sorry. Please.*

Nnasa holds her spear tip at Sangee's wide throat.

"Don't. Don't come any closer. You're one of them now."

"N-oh," Sangee says, struggling with the sounds. An outstretched tentacle gently brushes her sister's cheek before moving to draw a word into Nnasa's skin: *sister, my only sister.*

Nnasa draws back and Sangee closes the new space. Her younger sister's eyes dart to the side: the other wahinaq are watching. Watching their new leader and waiting to see a demonstration of her leadership, her hate.

The spear flies.

Sangee's mind tells her to let the spear pierce her. Make a dead beast of herself. What else did she have? No mother or sister, no tribe. But her instincts pull her to the left just in time, forcing the spear to glance off her shoulder. Sangee lunges, catching Nnasa around the waist in her mouth and pinning her to the ground. Nnasa screams out a single word. A twang of taut sinew hissing fills the air for a breath.

Sangee curls over Nnasa like a nautilus as a forest of arrows fill her hide. Rivulets of inky blood splash from her opened flesh, dripping down Sangee's shoulders and ribs, striping the rich ruddy color of Nnasa's skin black.

Tears wash away the blood splatter on Nnasa's face. "No . . . why?"

Sangee feels the arrowheads lodge deep within her muscles, radiating agonizing heat with every bodily twitch. Nnasa reaches out a fearful hand, touching Sangee's face. *Do I still look like myself,* Sangee wonders. Her mother's eyes, her great ama's jaw. *Or do I look like them? Or like no one?*

"I'm sorry," Nnasa's says, strangled. "I can't. I don't want the ice. I don't want the sea."

Sangee embraces Nnasa with every bit of her body she can, tendrils winding around her, weaving to hold her close. She embraces her all the way down to the heart, to the vein.

Sulfur and sweetness, salt and blood. A familiar scent but just off, not hers. Nnasa pushes Sangee back and then she sees it: a glint of opalescence on her younger sister's neck like the inside of a shell.

The color of change, the scent of a shift.

The shining beginning of her chrysalis.

"I wanted the stars, Sangee. I wanted the sun . . ."

Sangee cups her sister's neck, rocks her in her arms. The frothy tide pulls in around them like a warm blanket. The other wahinaq back off, angry, confused, and fearful. Behind her, more qalipuk breach into the shallows to observe their union. The sun beats down on them all, seabirds and the salt, the two tribes and the watery blood between them. The sisters remain locked in an embrace, mourning in the foam, knowing their paths are set for them, their wills be damned.

As the sun sets, the wahinaq sing their sorrows and pluck the arrows from Sangee's body, watching in awe as her tentacles knit the wounds closed of their own accord. From the deep, the qalipuk follow along with their own wordless psalms, voices floating off the water, a song of mourning and a song of birth, resounding out into the ocean past the seamounts where more qalipuk swam and sang in reply.

Like their mothers, they would forge a home in the world they had and in the bodies they were given, no matter the shape. Together, the two peoples sing, down into the heart of the sea and up into the expanse of the sky, where the stars lie waiting and distant suns rest, pulsing brilliantly like hearts in the darkness.

Hei Au

• BRUCE KA'IMI WATSON and PŌKI'I SETO •

Hei Au Rapture

• BRUCE KA'IMI WATSON and PŌKI'I SETO •

RAPTURE
PĀ MAI AUWĒ
E MAU NĀ HANAUNA Ē
KĀOHI MAI I NĀ IWI
NO KE ONE HĀNAU PONO'Ī

'OIAI I HĀNAU NA KA 'ĀINA
HE 'ĀINA IA LĀ
A HE 'ĀINA ALOHA MAU A MAU
HEI AU I KE AHO LĀ
ME HE KĀULA
I HO'OHEI NŌ A PA'A

PĀ MAI AUWĒ
OLA NŌ AU IĀ 'OE
'ONIPA'A LĀ HAWAI'I
KŌ KĀNAKA PONO'Ī

'OIAI I HĀNAU NA KA 'ĀINA
HE 'ĀINA IA LĀ
HE ALOHA 'ĀINA A KAU Ā KAU
HEI AU I KE AHO LĀ
ME HE KĀULA
I HO'OHEI NŌ A PA'A

'ĀINA ALOHA NO KE ALOHA 'ĀINA
ALOHA 'ĀINA NO KE 'ĀINA ALOHA

He Moʻolelo no ʻAilāʻau

• KĀKAU ʻIA E J. HAUʻOLI LORENZO-ELARCO •

I Kuaihelani lā i hoʻā ʻia ai ke ahi
Ke ahi ʻai humuhumu i ka nahele.
Hele a ʻāluku i ka ʻāina,
Ka ʻāina hoʻi o Puna.
I Puna nō i lapalapa ai,
ʻAi a pau ka lāʻau.
ʻO ʻAilāʻau nō ia ahi.
Ke ahi o Halemaʻumaʻu ka lua.
He lua naʻe i hiki mai,
Mai Kahiki mai i holo mai.
Holo mai Pele mai
Mai ka ʻāina o kona kupuna
He puna ʻo ʻAilāʻau.
ʻAi ka wahine a pau ia lāʻau
Lālau a kīpaku ʻia.
Pakupaku ʻia ʻAilāʻau
Au aku Pele i ia hale hou.
ʻO Halemaʻumaʻu kona hale ia.

E kuʻu wahi mea heluhelu ē, he moʻolelo kēia no ka hū ʻana aʻe o ka pele ma ke kūlanakauhale ʻo Leilani, ma Pāhoa, Puna, Hawaiʻi. Na ʻAilāʻau ia hana, ʻo ia ka ʻaihumuhumu i ka nahele, ka ʻālukuluku i ka ʻāina, ka heʻaheʻa i ka lani. Ua hānau ʻia ʻo ia i Kuaihelani, a he makua kāne no Kūwahailo, ka makua kāne hoʻi o ka wahine ʻai honua. Ma mua loa o ko Pele mā hiki ʻana mai i Hawaiʻi nei a me ko lākou noho ʻana i Halemaʻumaʻu, no ʻAilāʻau ia hale. Kīpaku ʻia akula ʻo ʻAilāʻau, a lilo ʻo Halemaʻumaʻu iā Pele. Mai ia wā mai, ua noho malū ʻo ʻAilāʻau me ka ʻike ʻole ʻia e Pele mā a hiki loa i ka wā i puka hou aʻe ai ʻo ia i ka M.H. 2018. Ma muli o ia hū hou ʻana aʻe i hana ʻia ai kekahi puʻu ahi hou loa, ʻo ia hoʻi ka mea i kapa ʻia ai ʻo Ahuʻailāʻau, a he inoa hoʻohanohano ia no kona mana. Nona hoʻi kēia moʻolelo.

I ka lā 3 o Mei, i ka M.H. 2018, ma ka mokupuni o Hawaiʻi, nenea wale ana nō ka poʻe kamaʻāina i ke ʻano nohona o Hawaiʻi nei, a neinei aʻela ke ōlaʻi. Maʻa hoʻi ia poʻe kamaʻāina i ke ōlaʻi, ʻoiai no Pele nō hoʻi kēia moku ola. Eia naʻe, ua ʻano ʻokoʻa iki ia ōlaʻi ʻana. ʻO ia mea ʻokoʻa, ʻo ia hoʻi, ua lohe ʻia ke kanikani nakanaka e hū aʻe ana mai lalo loa mai o ka honua. A laila, māwae aʻela ka honua ma ke alanui Luana, ma Leilani, Pāhoa. Hū aʻela ka pele, a mai ia hū ʻana aʻe, puka aʻela kekahi kino nui a weliweli hoʻi.

He ʻelekū kona kino, a he kīwaʻawaʻa kona ʻili me he ʻaʻā lā. He mahiole ko ke poʻo. ʻO ia mahiole e kau kehakeha ana, me he mea lā, he pele nō hoʻi nā hulu e hū aʻe ana mai ka mahiole mai. He ʻahu ʻula ko ka poʻohiwi. ʻO ia ʻahu ʻula hoʻi e kau hiehie ana ma kona poʻohiwi, me he mea lā, he pāhoehoe nō hoʻi ia e kahe mālie ana mai kona poʻohiwi a i ka honua. He lei niho palaoa ko ka ʻāʻī. ʻO ia lei e pāpahi ana i ka ʻāʻī, me he mea lā, ʻaʻole ia he niho palaoa, akā he ula ahi kāoko ia e puʻeʻena ana.

Kū haʻaheo aʻela ia kino mai ka honua mai a kilo akula iā luna i ka lani, a huli aʻela ia a nānā aku iā Kīlauea. Hanu ihola, a pohā akula kona leo oli;

Hulihia ka mauna,
Wela i ke ahi,
Ke ahi hoʻi a ʻAilāʻau,
Wela nopu ka uka,
Ma kahi Hanalei,
Pōhaku kai o Kū ka lā i uka,
Ka ʻiʻini o ka lae,
Kahi ka lua.

Iā ia e ʻai haʻa ana, kāia haʻakei akula iā Halemaʻumaʻu, iā Pele mā hoʻi. A keʻehi kalaʻihi ʻo ia i ka honua, a naue ka honua. I kēlā me kēia manawa i keʻehi ʻia ai ka honua, hoʻomaka e hoʻomāwae aʻela i ka ʻāina, a mai ia māwae nō e puka aʻe ai kekahi ahi likoliko o ka wela.

Ma Halema'uma'u, nenea ho'i 'o Pele mā i ka lua pele e puapua'i a'e ana, a i ka pa'ē 'ana mai o ia leo a me ka neinei 'ana o ka 'āina, pi'oloke nō ho'i ko lākou na'au. "Na wai kā ho'i ia hua 'ōlelo hemahema me ke ōla'i 'ana o ka honua? 'A'ohe ona 'ike i ka mea pololei o Lohi'au," i puoho a'e ai 'o Hi'iakaikapoliopele.

"Tsā! He leo kama'āina nō paha ia. 'O ia nō ho'i ke kupu'eu o ke ahi. 'A'ohe ona like iki me a'u. 'O ia ala ke kauā, a 'o wau nō ke ali'i. He kūlou wale kāna i mua o'u. 'O 'Ailā'au nō ia!" Mai kona wahi e noho ana i me'eu a'e ai 'o Pele, a kilo pono aku ma kahi o 'Ailā'au, a hāpai a'ela 'o ia i ka leo oli, penei;

> No Popopo ka 'ai lā'au,
> Kahi noho 'ia e 'Elepaio,
> Eia lā ho'i 'o Naio,
> I ka nā'ele'ele o uka,
> Kolo a'ela 'o Huhu,
> I ka hale o 'Oke,
> He hale ia no Huhuhu,
> Kūkulu 'ia e 'Ulupio,
> 'O 'oe nō kona ali'i,
> Ka 'ai lā'au ho'i o Popopo.

Pā akula ka leo oli o ua wahine 'ai honua nei i ka pepeiao o ua mea 'ai lā'au lā, a ha'ano'u hou 'o 'Ailā'au i ke oli, penei;

> No 'Ālukuluku ka 'ai lā'au,
> I uka o Pauhe'ahe'a,
> Aia lā i Pu'uahu'ula,
> ka 'āina mahi 'ole,
> A i kai o Palaoa,
> Pā'ani a'ela 'o Pu'ōpu'ō,
> I Nō'ā ku'u hale,
> He hale ia no Hōlapu,
> Kūkulu 'ia e 'Ulawena,
> 'O wau nō kona ali'i,
> Ke ahi 'ā o Humuhumu.

Pau ke oli i ka ha'ano'u 'ia, nahae 'ino a'ela ka 'āina, a hua'i a'ela ka pele mai ka māwae mai. 'Ike akula 'o Pele i ka uahi pele e pōnulu loa ana, a me ka ʻōwena o ka lani i ke ahi a ʻAilāʻau. Kēnā akula ʻo Pele iā Hiʻiakawāwahihonua, ka māhoe hoʻi o Hiʻiakawāwahilani, e hoʻomāwae ʻāina i ala holo pele ma lalo o ka honua nona e holo koke iō ʻAilāʻau.

Lele koke akula ʻo Hiʻiakawāwahihonua i ka hana e hoʻokō ai i ke kēnā a kona kaikuaʻana, a ʻo ka hele akula nō ia i mua o Hiʻiakanohoana, a noi akula iā ia e ʻae ʻo ia i kona komo ʻana i loko o ka luakele ma Halemaʻumaʻu i kapa ʻia ai ʻo Kahakakīloa. I laila nō i waiho ʻia ai nā mea waiwai loa o Pele mā, a no Hiʻiakanohoana ke kuleana kiaʻi. ʻAe koke ʻia ʻo ia a komo akula. Kiʻi ʻia ka ipu heke kupaianaha ʻo Paʻipaʻihonua. Na Hiʻiakaikapoliopele i aʻo aku iā ia i ke paʻi ipu. ʻO ke kumu hoʻi, no Hiʻiakawāwahihonua ke kuleana kiaʻi māwae a me ke kiaʻi ala holo pele i hana ʻia e Pele ma lalo o ka honua, a ua hiki nō iā ia ke hoʻomāwae i ka ʻāina ke kauoha ʻia e Pele. Me Paʻipaʻihonua nō ʻo ia i kia iho ai i kona mana hoʻomāwae ʻāina. No laila, kiʻi ʻo Hiʻiakawāwahihonua iā Paʻipaʻihonua, a noho nani ihola ua Hiʻiaka nei i mua o Pele mā, a ʻo ka hula noho kāna i hana ai.

Mai lalo mai nō ke ahi,
Ke ahi ola o ka honua,
I ka mole o ka ʻāina,
Kahi ʻike ʻole ʻia ka ʻenaʻena,
Kapalulu nā makani paio,
Kaʻulī ka uē o Kahuna,
Pāluku ka pali kapu moho aliʻi,
Wili ʻia e ka wahine kapu,
Uʻina ke kū pīnaʻi,
Pāpaʻaʻina ka uē o ke aloha,
Puapuaʻi ka puʻu i uka,
ʻŌpaʻipaʻi iho nā huku,
Puhi mau aʻe ka uahi o ka lua,
Ka lua ʻena o ka manu,
Kuʻi ana ke kākoʻi,
A kani aʻe ke kōlea,
Hiolo ihola ka papa hale,

Kī ka lau ea o ka maʻumaʻu,
Luaʻi hū ola ka honua!

I kēlā me kēia paʻi ʻana o Hiʻiakawāwahihonua iā
Paʻipaʻihonua ma ka ʻāina, haʻalulu ka honua i ka ōlaʻilaʻi, a wāwahi
iki aʻela ka honua ma lalo ona. A pau ia hula ʻana, a he ala holo pele
ko lalo o ia ipu heke i kuʻi ai. ʻO kekahi puka o ia ala, aia nō ma
Kīlauea, a ʻo ka puka ʻē aʻe, aia nō ma lalo o Ahuʻailāʻau. A lawa
kūpono hoʻi, lele koke akula ʻo Pele i loko o ia ala holo pele me ka
lawe pū ʻana i ka pele a pau loa mai loko mai o Halemaʻumaʻu. Heʻe
ana ʻo Pele i luna o ka pele ma lalo o ka honua, me he mea lā, aia nō
ʻo ia i kai i ka heʻe nalu. ʻO ia ke kumu i kapa ʻia ai ia ala holo pele ʻo
Kawahineheʻepele. Pau ka pele i ka lawe ʻia, a lele ihola ʻo Hiʻiaka
mā i loko o Kawahineheʻepele no ka hahai ʻana i ke kaikuaʻana.

Ua hiki nō iā ʻAilāʻau ke ʻike i ka hiki koke ʻana o Pele ma
muli o ka neinei loa ʻana o ka honua, a hoʻomākaukau ʻo ia iā ia iho.
Mai kona lima ponoʻī mai nō i puka aʻe ai i newa hālelo. He ʻaʻā ke
poʻo o ia newa, a he lelekepue ke kūʻau, a me he mea lā, he pele ko
loko o ia newa, no ka mea, he mau nakanaka kona e makali ana. ʻO
Kūkamakalukulauahi ka inoa o ia newa kupaianaha. He pili nō me
Kūkaʻōʻō, ka lāʻau pālau a Kamaakamahiʻai. Koali ana ʻo ʻAilāʻau iā
Kūkamakalukulauahi i luna o kona poʻo i kona kali ʻana iā Pele.

Lele ʻino aʻela ʻo Pele mai Kawahineheʻepele aku a hoʻouka
koke akula ʻo ia iā ʻAilāʻau, a kī pele akula ʻo ia iā ʻAilāʻau. Hahau
wale aku nō ua ʻAilāʻau nei i ka pele me kāna newa.

Hāpai aʻela ʻo Pele i kekahi oli, penei;
ʻAuhea wale ʻoe e ka ʻai lāʻau,
Ka lāʻau noho kiʻo o ka manu,
Ka lāʻau nalinali a ka ʻiole,
Ka lāʻau huhuhu a ka naio,
Ka lāʻau a ka lukuʻōhiʻa,
Ka lāʻau a ka huliʻōhiʻa,
Ka lāʻau ū wai i Kūlanihākoʻi,
He ʻōwena wale ke ahi ou,
A ʻo ka makali nō hoʻi koʻu.

Pane akula ʻo ʻAilāʻau me ke oli. ʻAʻole nō naʻe iā Pele kēia oli, i kekahi moʻo nō ia, penei;

Aia i Kīlauea kuʻu moʻo
ʻO Kanihiō kuʻu moʻo ia.
Kuʻu moʻo piʻi kumu,
Kuʻu moʻo noho lālā,
Kuʻu moʻo heʻe puka,
Kuʻu moʻo hoʻopiha lua i ka walewale.
E maʻūmaʻū ka ʻāina!
No kāua nō ia hale.

Pau kona oli, a hoʻouka hou akula ʻo Pele, a no kona noke mau i ka hakakā, ʻaʻohe ona ʻike i ka hana ma Halemaʻumaʻu.

E kuʻu wahi mea heluhelu, e haʻalele kāua iā lāua e kaua ana, a e nānā i ia hana ma Halemaʻumaʻu. Ma mua naʻe o ka hele ʻana i Halemaʻumaʻu, he mea nui kēia moʻolelo hoʻākāka.

No Kanihiō, He Moʻo

Ma hope o ke kīpaku ʻia ʻana o ʻAilāʻau e Pele, peʻe ʻo ia i loko o nā ala holo pele ona i hana ai. I loko o kekahi ala holo pele, ua hālana aʻe nō ka wai, a lilo ia ʻo ia kahi i noho ai kekahi moʻo, ʻo Kanihiō ia. ʻO ua Kanihiō nei ke keiki kāne a Kanikū lāua ʻo Kanimoe, nā moʻo kiaʻi i ka loko iʻa ʻo Wainānāliʻi, Kona. I ka wā ma mua, ua ʻono loa nō ʻo Pele i ka iʻa mai Wainānāliʻi mai, a no ia kumu, ʻai nō ʻo Pele i ia loko iʻa. Ua ʻike akula nā moʻo kiaʻi i ka hiki pololei ʻana mai o Pele i Wainānāliʻi. ʻOiai he mau kiaʻi hemo ʻole ʻo Kanikū lāua ʻo Kanimoe no ia loko iʻa, ʻaʻohe o lāua haʻalele i ia wahi, a ua kūpaʻa lāua i ke alo o Pele. Ma mua o ka hōʻea ʻana mai o Pele, hoʻonoho nā mākua moʻo i kā lāua keiki moʻo i loko o kekahi waʻa. Kāhea akula ʻo Kanikū i makani e puewa aku i ka waʻa o kāna keiki. Ua kapa ʻia ia makani ʻo Kanikū no ia moʻo. I ka holo ʻana o kona waʻa, huli aʻela ʻo Kanihiō a nānā aku iā Wainānāliʻi a me kona mau mākua, a ʻike maka akula ʻo ia i ka pau ʻana o kona mau mākua a me kona ʻāina i ka neʻepapa ʻia.

Holo akula nō ka waʻa ma waho aku o ke kapa kai a i Kaʻū. I ka hiki ʻana aku i laila, hei ʻia nō ka waʻa e ke kai holo ʻo Kawili, a lawe ʻia akula kona waʻa a i waho aku o Ka Lae, kahi i launa ai ʻo Kawili me ke kai holo ʻo Halaʻea, a pae akula i uka ma ke kahakai i kapa ʻia ai ʻo Kamilopaealiʻi.

I ka pae ʻana i uka, noho akula ʻo ia i ke one a ʻo ka uē nō kāna.

Auē e kuʻu mau mākua,
E Kanikū,
E Kanimoe,
Ua hala,
Ua pōhaku,
Ua pau i ka wahine ʻono iʻa,
Auē, e Wainānāliʻi,
Ua ʻai ʻia ka iʻa,
Ua pau ka wai,
Ua pau ke kai,
E kani ē,
E kani mau.

Pau kona uē ʻana, kū aʻela kekahi mea i mua ona. ʻO ia hoʻi ʻo Kūmauna, ke akua ua o Hīlea. "Tsā! ʻO wai kā hoʻi ʻoe ʻo ka uē? Ua ʻike maka ʻia kou pae ʻana mai ma kēia pae aliʻi. ʻAʻohe ou kuleana ma kēia one!"

"'O wau ʻo Kanihiō, ke keiki kāne a Kanikū lāua ʻo Kanimoe, nā kiaʻi o Wainānāliʻi. Ua ʻono ka wahine ʻai honua i ka iʻa Wainānāliʻi, a no kona pōloli, ua pau kuʻu ʻāina me nā mākua i ka ʻai ʻia."

Ua minamina nui ʻo Kūmauna i ia moʻo. "E Kanihiō ē, e kala mai ʻoe i ke kaikamahine aʻu i kona pōloli nui. Naʻu nō e hānai aku iā ʻoe, a nāu hoʻi e kiaʻi i koʻu kiʻo wai, e like me ke kiaʻi ʻana o kou mau mākua iā Wainānāliʻi. Inā make wai paha kekahi malihini, nāu hoʻi e alakaʻi iā ia i ke kiʻo wai o lalo. I laila nō e hoʻomaʻemaʻe ʻia ai kona mau lima, kona alo, a me kona mau wāwae. Pau i ka hoʻomaʻemaʻe ʻia, piʻi aʻe i uka i ke kiʻo wai o luna a inu i ka wai huʻihuʻi a kena ka puʻu." A pēlā nō i lilo ai ua Kanihiō nei ʻo ia ke kiaʻi o nā kiʻo wai a me ka mea kōkua iā Kūmauna i kona hānai ʻana i ka poʻe o Hīlea i ka ua.

I kekahi lā, ua kānalua loa nō kekahi haole i ka mana o Kūmauna, a no kona kānalua, hele akula 'o ia i ke kino pōhaku o Kūmauna e noho ana ma ke ka'e o ke ki'o wai o luna. Kī pū akula ke kānalua i ka pōhaku, a lele a'ela 'elua 'āpana pōhaku li'ili'i mai ke kino pōhaku mai o Kūmauna. Pi'i a'ela ka inaina o Kūmauna, a hālana a'ela ke kahawai a holo i ka hale o ia haole, a pau kona hale. Ua mana'o nō 'o Kūmauna, 'a'ole nō i hō'ihi ka po'e iā ia, a no ia kumu, ha'alele 'o ia iā Ka'ū. 'A'ole nō 'o ia i ho'i hou aku a hiki loa i kēia mau lā. 'Ike akula 'o Kanihiō i ka ha'alele 'ana o kona kahu, a 'imi akula 'o ia i nā 'āpana pōhaku o Kūmauna. Ua loa'a iā ia kekahi 'āpana pōhaku, a mālama ihola. 'O kekahi, aia nō ma ka Hale Hō'ike'ike o Kamehameha i kēia mau lā. 'Oiai ua ha'alele kona kahu, ha'alele nō ho'i 'o ia.

Ha'alele akula 'o Kanihiō iā Ka'ū a hō'ea i Puna, a noho ihola 'o ia i loko o kekahi ala holo pele kahiko loa piha i ka wai. A 'o ia ala holo pele nō i launa ai me 'Ailā'au ma hope o kona kīpaku 'ia e Pele. Ua noho pū 'o 'Ailā'au lāua 'o Kanihiō, 'oiai he 'ai lā'au maoli nō lāua. I ko lāua noho pū 'ana, ho'olālā 'ia nō ka ho'okahuli hou 'ana iā Pele.

E ka mea heluhelu, 'oiai ua pa'a ke kahua, e ho'i hou kāua i Halema'uma'u a e 'ike i nā hanana ma laila.

Iā Pele lāua 'o 'Ailā'au e kaua ana, a ua pau loa nō ka pele i loko o ka lua pele, hele akula 'o Kanihiō iō Kīlauea, a kū a'ela 'o ia ma ke ka'e o ka lua. A hāpai a'ela 'o ia i ka 'āpana pōhaku o Kūmauna i ka lani, a oli 'o ia, penei;

'O wai i ta wai, wai
Mo'o i ta wai, wai
Walewale waiwai
He wale i ta wai, wai
Mo'o walewale waiwai
He hale ma'ū i ta wai, wai

A helele'i maila ka ua, a kahe ihola ka walewale mai ke kino mai o ua Kanihiō nei, a piha ka lua. 'Oiai ua hihia loa nō 'o Pele mā i ka hakakā ahi 'ana me 'Ailā'au, 'a'ohe o lākou 'ike i ia hana a Kanihiō.

I ke kaua ʻana o Pele me ʻAilāʻau, ua ʻoi loa aku nō ka mana o Pele i ke ahi a me ka pele ma mua o ʻAilāʻau. Neʻe ʻo Pele, neʻe hoʻi ka pele. Akā naʻe, ua ikaika loa nō ka ʻili o ʻAilāʻau. ʻOʻole ʻa maoli nō kona ʻili, no ka mea, he ʻaʻā nō kona ʻano. No ia kumu, ua paʻakikī loa nō ka hōʻeha ʻana iā ia. Ua hehi ʻo Pele i ka honua me kona wāwae a huaʻi koke aʻela ka pele, a kī pele ʻia aʻela ʻo ʻAilāʻau a hoʻolele ʻia aʻela i luna loa i ka lani. Hoʻi a pā ihola kona alo i ka honua, a kī pele hou ʻo Pele iā ia. Eia nō naʻe, kū koke aʻela ʻo ʻAilāʻau a ʻakaʻaka me ka hoʻohenehene ʻana aku iā Pele, me he mea lā, he mea ʻole ia kī pele ʻia.

"Tsā! ʻO ʻoe kā ia wahine ʻai lepo?!"

Wela loa aʻela ka huhū o Pele a kī pele hou akula ʻo ia iā ʻAilāʻau, a ʻo ka hahau wale akula nō ia o ʻAilāʻau i kāna newa.

Hala aʻela kekahi mau anahulu i ko lāua kaua ʻana a ua hele a luhi loa ʻo Pele. Ma ko lāua kaua ʻana, ʻaʻole nō i hoʻokuʻi iki ʻo ʻAilāʻau iā Pele. Kali ʻo ia a luhi loa ʻo Pele, a laila hoʻi, kiola hou aʻela ʻo ʻAilāʻau iā Kūmakalukulauahi a ʻōlelo akula, "Naʻi ʻia ʻo Halemaʻumaʻu." Hoʻokuʻu ʻia akula ʻo Kūmakalukulauahi, a me ke kani kīkē ʻalāna i pā ikaika ai i ka ʻōpū o Pele, a hoʻi hou akula kāna newa i kona lima

Ua hele a nāwaliwali loa nō ʻo Pele i ka ʻeha. I ka ʻike ʻana aku i ia ʻeha o ko lākou kuaʻana, kiʻi koke ʻo Hiʻiaka mā iā Pele. Hoʻokuʻu hou akula ʻo ia i kāna newa iā lākou. Kāhea koke akula ʻo Hiʻiakaikaʻulu, a puka honua aʻela kekahi kumu ʻulu mai ka honua mai, a wehe aʻela kona kumu, a komo lākou a pau i loko no ka hoʻopakele ʻana i ke kuʻi ʻia e Kūmakalukulauahi. ʻAkaʻaka aʻela ʻo ʻAilāʻau, a ʻoliʻoli ʻo ia i ke eo ʻana o Pele.

Hele akula ʻo ia i Halemaʻumaʻu e launa pū me Kanihiō. ʻŌlelo hou akula ʻo ia, "Ua ʻai ʻia ʻo Halemaʻumaʻu." Akā, ua makemake ʻo ia e hoʻi i ka puʻu hou ona i hana aku ai, ʻoiai he hōʻailona lanakila ia. No laila, ua hoʻoholo ʻia, ʻo Kanihiō nō ke kiaʻi o ke kiʻo wai walewale ma Halemaʻumaʻu, a e noho ana ʻo ia ma Ahuʻailāʻau.

Ua hāmaʻomaʻo lahilahi ka wai ma Halemaʻumaʻu a ua ʻano wela loa nō, no ka mea, he pele ko lalo loa, a ʻo ia ka mea i ho'omehana ai i ia wai. No ia kumu i kapa 'ia ai ia ki'o 'o Kawalewalewelaokamo'o. 'Oiai na'e, ua noho pū 'o Kanihiō me 'Ailā'au, ua ma'a loa nō 'o ia i ka wela i ho'ohahana ai mai ke kino mai o 'Ailā'au.

No ka eo 'ana o Pele, hele akula lāua i ka 'ai lā'au. 'Oiai lāua e 'ai ana, e nānā kāua i ka hana a Hi'iaka mā. Ma hope o ke komo 'ana i ke kumu lā'au ulu, puka hou a'ela lākou ma kekahi kumu 'ulu ma kai, ma Nanahuki. Ua palapū a nāpele loa nō 'o Pele i kona holopapa loa 'ia e 'Ailā'au. Ua lele koke a'ela kona mau kaikaina i ka 'oihana lā'au lapa'au i mea e hō'ola hou ai a e ho'oikaika hou ai i kona kino. Ho'omākaukau 'ia kahi e moe ai. Ma lalo loa, 'o ia ka lā'ī 'ōma'oma'o i ki'i 'ia e Hi'iakaikalā'ī. A laila, ua kuapapa 'ia ka 'uluhe a me ka 'ama'u e Hi'iakaika'uluhe lāua 'o Hi'iakaikeama'u. Ho'onoho 'ia nā lā'au lapa'au a puni o ko lākou kaikua'ana e Hi'iakaikapopolo, Hi'iakaikanoni, Hi'iakaikekō, Hi'iakaika'awapuhi, a me Hi'iakaikamamaki. Na Hi'iakaikamailekūhonua, Hi'iakaikape'ahi, Hi'iakaikahinano, Hi'iakaikealahe'e a me Hi'iakaika'iliahi i ho'ōnaona i kona wahi i moe ai. A laila, lawe 'ia nō ho'i e Hi'iakaikamamaki kekahi apu me ka wai hou, ka mamaki, a me ka pa'akai, a hānai akula iā ia. Pau kona inu 'ana, a moe ihola.

Nīnau akula 'o Hi'iakaika'ale'ī, "Auē, he aha lā ho'i kā kākou hana?"

"He paio mau nō!" i pane koke ai 'o Hi'iakakapu'ena'ena.

"'Ē, 'o ka paio ho'i kā kākou! E lilo ana nō nā iwi o ia po'e 'aihue 'o ia ka wāhie no kā kākou ahi!" i 'uwā ai 'o Hi'iakaika'akoko.

"Kōkua! Kōkua!" i pane mai ai 'o Hi'iakaika'ae.

"A pehea?" wahi a Hi'iakaikauhi.

"Pehea kā ho'i!" i 'ōlelo aku ai 'o Hi'iakaika'ōhelo.

"E kū ho'i kākou me ka naue 'ole! 'O ke 'ano o ko kākou kū 'ana, he akamai! 'A'ole ia he kū koke, 'oiai 'o ka hiolo wale nō ka hopena," i 'ōlelo aku ai 'o Hi'iakaikapoliopele.

Moe wale ihola nō 'o Pele a hala akula kekahi manawa, a 'ōlelo akula. "'Ae like nō wau i kā ku'u Poli. E akamai kākou, a e 'imi kākou i ia ala akamai. Na wai ho'i ka 'ole o ke akamai? He alanui i maʻa i ka hele ʻia e ko kākou kaikuaʻana. ʻO ia hoʻi ʻo Kapoʻulakīnaʻu. Naʻu hoʻi e ʻimi aku iā ia e noi mai i kōkua.”

"A pehea ana lā ʻoe e ʻimi aku ai iā ia, ʻoiai ua paʻa nō ʻoe i ka moe?” i nīnau aku ai ʻo Hiʻiakanoholae.

"Malia, e hoʻouna ʻia nō paha ʻo Hiʻiakaikapoliopele?” i hāpai aʻe ai ʻo Hiʻiakanoholani.

"ʻAʻole paha. Ua ʻāpiki loa nō ko kākou kaikuaʻana. Aia lā ʻo ia e peʻe nei. ʻO wau wale nō paha ke ʻimi aku iā ia. E paʻa nō koʻu kino i ka moe, a haʻalele ana ka ʻuhane oʻu, a lele aʻela i ka lani lā e ʻimi aku ai i ke kaikuaʻana o kākou. Na ʻoukou nō e hoʻokapu i koʻu wahi kino e moe nei a hiki i koʻu wā e hoʻi hou mai ai. ʻAʻohe mea e hoʻāla hou mai ai iaʻu.”

ʻAe maila nō hoʻi ʻo Hiʻiaka mā. Ua moe ihola ʻo Pele, a hele maila nā lihilihi o ʻĀwihikalani a luluʻu i ka nipo a ka hiamoe. Hala akula kekahi manawa, a hāʻule i ka hiamoe. Lele aʻela kona ʻuhane i luna loa o kona kino. Huli aʻela ʻo ia a nānā akula i kona kino e moe nei me kona poʻe kaikaina e kū kiaʻi ana. A laila, huli hou aku ʻo ia a ʻimi hele i kona kaikuaʻana. Iā ia nō e lelele ana i ka lani, oli akula ʻo ia i kekahi oli kāhea, penei;

E Kapo,
Ka ʻula,
E ala ʻoe e Kapoʻula.
E Kapo,
Ka ʻula,
Ke kīnaʻu,
Eō mai e Kapoʻulakīnaʻu.
E Kapo,
ka lei,
Lei ʻia ʻo Kapolei.
E Kapo,
ke kohe,
Ka lepelepe,
E aloha mai ʻoe e Kapokohelepelepe.
E Kapo,
Ka maʻi,

Ka lele,
E lele aʻe ʻoe e Kapomaʻilele.
E Kapo,
Ke kohe,
Ka lele,
E lele aʻe ʻoe e Kapokohelele.
ʻAuhea ʻoe e Kapo ka wahine
Ka wahine kālaipāhoa.

Iā ia e lelele ana i uka o Keauhou, Mauna Loa, kū honua aʻela kekahi puʻu mai ka ʻāina mai. He puʻu kiʻekiʻe loa nō ia ma luna aʻe nei o nā kumu lāʻau. Kūlou ihola nā kumu lāʻau ma luna o ia puʻu a ʻike ʻia maila kekahi hale, a ʻo ka maopopo koke ihola nō ia iā Pele, ʻo ia ka hale o kona kaikuaʻana.

Iho ʻo Peleʻuhane a kū i mua o ka hale. He hale hulu uliuli nō ia, he mau hulu ia o ka ʻalalā. A ʻo ia nō kekahi mea a Pele i ʻike leʻa ai, ʻo ia nō ka hale o kona kaikuaʻana, no ka mea, he kahu ʻo Kapo i nā manu ʻalalā, a ʻo lākou hoʻi kāna poʻe ʻelele. Ma kona kū ʻana i mua o ka pā hale, oli kāhea akula ʻo Pele, penei:
E kuʻu kuaʻana,
E Kapo,
Kapoʻula,
Kapoʻulakīnaʻu,
Kapolei,
Kapokohelepelepe,
Kapomaʻilele,
Kapokohelele,
E ka wahine kālaipāhoa.
I ʻaneʻi au,
I mua ʻoe.
Ua ʻai ʻia ka lāʻau,
A ua hulihia ka mauna,
Noho walewale ʻia e ka moʻo.
I hale noʻu,
I puʻuhonua no kākou,
E aloha mai, e aloha mai.

Eō mai ē!

A pane koke maila kekahi leo no loko mai o ka hale, penei;

E ku'u kaikaina ē,

E Pele,

Pelehonuamea,

Pelewena'ula,

Pelekauahi,

Pelekahū,

Peleikapāhoehoe,

Peleika'a'ā,

Peleikeahilapalapa,

Ke ahi 'ai honua,

Ka wahine o ka lua,

Mai, mai, e komo mai,

Ka pu'uhonua 'alalā,

I Haleuliuli nei,

Aloha mai!

Komo akula 'o Pele i loko o ka hale, a 'o ka honi a'ela nō ia o lāua. Noho pū lāua ma luna o kekahi nu'a moena pāwehe makaloa.

"He aha lā ho'i kēia huaka'i 'o ka 'imi 'ana mai ia'u?" i nīnau ai ka wahine o Haleuliuli.

"I 'ane'i au i 'imi aku ai iā 'oe i kōkua no ka 'ohana," i pane ai ka wahine o Halema'uma'u, a ho'omau 'o ia,"Ua ola a'e nō 'o 'Ailā'au, ka 'aihumuhumu o ka nahele. Ua pu'u a'ela ke ahi honua. He kāne 'o ia na Kanihiō, ka mo'o keiki a Kanikū lāua 'o Kanimoe. Na lāua ho'i i kā'ili i ko mākou hale. Ua pau ho'i ka pele o ka lua, a 'o ka walewale mo'o ka mea e puapua'i nei."

"Auē, e ku'u Pele ē, 'a'ohe o'u mana e kaua iā lāua. Nou wale nō ia kuleana. Nāu i 'ai hamu i ke ahi o 'Ailā'au, a nāu ho'i i 'ai i ka i'a a Kanihiō. Eia nō na'e, e lawe aku 'oe i kēia wahi mea hune, malia he mea kōkua iā 'oe."

Ua ki'i maila 'o Kapo i kekahi 'umeke li'ili'i i ho'opa'a 'ia i loko o kekahi kōkō e kau ana ma kekahi kā 'umeke, a hu'e a'ela nō 'o ia i ke po'i. Aia nō i loko o ia 'umeke kekahi mau māmala lā'au he nui. Ki'i akula 'o Kapo i kekahi a hā'awi pono akula iā Pele.

A'oa'o akula 'o Kapo iā Pele, "He māmala nō ho'i kēia mai Kālaipāhoa mai, no Mauna Loa, Moloka'i. He lā'au make ia, no laila, e mālama pono i nā lima. Inā kui 'ia nō 'o 'Ailā'au e kēia wahi māmala, he make nō ka hopena. 'A'ole nō paha lawa ka 'awa o ia māmala e ho'omake koke aku ai iā ia, eia na'e, e make pupū ana nō me ka walania loa. Ua lawa kūpono nō paha e ho'onāwaliwali iho i kona kino. A laila, e na'i aku 'oe iā ia. E maka'ala na'e o kui 'ia auane'i 'oe."

"Pehea lā e ho'okui 'ia ai 'o 'Ailā'au? He 'a'ā pa'a loa kona 'ili," i nīnau aku ai 'o Pele.

"Pehea lā ho'i? Nou nō ke kuleana e no'ono'o. E lele a ho'i a'e 'oe i kou kino pono'ī," i kuhikuhi aku ai 'o Kapo.

Honi nō ho'i lāua, a ha'alele koke akula nō 'o Pele. Komo hou akula nō 'o Pele i kona kino maoli i kia'i 'ia e kona po'e kaikaina, a 'o ka puoho a'ela nō ia. Pū'iwa a'ela nō 'o Hi'iaka mā i ka ho'i hou 'ana mai o ke kaikua'ana. He anahulu nō ka lō'ihi o kona moe 'ana. Wehewehe akula 'o Pele i nā mea a ko lākou kaikua'ana i kuhikuhi aku nei no ka māmala a Kālaipāhoa.

"He mana'o maika'i nō ia! Eia kā, i hea hā ho'i ia wahi māmala?" i pane aku nei 'o Hi'iakapaikauhele.

Pau kona nīnau 'ana, 'emo 'ole a lele ihola kekahi manu 'alalā iā lākou a waiho 'ia kekahi 'umeke i ka wāwae o Pele. Ki'i maila 'o Pele i ka 'umeke, a hu'e a'ela i ke po'i, a he māmala ko loko. 'Alalā a'ela ia manu uliuli, ho'i akula i kona kahu.

"Tsā! He mea 'ole ho'i kēnā wahi mea hunehune!" i puoho a'ela 'o Hi'iakaka'alawamaka.

"'O ia nō paha ka mea e ho'omake ana iā 'Ailā'au?" i 'ōlelo a'ela 'o Hi'iaka'ōpio

"Auē kā ho'i e kaina mā, nui ke kānalua i ka mana o ko kākou kaikua'ana. E kūkākūkā kākou i ko kākou ho'i hou 'ana i ke alo o 'Ailā'au. Pehea ana lā e ho'okui 'ia ai 'o ia ala?"

"He mana'o ko'u," wahi a Hi'iakakupu'ano'ano. "Na'u e lawe i ka māmala." No ua Hi'i nei ke kuleana ho'olū a ho'okupu 'ano'ano ho'i ma hope o ka hū 'ana o Pele i ola hou ka nahele. Ua kāhiko 'ia 'o ia e nā lei 'ano'ano like 'ole, 'o ka wiliwili 'oe, 'o ka

'a'ali'i 'oe, 'o ke kukui 'oe, 'o ke koa 'oe, 'o ka 'ōhi'a 'oe, a ia 'ano
hou aku. Ho'omau akula ua Hi'i lā, "E ho'onoho 'ia ana kekahi
'ano'ano ma ke ala o 'Ailā'au, a e ho'okupu 'ia ana ka 'ano'ano a ulu
a'ela kekahi 'ōhi'a nani lua 'ole a puni o ia māmala. E 'ike aku ana 'o
ia i ka nani o ia 'ōhi'a, a e moni ana nō kona ha'ae ke nānā aku i ia
lā'au, a laila, 'o ka 'ai 'ana kāna."

    "'O ia!" wahi a Hi'iakalei'ia, "Akā, pehea ana 'oe e ho'okupu
a'e ai i ia 'ano'ano me ka māmala me ka 'ike 'ole 'ia e 'Ailā'au?"

    "Me ka 'ēheu nō o ka pō a me ka uhi o ka uahi pele," i
ho'opuka a'ela 'o Pele, "Na'u ho'i e alaka'i iā 'oe, e ku'u
Hi'iakakupu'ano'ano, ma ko'u 'ano uahi pele, a 'a'ohe ona 'ike iā
'oe." Hā'awi akula 'o Pele i ka māmala iā Hi'iakakupu'ano'ano me
ka 'ōlelo 'ana, "Iā 'oe ko kākou ola."

    Ua pō ke ao, a ia pō nō i ho'opolalauahi a'e ai 'o Pele ma
kona kino uahi pele. Ua mākaukau nō nā mea a pau, a 'o ia nō ka wā
a Hi'iakakupu'ano'ano i hele aku ai me ke kino uahi pele o kona
kaikua'ana a hiki loa i Pāhoa. Iā ia ma Pāhoa, 'ike le'a 'ia ka wena
'ula o ka lani ma kahi e pā'ina ana 'o 'Ailā'au. Eia na'e, he mea 'ole
ia na Hi'iakakupu'ano'ano, 'oiai ua ku'upau aku 'o ia i kona kuleana
a hō'ea i kahi kūpono e ho'okupu a'e ai i ka 'ano'ano. Ki'i a'ela nō 'o
Hi'iakakupu'ano'ano i 'ano'ano 'ōhi'a ka'a nemo, a honi akula. Noho
kukuli ihola 'o ia ma ka lepo a kanu i ka 'ano'ano i ka 'āina. A laila,
hele a kokoke loa kona waha i ka lepo me he mea lā, e honi 'ia ana ka
'āina, a pule akula 'o ia me ka leo polinahe.

    E ola ē, e ola nui ē
    E kupu ē, e kupu a'e nei,
    E ka 'ano'ano ē,
    I ho'onoho 'ia ma ka 'āina,
    I haokanu 'ia ka papa lepo,
    I pūlama 'ia e Welahonua,
    I hānai 'ia e Kaualani.
    'Ōilo ka pulapula,
    Heu a'e ka lau iki,
    I ka malu o Kūkawowo,
    E kolo nō ke ēwe,

A paʻa honua ke kumu,
E kīkoʻo lani ka lālā,
A hoʻomalu ka paʻa lalo.
E ola, e ola, e kupu aʻe nō!
A kupu aʻela ka ʻanoʻano. Hoʻomau akula nō ʻo
Hiʻiakakupuʻanoʻano i ke oli, a i ka nui ʻana aʻe o ka lāʻau, i nui pū
aʻe ai kona leo oli. Ke kīkoʻo aʻe nō ke kiʻekiʻe o ke kumu lāʻau,
hoʻomalolo iki maila ke oli ʻana, a kiʻi ʻia ka māmala mai ka ʻumeke
mai. Hoʻokomo ʻia ka māmala ma kahi e ʻāmana ai ke kupu kumu
lāʻau. Pau i ka waiho ʻia, a hoʻomau ʻia ke oli, a hoʻoulu hou aʻela ke
kumu ʻōhiʻa me ka ʻāwili pū ʻia ʻana o nā mana, a hūnā ka māmala
kālaipāhoa i loko o ke kumu.

Hoʻomau akula nō ʻo Hiʻiakakupuʻanoʻano i kona oli ʻana a
kūpono ke kiʻekiʻe o ke kumu lāʻau, he kaʻau kapuaʻi a ʻoi loa aʻe ke
kiʻekiʻe, a he kāuna anana ka laulā o ke kumu. Ua ʻeu i ka lehua
ʻākepa, ʻo ia ka lehua kohu like me ka manu ʻākepa. Hōpoe aʻe nā
lehua, me he mea lā, muimui ana ia manu ʻākepa i ke kumu lehua, ʻo
ia hoʻi he ʻalani a ʻulaʻula hoʻi nā lihilihi, a he kohu hoʻi me ke ahi, ke
nānā aku. No ia kumu i kapa ʻia ai ke kumu ʻo Lehualihilihilapaahi.
Honi akula ke kaikamahine lei ʻanoʻano iā Lehualihilihilapaahi, a ʻo
ka hoʻi hou akula nō ia i Nanahuki. I kona hoʻi hou ʻana,
hoʻomaopopo akula nō ʻo ia iā Pele mā no ka hoʻokō ʻia o kona
kuleana.

Iā ia nō i mua o Pele, hoʻolei akula ʻo ia i kekahi mau lei
lehua ʻākepa mai Lehualihilihilapaahi mai. Ua makaʻala ʻo ia e kau
ʻole i kona mau lima i luna aʻe o ke poʻo o kona kaikuaʻana. I kona
hoʻolei ʻana, hoʻomaka ke oli ʻana, a ua komo pū nō ʻo Hiʻiaka mā i
ke oli pū, penei;
He lei ē,
He lei hoʻi,
He lei poʻo,
He lei pāpahi,
He lei kau i ka umauma,
He lei kāhiko i ke kino,
He lei ahi,

He lei lehua,

He lei lehua lihilihi lapa ahi,

He lei ia no ke kua'ana.

Honi lāua, a aloha aku 'o Pele i kona po'e kaikaina a pau, a ha'alele a'ela 'o Pele i kona po'e kaikaina ma kona kino he uahi pele no ka hele 'ana iō 'Ailā'au. Hō'ea akula 'o ia ma kahi o Lehualihilihilapaahi e kū ki'eki'e ana. I ka pā 'ana mai o ka makani, kapalili a'ela nā lihilihi lehua, a me he mea lā, he ahi ia e lapalapa a'e ana. Huli akula 'o ia a nānā iā Ahu'ailā'au, kahi ho'i e hula ana 'o ia a puni kona ahu.

Kū ha'aheo a'ela 'o Pele me ke kāhea 'ana aku iā 'Ailā'au, "E 'Ailā'au ē, pōloli paha 'oe? 'A'ohe huna 'ai a ka 'iole. 'O ka hue wale ho'i ka 'ai. He 'ai, he 'ai nō i 'ane'i mai. Mai, mai. 'O kou iwi wale ka 'ai!"

A hāpai 'ia kēia oli pololei a Lohi'au, penei;

Hulihia ka mauna, wela i ke ahi,

Wela nopu i ka uka o Kuiihanalei

Ke 'ā pōhaku, pu'u lele mai i uka o Kekāko'i,

Ka maiau pololei kani le'ale'a,

Ka hinihini kani kua mauna,

Ka māpu leo nui, leo kohākohā,

O kanaka loloa o ka mauna,

Kūpulupulu i ka nahele,

'O nā akua mai ka wao kele . . .

Pa'ē maila nā hua oli iā 'Ailā'au, a 'o ka holo akula nō ia i mua o ia wahine me ka pehi wale 'ana aku i kāna newa 'a'ā. 'A'ole nō na'e i pau ke oli a ka wahine, akā ua 'onipa'a 'o ia me ka luliluli 'ole a i 'ane ho'opā aku ka newa iā ia. Kiani akula ka lima o Pele i ka newa a ho'olele 'ia i luna lilo. Hū a'ela ka inaina o ua 'Ailā'au nei a noke mau 'o ia i ka holo i mua o Pele me ka 'ai pau 'ana i ka nahele i mua ona. Hiki 'o ia ala i mua o Pele a lele a'ela 'o Pele i luna a i hope ho'i o Lehualihilihilapaahi, a 'o ka 'ai ihola nō ia o 'Ailā'au i ia 'ōhi'a lehua me ka māmala kālaipāhoa i kona noke mau 'ana iā Pele. 'Emo 'ole a ho'okū 'o 'Ailā'au no ka 'eha'eha o kona 'ōpū a me ke kīkani ho'i o kona houpo, a hā'ule ihola 'o ia i ka honua, ua hinapē a hākalalū hoʻi ʻo ia. Holo akula ʻo Pele me ka hoʻopā paʻa ʻana aku i ka honua, a mai lalo mai kona lima a i luna a kuʻi lua akula ʻo Pele i ke alo o ʻAilāʻau me ka mana nui o ke ahi o Kīlauea, a hoʻolele aʻela ʻo ʻAilāʻau i luna loa. Hāʻule hou ihola ʻo ia ma kahi o Ahuʻailāʻau. Holo hou akula ʻo Pele iō ʻAilāʻau, a i ka ʻike ʻana aku o ua ʻAilāʻau lā i ka holo wikiwiki ʻana o Pele, kokolo ʻo ia a hoʻi hou akula i loko o ka puka ona i puka mua aʻe ai, a nalo me he ilo lā.

ʻOiai ua ʻauheʻe wale akula ʻo ʻAilāʻau, kia hou ʻo Pele i kona wahi hale. Holo pololei akula ʻo ia i ke kaʻe o Halemaʻumaʻu a nānā iā lalo. I kona hiki ʻana i Halemaʻumaʻu, ʻike akula ʻo ia iā Kanihiō e nanea ana i ka wai walewale wela, ʻo ka inaina aʻela nō ia i ka ʻike maka ʻana i ka haʻakei o ia moʻo i kona wahi home ponoʻī, a oli akula, penei;

> Hulihia ka mauna
> Wela i ke ahi a ka wahine
> Hū aʻe ka pele
> Hoʻopaila ʻia ka wai
> A miki aʻe ka walewale
> A pau moʻa ka moʻo

A ōlaʻi hou ka honua, a hoʻowela ʻia ka wai e ka hū ʻana aʻe o ka pele mai lalo mai o ka honua. Ua ʻike ʻo Kanihiō i ka puapuaʻi ʻana o ia walewale, a lele aʻela ʻo ia me ke kolo wikiwiki ʻana aʻe i ke alo lua pele a hoʻi hou akula ʻo ia i ka nahele. Pahū aʻela ka honua a pau ka wai walewale, a ʻo ka pele wale nō ka mea e puapuaʻi nei. Ua hoʻi nō ʻo Pele.

Kāhea akula ʻo Pele i kona poʻe pōkiʻi me ke oli;

> E hoʻi, e hoʻi,
> E hoʻi mai ē,
> I ko kākou hale ē,
> I Halemaʻumaʻu ē
> Hale wela i ke ahi ē.
> No kākou nō kēia hale ē.
> Lapalapa mau ē.

A ʻo ka hoʻi hou maila nō ia o Hiʻiaka mā i Halemaʻumaʻu, a ʻo ka hula ihola nō ia o lākou me ke ahi lapalapa o Kīlauea.

Iā lākou e hoʻolauleʻa ana, hoʻi ʻo Hiʻiakanohoana i Kahakakīloa. I kona nānā ʻana i nā mea a pau i loko o ia ana, pūʻiwa aʻela ʻo ia i ka ʻike ʻole ʻia o kekahi mau mea koʻikoʻi, ʻo ia hoʻi ʻo ʻAunaki a me ʻAulima, nā lāʻau hana ahi a Lonomakua, nāna hoʻi i aʻo aku iā Pele i ka hana ahi. "Auē, auē," i uē aʻela ʻo ia. Pau koke ka hula ʻana o Pele mā, a huli a nānā aku iā Hiʻiakanohoana.

"Auē, ua pau ʻo ʻAunaki a me Aulima!"

"Tsa!" i hoʻopuka aʻela ʻo Pele, "Ua pau nō paha i ka hoʻopulu ʻia e ka walewale. He ʻaihue, he ʻaihue! He moʻo ʻaihue nō! E ʻimi aʻe kākou iā Kanihiō, a hoʻihoʻi ʻia nā lāʻau a ko kākou ahi, a e lilo ana ka iwi a Kanihiō ʻo ia kā kākou wahie!"

ʻAʻole i pau.

Ka Lupe O Kawelo

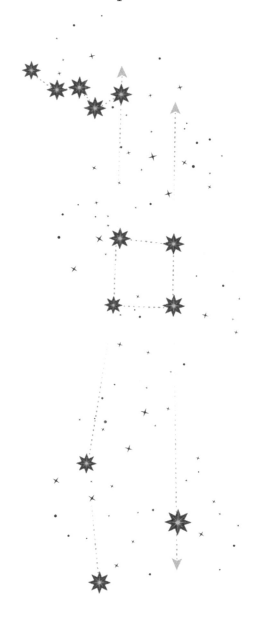

Rasha Abdulhadi is a queer Palestinian Southerner who cut their teeth organizing on the southsides of Chicago and Atlanta. Rasha's writing has appeared in *Mslexia, Strange Horizons, Shade Journal, Plume, Mizna, Room, |tap| magazine, Beltway Poetry,* and *Lambda Literary.* Their work is anthologized in *Essential Voices: A COVID-19 Anthology* (forthcoming), *Unfettered Hexes, Halal if You Hear Me, Stoked Words,* and the Hugo-nominated collection *Luminescent Threads: Connections to Octavia Butler.* A fiber artist, poet, and speculative fiction writer and editor, Rasha is a member of Justice for Muslims Collective and Alternate ROOTS. Their new chapbook is *who is owed springtime.*

A. A. Attanasio: I'm a novelist and student of the imagination living in Honolulu. Fantasies, visions, hallucinations, or whatever we call those irrational powers that illuminate our inner life fascinate me. I'm particularly intrigued by the creative intelligence that scripts our dreams. And I love carrying this soulful energy outside my mind into the one form that most precisely defines who we are: story.

Sara Backer's Elgin-nominated first book of poetry, *Such Luck* (Flowstone Press 2019), follows two poetry chapbooks: *Scavenger Hunt* (dancing girl press) and *Bicycle Lotus* (Left Fork), which won the Turtle Island Poetry Prize. Her speculative poems have appeared in *Abyss & Apex, Asimov's, Bracken, Crannóg, Dreams & Nightmares, ETTT, Liminality, The Pedestal, Polu Texni, Silver Blade, Space and Time, Star*Line,* and *Strange Horizons.* She has also placed non-genre poems in over 100 journals which include *Slant, Tar River Poetry, Cut Bank, Poetry,* and *Kenyon Review.*

Joshua Beggs is a 2019 graduate from Hendrix College and a current MD candidate at Kansas University Medical Center, with previous publications including appearances in *MAYDAY, Fleas on the Dog,* and *Chestnut Review.* In his free time, he volunteers as a Spanish interpreter at his local free clinic, makes a podcast (which his mom says is awesome), and maintains his very creatively named website, joshuabeggs.com.

Ahimsa Timoteo Bodhrán is a multimedia artist, activist/organizer, critic, and educator. A Tulsa Artist Fellow and National Endowment for the Arts Fellow, he is the author of *Archipiélagos; Antes y después del Bronx: Lenapehoking;* and *South Bronx Breathing Lessons;* editor of the international queer Indigenous issue of *Yellow Medicine Review;* and co-editor of the Native dance/movement/performance issue of *Movement Research Performance Journal.* He has received scholarships/fellowships from the Voices of Our Nations Arts Foundation, CantoMundo, Radius of Arab American Writers, Macondo, and Lambda Literary. His work appears throughout the Pacific, Australia, Asia, the Américas, Africa, Europe, and the Arab world.

Donald Carreira Ching was born and raised in Kahaluʻu, on the island of Oʻahu, Hawaiʻi. His work has been published in national and international publications. In 2015, his debut novel, *Between Sky and Sea: A Family's Struggle,* was published by Bamboo Ridge Press.

Melissa Chimera is a conservationist and Hawaiʻi Island artist of Lebanese and Filipino ancestry. She studied natural resources management at the University of Hawaiʻi and worked for two decades as a conservation manager. Her paintings, textiles, and installations are research-based and investigate species extinction, globalization, and human migration. She has exhibited in the U.S., Asia, and the Middle East and is the recipient of the Catherine E. B. Cox Award and finalist for the Lange-Taylor Prize. Her work resides in the Arab American National Museum, the Honolulu Museum of Art, and the Hawaiʻi State Foundation of Culture and the Arts.

Timothy Dyke lives in Makiki with parrots. He has published two books of poetry and one chapbook with Tinfish Press. He has an MFA in Creative Writing from the University of Arizona, and he teaches English to high school students in Honolulu.

Solomon Robert Nui Enos is a Native Hawaiian artist, illustrator, and visionary. Born and raised in Mākaha Valley (Oʻahu, Hawaiʻi), Solomon hails from the well-known Enos ʻohana. Solomon has been making art for more than 30 years and he is adept at artistic expression in a wide variety of media including oil paintings, book illustrations, murals, and game design. Solomon's art expresses an informed aspirational vision of the world at its best via contemporary and traditional art that leans towards Sci-Fi and Fantasy. Recent clients include the Smithsonian, Google, Pixar, Vans, and Disney.

Brady Evans is a comic artist and illustrator born, raised, and working in Honolulu, Hawai'i. With a strong interest in manga and other forms of sequential imagery and storytelling, he enjoys creating stories and characters that draw on folklore from around the world as well as his own experiences and family stories.

Joy Gold: Born and raised near the piko of O'ahu, Wahiawa, I've been writing on and off since small kid time. "Po-Ho, Waste Time," published in the *Hawaii Review*, emerged decades ago from Eric Chock's creative writing class. A few years later, "Sansei" was published in *Ricepaper*, a Canadian-Asian literary and arts magazine. Many thanks to Bamboo Ridge and da Buckaroo's writing prompts for getting me back in the saddle to write, write, write!

Jennifer Hasegawa is a Pushcart Prize-nominated poet who has sold funeral insurance door-to-door and had her suitcase stolen from a plastic surgery clinic in Paraguay. The manuscript for her book of poetry, *La Chica's Field Guide to Banzai Living* (Omnidawn), won the Joseph Henry Jackson Literary Award and the book itself was longlisted for The Believer Book Award in Poetry. Her work has appeared in *The Adroit Journal, Bennington Review, jubilat, Tule Review,* and *Vallum*. Hasegawa was born and raised in Hilo, Hawai'i and lives in San Francisco.

Scott Kikkawa has an Elliot Cades Award for Literature for writing stories about a Nisei cop who drank on duty and chain-smoked his way through his homicide cases in Territorial Hawai'i. He's received no awards that anyone outside the U.S. government has ever heard of for staying sober at work and sleepwalking through his real-life cases. He's lucky as hell that Bamboo Ridge has taken a chance on his detective fiction and given him a platform for his bile and spleen in a monotone narrative.

Kalehua Kim is a poet living in the Seattle area. Born of Hawaiian, Chinese, Filipino, and Portuguese descent, her multicultural background informs much of her work. A finalist for the James Welch Prize for Indigenous Poets, her poems have appeared in *Poetry Northwest, Belletrist, Panoply,* and *'Ōiwi: A Native Hawaiian Journal.*

Juliet S. Kono finds every day a gift in this extraordinary time. She wishes everyone safe and well.

Gabi Lardies is a writer from Aotearoa New Zealand. Online, Gabi has recently published "Big-Nosed Women" on *The Spinoff,* "structure's surface skin" for *RM Gallery,* and "Embracing Freaky Futures" on *Designers Speak (Up).* In print, this year, she has published in *The JavaScript* Issue 11, *Dwelling in the Margins: Art Publishing in Aotearoa,* and the *Poetry New Zealand Yearbook 2021.* Gabi holds a Masters of Fine Arts (First Class), a Graduate Diploma in Sociology and Creative Writing, and a Bachelor of Communication Design. You can find Gabi on Instagram (@bb_geep) or online (art.gabi-lardies.com).

Sloane Leong is a cartoonist, artist, and writer of Hawaiian, Chinese, Mexican, Native American, and European ancestries. She's written and drawn two acclaimed graphic novels, *Prism Stalker* and *A Map to the Sun,* and has short fiction credits with *Fireside Magazine, Dark Matter Magazine,* and *Entropy Magazine.* She was raised on Maui and is currently living on Chinook land near what is known as Portland, Oregon.

Jason Edward Lewis writes about technology and culture. At times as a poet, at times as a scholar, at times as a tool-maker. Online at jasonlewis.org.

J. Hauʻoli Lorenzo-Elarco was raised by the Kīpuʻupuʻu rain in the mountainous lands of Waimea, Hawaiʻi. He currently resides in Waialua, Oʻahu. Hauʻoli is an Instructor of Hawaiian Language at Honolulu Community College. One of the courses he teaches focuses on Hawaiian literature in ʻōlelo Hawaiʻi and English. An important goal of this course is to draw inspiration from these moʻolelo (stories) to write about our own contemporary experiences in Hawaiʻi. This course inspired *He Moʻolelo No ʻAilāʻau.*

Darrell H. Y. Lum once attempted to trap nuisance geckos who inhabited the kitchen ceiling with Hoy Hoy Trap-A-Roach taped to the ceiling. Nevah work. Now guests always ask, "How come get one roach trap on your ceiling?"

Wing Tek Lum is a Honolulu businessman and poet. Bamboo Ridge Press published his two collections of poetry, *Expounding the Doubtful Points* (1987) and *The Nanjing Massacre: Poems* (2012).

Kahealani Mahone-Brooks was born and raised on Oʻahu. She is a mother, Hawaiʻi kiaʻi, mixed Kanaka, and self-taught artist. She currently resides on Hawaiʻi Island, where she and her ʻohana are developing a self-sustaining farm, and where she also runs a small online art shop. You can find her on Instagram at @kahea.mana.hina or online at https://kaheamanahina.bigcartel.com/.

Brandy Nālani McDougall (Kanaka ʻŌiwi) is a poet, scholar, mother, and aloha ʻāina originally from Aʻapueo, Maui, and now living with her ʻohana in ʻAiea, Oʻahu. She is an associate professor specializing in Indigenous Studies in the University of Hawaiʻi at Mānoa's American Studies department. Her poetry collection, *ʻĀina Hānau, Birth Lands*, is forthcoming from the University of Arizona Press in 2023.

Chris McKinney was born in Honolulu and grew up in Kahaluʻu on the island of Oʻahu. He is the author of *Midnight, Water City*, book one of the Water City trilogy. He has written six other novels: *The Tattoo, The Queen of Tears, Bolohead Row, Mililani Mauka, Boi No Good*, and *Yakudoshi: Age of Calamity*.

Veronica Montes is the author of the award-winning chapbook *The Conquered Sits at the Bus Stop, Waiting* (Black Lawrence Press 2020) and *Benedicta Takes Wing & Other Stories* (Philippine American Literary House 2018). Her fiction has been published in anthologies including *Contemporary Fiction by Filipinos in America* and *Growing Up Filipino*, and in journals including *Bamboo Ridge* (Issue 89), *Wigleaf, SmokeLong Quarterly,* and many others.

Jocelyn Kapumealani Ng is a queer multi-dimensional creative of Hawaiian, Chinese, Japanese, and Portuguese descent. The fluidity of her art blends award-winning spoken word poetry, special effects make-up, theater performance, photography, and fabrication to navigate themes of queerness, indigenous culture, womxn issues, and the representation of under-represented narratives.

Born and raised on Kaua'i, **Kēhau Noe** is pursuing a doctorate in Computer Science with a focus in computer interaction and immersive technology. Her passion is in creative media; however, before learning programming and digital art, her first love was drawing comics. Noe enjoys the fantastic, believing that sometimes it takes extraordinary contexts to understand things that can't just be plainly said.

Rainie Oet is a nonbinary, transfeminine writer of poetry and fiction for adults and younger readers. Her third poetry book, *Glorious Veils of Diane,* was published by Carnegie Mellon University Press in 2021. Their picture book, *The Birthday Party*, is forthcoming from Astra Young Readers in 2023. She received an MFA in Poetry from Syracuse University, where she was awarded the Shirley Jackson Prize in Fiction. Read more of their work at rainieoet.com.

Kalani (Lauren) Nicolle Padilla was raised on O'ahu, in Mililani, the descendant of immigrants from Ilocos Norte. Since moving to Spokane, Washington, for school, her writing practice and soul have been nourished by deep roots in both the islands and the Pacific Northwest. Kalani is currently a graduate student of Poetry and teacher of writing at the University of Montana in Missoula. She hopes her creative and academic pursuits bring her home one day.

Lehua Parker writes speculative fiction for kids and adults, often set in her native Hawai'i. Her award-winning works include the *Niuhi Shark Saga* trilogy, *Lauele Fractured Folktales*, and *Chicken Skin Stories*. *One Boy, No Water (Niuhi Shark Saga #1)*, was a 2017 Hawaii Children's Choice Nene Award Nominee.

A Kamehameha Schools graduate, Lehua frequently speaks at conferences and symposiums about the need for authentic voices and representation in media. She is also a freelance editor and story consultant. Now living in the high Rocky Mountains, during the snowy winters, she dreams of the beach. Connect with her at https://www.lehuaparker.com.

Craig Santos Perez is a CHamoru originally from Guam. He is the author of five books of poetry and the co-editor of five anthologies. He is a professor in the English department at the University of Hawaiʻi at Mānoa.

Yasmine Romero is an Associate Professor of English at the University of Hawaiʻi–West Oʻahu. She grew up in Saipan of the Northern Marianas Islands and Boise, Idaho. Her forthcoming book, *Moving Across Whirlpools: Intersectionality in Writing and Language Studies,* combines her research interests in intersectionality, critical narrative studies, and translingualism. Currently, she is researching intersections across teacher training, language attitudes towards Pidgin and English, and language policies in K–12 schools in Hawaiʻi. She is also working on a short story collection of feminist revisions of legends and faerytales.

John P. Rosa grew up in Kaimukī and Kāneʻohe on the island of Oʻahu. He is the author of *Local Story: The Massie-Kahahawai Case and the Culture of History* (University of Hawaiʻi Press 2014).

Normie Salvador is a disabled Filipino-American who taught poetry at University of Hawaiʻi at Mānoa and composition, creative writing, short story and novel classes at Kapiʻolani Community College, and also oversaw *Ka Hue Anahā: Journal of Academic Research and Writing* as its faculty advisor. He is now a freelance editor. Tinfish Press published his poetry chapbook, *Philter* (2003). His most recent works have appeared in *Bamboo Ridge* and *Wordgathering.* His pandemic hobbies are reading Japanese light novel translations, being the gamemaster for a 2-year-long Dungeons & Dragons campaign, and restoring wooden bowls bought from thrift stores.

Misty-Lynn Sanico lives and writes in downtown Honolulu near a crossroad where the winds pause at a traffic light and spill out their carried sounds of church bells and the whispers of historic buildings.

I was born on the island of Oʻahu and raised in the shades of the coconut grove of Pōkaʻī. My name is **Pōkiʻi Seto**, a native of Waiʻanae and a child of Hawaiʻi. ʻIke is my guide and ʻōlelo is the medium in which I am able to pass it to the generations. Ola i ka ʻōlelo. Ola hoʻi i ka Hawaiʻi.

Ngaio Simmons (she/her) is a queer writer and performer with a degree in English from the University of Hawaiʻi at Mānoa. Writing from the diaspora as a Māori poet born and raised away from Aotearoa, her work digs into such themes as diaspora, identity conflict, and home. Her work has been featured in *Public Journal, Flux Hawaiʻi, Contemporary Verse, Tayo Literary Magazine, Hawaiʻi Review,* and *Ora Nui.*

Zoe C. Sims was born and raised in Kona, Hawaiʻi. She studied ecology and writing at Princeton University, graduating in 2017. She now lives, works, and tries to grow backyard vegetables in Honolulu, Oʻahu. Website: zoesims.net.

Joseph Stanton has lived in Hawaiʻi since 1972. His books of poems are *Moving Pictures, Things Seen, A Field Guide to the Wildlife of Suburban Oʻahu, Imaginary Museum, Cardinal Points,* and *What the Kite Thinks: A Linked Poem.* His poems have appeared in *Bamboo Ridge, Poetry, Harvard Review, New Letters, Antioch Review, New York Quarterly,* and many other magazines. He is Professor Emeritus of American Studies and Art History at UH Mānoa.

Lehua M. Taitano is a queer CHamoru writer and interdisciplinary artist from Yigu, Guåhan (Guam), familian Kabesa yan Kuetu, and co-founder of Art 25: Art in the Twenty-fifth Century. She is the author of *Inside Me an Island* and *A Bell Made of Stones.* Taitano's work investigates modern indigeneity, decolonization, and cultural identity in the context of diaspora.

My name is **Delaina Thomas**. I was born in Pālolo and am a Roosevelt grad. Most of my adult life I've spent in Upcountry Maui. I've returned to Honolulu to care for my parents. I have an MFA from UC Irvine.

Blaine Namahana Tolentino lives and works in Honolulu on Oʻahu. She is the co-editor of *The Hawaiian Journal of History* and an editor for Awaiaulu. Her poems have been published in *Trout* (2008), *ʻŌiwi: A Native Hawaiian Journal* (2010), *Whetu Moana* (2010), *JAAM*

(2011), and *Flux Magazine* (2017). In 2020, University of Hawaiʻi Press published her Hawaiian translation, *ʻO Manu, ke Keiki Aloha Manu*, originally written in English by Caren Loebel-Fried. Written with Kauʻi Sai-Dudoit, the article "Aloha ʻĀina: From the Historical Record" will appear in a forthcoming anthology from the Hawaiʻinuiākea Monograph series in 2023.

"Da Pidgin Guerrilla" **Lee A. Tonouchi**'s most recentest book wuz his children's picture book *Okinawan Princess: Da Legend of Hajichi Tattoos* with artist Laura Kina that won one 2020 Skipping Stones Honor Award. His Pidgin poetry collection *Significant Moments in da Life of Oriental Faddah and Son* won da 2013 Association for Asian American Studies Book Award. His oddah books include *Da Word*, *Living Pidgin*, *Da Kine Dictionary*, and *Buss Laugh*. He had a buncha plays produced before by Kumu Kahua Theatre, da Honolulu Theatre for Youth, and East West Players. An'den he's also one food critic for frolichawaii.com.

Aldric Ulep is pursuing an MFA in Creative Writing from the Rainier Writing Workshop at Pacific Lutheran University. He works with The Speakeasy Project, a literary arts organization and talent agency. His writing can be found or is forthcoming in *Beloit Poetry Journal*, *Tinfish*, *Bamboo Ridge*, and *Witty Partition*. He lives and writes in Pearl City, Hawaiʻi.

Don Wallace is editor of *The Hawaiʻi Review of Books* and contributing editor of *HONOLULU Magazine*. Books: *The French House, One Great Game*, and *Hot Water*. Essays and stories: *Harper's, The New York Times, The Wall Street Journal, The Surfer's Journal, Bamboo Ridge, Snake Nation Review, Fast Company*, etc. Documentary (writer): *Those Who Came Before: The Musical Journey of Eddie Kamae*. Awards: Loretta D. Petrie Award, Pluma de Plata. Body of Work: Society of Professional Journalists. More at donwallacewriter.com. He lives on Oʻahu with his wife, writer Mindy Eun Soo Pennybacker.

Aloha. I am from the island of Oʻahu, my family lives in the valley of Pālolo and I spend much time in the Tuahine rain that falls upon the university in Mānoa. I am **Bruce Kaʻimi Watson**. I am Kaʻimi, an ʻŌiwi philosopher and historian in an occupied nation.

Tama Wise is a Māori author of Ngāpuhi descent. He was influenced by growing up with hip hop culture, one of a generation of urban Polynesians searching for identity. In his teens, he was drawn to what little fiction he could find that addressed race, sexuality, and poverty in an urban setting. Since then he has told stories of this world and others, weaving love, life, and a Māori view of things.

Tama has been published in *Huia Short Stories 7: Contemporary Māori Fiction* and in the *Yellow Medicine Review*. His novel *Street Dreams* was released by Bold Strokes Books.

Hana Yoshihata is a painter and illustrator from Hawai'i Island who draws inspiration from the stars, sea, land, people, and stories around her. Much of her current work explores her experiences sailing around the world on voyaging canoes, with a focus on honoring our intrinsic human connections to nature, the cosmos and each other. Hana hopes her creations can help nurture these connections and imagine a kinder, more sustainable future for all.

Nā Hiku
setting

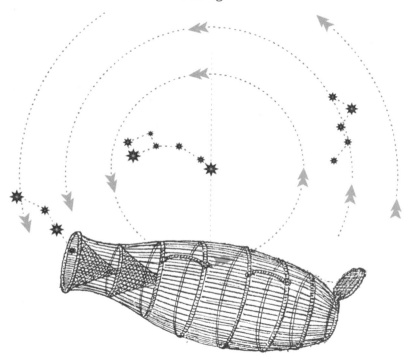